KISSING GALILEO

DEAR PROFESSOR BOOK #2

PENNY REID

WWW.PENNYREID.NINJA/NEWSLETTER/

COPYRIGHT

Legal Stuff: This book is a work of fiction. Names, characters, places, rants, facts, contrivances, and incidents are either the product of the author's questionable imagination or are used factitiously. Any resemblance to actual persons, living or dead or undead, events, and/or locales is entirely coincidental if not somewhat disturbing/concerning.

Caped Publishing

Made in the United States of America

Print Edition

CHAPTER 1

EMILY

Professor Hanover's eyes were affixed to his smartphone with the determined unsteadiness of a man who was exceedingly uncomfortable.

Meanwhile, I was in the precarious position of being naked.

Wait. Let me back up a second and explain. Most people aren't aware that there are five stages of naked for a woman.

The first, and most obvious of course, is just *buck-bare naked*. No clothes, no nothing. All skin.

The second stage is *virtually naked*. The nipples might be covered with a bit of sequin, but not always. Typically, all that is needed is a strategically placed triangle secured to the front lady parts by either adhesive or barely visible plastic string. Usually, the bottom is completely exposed.

Stage number three is *almost naked*. The boob—the nipple at a minimum—is scarcely veiled and panties of some kind are worn, frequently a G-string or floss-like thong.

Stage four is still a type of naked, but some would argue it may also venture into the not-technically-naked category.

We call it *transparently naked* and it normally involves a bra, panties, or lingerie of some sort. However—whatever the items—they are completely see-through, sheer lace. As such, very little is obstructing the eye from the skin beneath.

Finally, stage five just manages to cross the line from naked to not naked. It is being in a state of undress, donning conservative underthings—like an opaque nightie, or a long slip—and is commonly referred to as *disrobed*.

But back to me being naked in front of my professor.

I hadn't recognized him at first. I don't look at the faces of clients. I exit the session with a vague impression of a person like, "that guy who smelled like peanuts" or, "the really tall one who tried to touch my boob."

They—the men, and sometimes their second wives or mistresses—were always looking at my body, never my face or eyes. So looking directly at the customers seemed unnecessary.

Actually, let me amend that, they weren't looking *at me*. They were looking at what I was wearing. At first, when I started, I assumed they were assessing whether seven hundred dollars was too much to pay for a bra. But the longer I worked for the Pinkery as a lingerie model, the more I began to understand that the clients weren't concerned with money. They had plenty of money.

They were concerned with their own boredom.

Which meant I only ever noticed someone, really saw them, if they weren't looking at me. Victor Hanover—Dr. Hanover—my research methods professor, wasn't looking at me. He was looking at his cell. *Thank God.*

Because I was currently stage three naked. Also, randomly, I couldn't help but notice how huge his hands were, large with long fingers, which made his smartphone seem tiny and—

"Hello…?"

I blinked against the murkiness of mortified recognition and turned my attention to the only other person in the room. He was older than Dr. Hanover, nicely dressed, with silver hair at his temples. The unknown man was also smaller than my professor, but somehow his presence felt larger, suffocating.

I couldn't focus on this older man's face, but not for the usual reasons. I was distracted, too busy arbitrating the wrestling match between my shock and embarrassment. Embarrassment was winning.

"I said, could you turn?" he snapped.

I nodded, turned, happy to show them my basically bare backside if it gave me a moment to collect myself.

Dr. Hanover and this older man were sitting in a private room, my private room, at the Pinkery. As the most exclusive lingerie, fripperies, and accoutrements shop in New England, it required a membership and minimum monthly purchase guarantee for entry and continued access. I wasn't used to seeing anyone I knew in real life while at work. Neither my classmates nor my professors could afford the membership or the merchandise.

For that matter, the scraps of lace and silk were firmly out of my budget as well.

"What do you think, Victor?"

I swallowed, being careful to do so quietly. The last thing I wanted was to be the source of a cartoonish gulp while my professor contemplated my ass. He was looking at my ass. I was sure of it. I knew the precise moment his eyes lifted to my skin and I gritted my teeth, feeling the affliction of his gaze traveling lower, over my thighs.

Call it a sixth sense, call it intuition, but I always knew where the clients were looking. This uncanny ability usually came in handy as it meant I could focus my energy on highlighting that area, giving it the best light, angling my leg just so.

But not this time. This time I held perfectly still like I used to do when caught by my mother with my hand in the cookie jar. And by cookie jar, I mean my hand in my high school boyfriend's pants, in the back of my car on prom night.

My mother, God love her, tossed three condoms into the back seat and called over her shoulder, "You better get my daughter off before you come all over her car."

I hadn't inherited my mother's impressive talent for punch line delivery, but I had inherited her pragmatic nature. I'd always been more likely to freeze than flee, or fight, or flirt when faced with a mortifying situation.

Which was why I stood stock-still as I heard Professor Hanover clear his throat before saying, "I'm not sure where I should be looking."

"Oh for God's sake," the older man huffed with obvious impatience. "The model, Victor. Look at the model."

"Why? She's not for sale."

I closed my eyes, pressing my lips together. It was such a Dr. Hanover thing to say, much more in character than glaring uncomfortably at the screen of his smartphone.

Over the last two months of sitting through his course, I'd never once seen him uncomfortable, though I'd seen him glare plenty. Glare at students who took too long to answer. Glare at students who were obviously unprepared for class. Glare at students who couldn't quite grasp the concept of a split tailed T-test.

He glared all the time, in that exasperated "I'm so much smarter than you, you might as well be a single-celled organism in comparison" kind of way.

But uncomfortable? Never.

It was Dr. Havover's turn to sigh. "I don't know why you brought me."

The older man made a sniffing sound. "Is it so odd that I would want to spend time with my son?"

His. . . son? What? Wait. That's weird, right? Who would take their son to a lingerie shop? Or maybe this practice was all the rage and I was completely out of touch.

Victor made a scoffing sound, and I imagined he was rolling his eyes. I'd never seen him roll his eyes, he was far too enlightened for that, but for some reason I imagined him as rolling his eyes now.

"Fine. Lyla suggested it." The older man lowered his voice to a gruff whisper.

"Who's Lyla?"

"Victor . . ." The single word was ripe with warning.

"I'm sorry, is she one of your wives? I've lost count, so you can't expect me to remember names."

Now I rolled my lips between my teeth, because that was also a very Professor Hanover thing to say. The man was firmly in the asshole column, but his sarcastic sass always made me laugh (sometimes against my will). This meant I was frequently ducking my head and hiding behind my laptop during class.

It also meant that I never, ever, ever put myself in the position of being on the receiving end of his sarcasm. I knew the research methods textbooks so well, I probably could've taught the course at this point.

But back to the good professor and his mad dad.

"Don't I deserve happiness?" he ranted. "Don't I—"

Victor made another scoffing sound, raising his voice over his father's. "You want to keep looking for happiness between a woman's legs? Fine. Go for it. But don't fucking bring me here and expect father-son bonding time. Sitting in a bourgeois lingerie store, slobbering over a woman one third your age while your current wife—"

"You know we're engaged," his father thundered, and it sounded like he'd lunged to his feet.

"Whatever." Victor's voice also rose. "Current vagina of the moment—"

Whoa!

"Mr. Hanover," a woman's voice cut in, silencing both men.

But not just any woman's voice. Madame Purple, my boss, and a take-no-bullshit-or-prisoners kind of superwoman. She reported directly to the owner, Madame Pink.

At the sound of her voice I flinched, half turning on instinct. But then I stopped myself and offered just my profile. From my vantage point I could see the professor was standing, facing his father. Unable to help myself, I looked at him; I'd been so shocked by his presence earlier, I hadn't taken a moment to study the man.

Firstly, he looked pissed, his eyes flashing fire, his hands clenched into fists.

Secondly, I realized he wasn't in his usual baggy dad jeans and dorktastic, overly large, brown and yellow plaid button-down shirt. With a pocket protector. One shirttail tucked in, one shirttail flapping in the breeze.

No. Not today.

Today he was wearing a dark blue tailored suit that accentuated the upside-down triangle shape of his torso. It fit. He looked damn fine in it. It made him seem taller, bigger, stronger. . . or was it the waves of menace and fury? Or had he always been tall and strong?

Also, I'd never witnessed his hair anything other than flat and ignored. Not today. His hair was styled as though the man knew how to style it. However, he did don his usual thick horn-rimmed glasses. The effect of this makeover plus the glasses gave Victor Hanover a distinctly nerdy-sexy-Calvin Klein-model vibe that. . . well, it startled me.

He was still firmly in the asshole column, but now he was in the sexy asshole column.

"What?" Victor's dad didn't try to veil his impatience with my boss's interruption.

She smiled at the two men, her shimmery purple lipstick a gorgeous complement to her flawless brown skin. "You have a phone call."

"What?"

"A phone call."

Mr. Hanover straightened, his gaze flickering over her like he couldn't decide whether to be indignant or furious.

But before he could question Madame Purple further, she volunteered, "It's Madame Pink. She wishes to discuss the status of your membership."

Oh. Snap.

My eyes widened, but I caught the crack in my demeanor almost instantly. Schooling my expression, I gathered a silent breath. There was no three-strikes-and-you're-out policy at the Pinkery. You were out when Madame Pink said you were out. End of story. She never explained why. Once you were out, you could never get back in.

Mr. Hanover shifted restlessly on his feet. "I apologize if our raised voices caused any disturbance." It looked like the words poisoned him as he spoke them. I imagined this man rarely—if ever—apologized. This suspicion was confirmed as his son glanced between Madame Purple and his father, visibly confused, or astonished, or both.

"Please." Madame Purple widened her smile, stepping to one side and motioning to the door with a graceful movement of her hand. "After you."

Mr. Hanover slid his teeth to the side and sent his son a quick, incensed look. Then the man turned a rigid grin to my boss and gave her a little head nod, strolling unhurriedly out of the room while fiddling with a cuff link.

My boss gave Professor Hanover a whisper of a smile, then to me indicated with her chin toward the bar console in the corner. "Lavender, please pour a glass of scotch for your guest. And . . ." Her eyes moved back to him and she studied his openly bewildered expression for several beats before continuing, "And perhaps the black and red garter ensemble next."

I wanted to wince. I wanted to wince so hard. Or at the very least communicate my panic with a glance of extreme askance. It would be the most askance glance in the history of glances.

But I didn't. Mostly because I was frozen. But also because Madame Purple didn't give me the chance. She turned on her heel and left.

Oh jeez.

Well.

Okay then.

Here I go.

. . . I couldn't move.

But I had to move. I glanced at the camera, artfully hidden in the corner, and reminded myself of how much I wanted this job. For the record, it was a lot. *Think of your mom and all her therapy bills. Think of money. Money!*

That did it. Finally, I forced my feet to carry me toward the bar.

"Where are you going?" Professor Hanover's voice was heavily seasoned with suspicion; my steps faltered at his tone.

I didn't stop, though my gaze instinctively lifted and connected with his, causing my chest to tighten with dread. I ignored the sensation. Instead I focused on his frown. To my immense relief, I saw his gaze was cloudy with something like frustration, but definitely not recognition.

I motioned to the bar and continued toward it, saying nothing. If I could help it, I rarely spoke in front of clients, just what was required according to our guidelines. But beyond that, I wondered if Dr. Hanover was more likely to recognize my voice than my face.

I was quiet in class, answering succinctly whenever he called my name. And I typically wore a hat with my hair tucked up inside or pulled back in a ponytail. I also never wore makeup outside of work, mostly because makeup was expensive. In addition to inheriting my mother's pragmatism, I'd also inherited her frugal nature.

Flexing my fingers, I relaxed, realizing that the chances of him recognizing me were fairly low. He had, what? Over a hundred students in that lecture hall every week? And that was just my class.

Slowly, I placed my hands on the glassware, pleased to see they weren't shaking. I'd just removed the stopper to the decanter and released a steady breath when he spoke again.

"I'm sorry."

My fingers stilled, and I looked at him, discovering that my professor was strolling toward me. His hands in his pants pockets, his attention on the bar console. He stopped a few feet away while I tried to stand as nonchalantly as possible.

Have you ever tried to stand nonchalantly before? Like tried to be pointedly disinterested? Or "act normal"? It's impossible. It's like trying to pee on a target with an audience of five hundred nuns.

Not to mention, Victor Hanover had just apologized. To me. For what, I had no idea. The mere idea of the superior professor apologizing to anyone for anything had me questioning whether I was awake, or if this was a dream, or maybe I was high. I'd never touched drugs, but the possibility of being high felt more likely than Dr. Hanover apologizing.

"I'm sorry," he repeated, his voice softer, his gaze resting everywhere but on me. "My words were sarcastic and spoken in anger. They were meant to reflect how my father views women, and are not indicative of my own thoughts. He is a faithless taint, and should be despised. For the record, I do not share his—" Victor's eyes moved to the left, as though he were searching for the right words. "I do not share his lack of respect for other humans, especially female humans. Therefore, I'm sorry you heard it. But more than that, I'm sorry I said it."

Well . . . *huh.*

How about that?

Unable to tear my gaze away, I stared at him, openly examining my professor. His eyes were a dark color—maybe dark green, maybe brown, maybe indigo—it was hard to see them behind his glasses. His nose reminded me of Brad Pitt's or Chris Evans's nose, smaller than the average man nose, but strangely it worked for him. Victor's jaw was angular, strong, and covered in late afternoon scruff. He was probably one of those guys who had to shave twice a day.

Victor Hanover was so . . . odd.

And quite suddenly made enormously attractive by his apology.

This abrupt discovery of his attractiveness—especially relative to his previous plainness and firm placement in the asshole column—overwhelmed me. Maybe because I'd never been this close to him? Maybe because I'd never seen him impassioned? Maybe because I'd never seen him as anything other than dry, distracted, and aloof? Or maybe because I'd never looked at Professor Hanover before and thought of him as a man.

As brilliant? Yes. As funny and witty? Yes and yes. As a

sadist who enjoyed torturing his students and forcing them to learn all relevant applications of the chi-square test? Yes, yes, and yes.

But never as a man.

It was overwhelming. He was overwhelming. The crush alarm sounded between my ears and low in my stomach. My face flushed with heat and I swallowed a breath.

Ahhhhh crap. He's not even my type! He's too tall. He's too pretty. He's muscular. His hands are too big. Blarg!

He was still staring beyond me, lost in his own thoughts, which gave me a precious moment to compose myself. I needed it.

This wasn't good. I still had two months in this man's class and he called on every student at least once a week. He might not ever recognize me, but crushes made me tongue-tied and stupid. If I were tongue-tied and stupid for this man, he'd squash me like an ant.

Plus—hello—I was standing in the same room as him, stage three naked, lest I forget.

"What's your name?" He still hadn't looked directly at me.

"Lavender," I answered breathlessly without thinking. Had his voice always been so deliciously deep?

"No. What's your real name?"

I shook my head, my mouth forming a tight smile as I glanced quickly at the camera in the corner, then busied myself with making his drink.

He followed my gaze, then whispered, "We're being watched?"

I nodded, my smile growing a smidge more sincere as I held out the glass of liquor I'd just poured. After a short moment of hesitation, he accepted the glass, his fingers brushing against mine. A shiver raced down my spine at the contact. I ignored it, stepping, turning, and strolling away toward the open rack of lingerie.

Going through the motions, I decided I'd put the garter ensemble—which consisted of a red-and-black boned bustier with garter straps and thigh-high silk stockings—over the bra and thong I was already wearing.

I'd just finished rolling up the second stocking when he said, "You don't have to do that."

Looking to him, I lifted a questioning eyebrow. He'd stayed by the bar, one hand in his pocket, the other holding his drink. His posture was relaxed as he took another swallow of scotch, but he'd yet to meet my gaze.

"Do what?"

"Don't you have a robe?"

I straightened. "Do you want to see a robe?"

"Wouldn't you be more comfortable? If you were less . . ." He scratched the back of his neck, his attention on the wall behind me.

"Less?"

"If you were covered?"

I blinked at him and answered before I could think better of my response. "No. Would you?"

"You wouldn't?" Once again, he was strolling toward me, this time his gaze was on his drink. "It doesn't bother you? Being objectified?"

"Think of me as a clothes hanger." That's mostly how I thought about it.

He snorted an inelegant laugh, like I'd caught him completely off guard, his features twisting with amusement and disbelief. His gaze danced to mine for a split second, and then away.

"My imagination isn't that good," he said to his scotch.

"Fine. Then a mannequin."

Dr. Hanover's eyes flickered quickly over my form and he appeared to stand straighter, the muscle at his jaw jumping as he ground out, "My imagination isn't that good either."

Sensing his discomfort, I reached for a red, silk kimono and slipped it over my shoulders. "If you'd like to see a robe, I'll wear a robe."

"Do you get paid if you put on the robe?"

"Yes."

"But you don't like the robe?" His inquisitive stare was pointed at my forehead.

"It's a lovely robe," I deflected smoothly, but then stumbled over the next part, "W-would you like to touch it?"

Gah and drat. I had to ask.

Every time we put on a new layer, we were supposed to ask the client if they wanted to touch the item. And that meant he could basically touch me anywhere as I was covered from neck to ankle in red silk kimono.

Dr. Hanover drew in a slow breath, his gaze coming to my body, moving lower and lingering this time, as though now that I was no longer naked, he'd given himself permission to actually look at me. His stare moved slowly, caressing a path to my neck, jaw, to my hair where it rested over one shoulder.

Suddenly, his frown returned, and this time he looked thoughtful. He blinked.

And then his eyes shot to mine, growing at once cold and hot, and dread unfurled like a slithery beast in my belly.

He recognized me.

Or rather, he realized he knew me from somewhere, but hadn't quite figured out who I was. Which meant I had exactly two seconds to do something drastic.

Instead—big surprise—I froze.

"Wait a second." Dr. Hanover drew closer, until less than two feet separated us. Peripherally, on autopilot, I realized I could smell his cologne. He smelled great and I chastised myself for noticing that he smelled great. Especially now. I needed to act, and instead I was sniffing him.

Do something other than smell him!

His eyes were currently flickering over me with urgency, jumping from my breast to my lips to my neck to my eyes. And when they finally settled, I saw that his irises were dark green-ish blue.

That slithery beast of mortification punched me in the gut as my professor whispered, "I know you."

CHAPTER 2

EMILY

Dr. Hanover stared at me, his eyebrows pulling low on his forehead. Then he raised one. Then he raised the other. Then they pulled low again.

At odd intervals, he took a breath as though about to make a declaration. Instead of speaking, he breathed out, the thread of a thought or shadow of a suspicion evading him.

All the while I watched, waited with bated breath—with a stone cold façade—for my professor to place me.

After a full minute, maybe less, maybe more, he shook his head. "I know you." The words were an accusation, but they were also uncertain.

Inwardly, a wave of tentative relief loosened my mind enough that I realized, for maybe the first time in my life, my propensity to freeze had saved me. Now that my brain was thawing, it was also spinning. I needed to do something. Soon. I needed to distract him. I guestimated we had less than ten minutes left in this session.

"You think so?" I countered quietly, hoping my expression was as disinterested as I sounded. On a reckless hunch, I took a step closer. The back of his knuckles—of the hand holding his scotch—came in light contact with the fabric of the robe over my stomach.

He stiffened, his chin lifting, but he didn't step away. "What are you doing?"

"The kimono is a blend of vucana and spider silk. Isn't it soft?" My voice was just above a whisper.

"I thought we weren't allowed to touch." He unbent his index and middle fingers from his glass, catching a fold of the kimono between his fingers while also lightly brushing them against my stomach. The movement was so natural, felt so instinctual, I doubted he realized what he was doing.

"You're allowed to touch the material of our lingerie, with your fingers, anywhere except at the breast or . . ." I couldn't finish, my chest and throat wouldn't cooperate. I wasn't breathing hard, but I was out of breath.

This was so ridiculous. I'd said these words hundreds of times to hundreds of clients.

Before I could sort out the source of my anomalous behavior, Victor removed his other hand from his pocket and trailed a light fingertip along the edge of the robe at my neck, down the V to my chest between my breasts, then back up to my shoulder.

His eyes followed the movement of his finger as though entranced. "Like this?"

I nodded. My lips parted, but I was still unable to speak, and certainly not able to think.

Victor's gaze moved to my mouth, sharpened as his gentle touch skimmed down the silk at the back of my arm, to my waist, then hip, sending a cascade of goose bumps over my skin beneath the robe.

"I can only touch the material of what you wear?" His gaze narrowed, but not with suspicion. More like curiosity, as though he were asking me to read back the rules of a game.

I nodded again.

"Can you touch me?" Victor brushed the backs of his knuckles along the outside of my leg, and then used his fingertips to raise the fabric upward, the cool silk caressing my skin, the hem of the kimono lifting to my knee. His progress stopped at the curve of my bottom.

I shook my head, biting my bottom lip to keep from making a sound that would only embarrass me. A shock of heat radiated from my abdomen outward; I locked my knees so I wouldn't sway toward him; I curled my hands into fists so I wouldn't touch him. The room, everything in it except the man in front of me and his touch, faded into a shadowy nothingness.

"Is that why—" he started softly, tilting his head to the side as his dark eyes moved between mine. "Is that why you didn't want to be covered? By the robe? Because, if you're covered, I can touch you?"

I could only swallow and stare in response.

I wasn't panicked and I wasn't exactly frozen, I was too hot to be frozen. In truth, I was on fire. Everywhere. Yet the effect was still the same.

He was right, I preferred stage three garments. Stage three meant customers couldn't touch anywhere except the bra strap over the shoulder or clasp at the back. Everything else was off-limits or bare skin (so, again off-limits).

Looking was just looking. So what if these rich people saw me naked?

But touching? Nope. I wasn't a fan of strangers touching me and I believed that made me 100 percent normal. Except right now, I didn't mind being touched at all.

"How ironic." The side of his mouth curved just barely and the light in his eyes felt oddly esteeming, as though he'd discovered something wonderful about me. "The more you wear, the more vulnerable you become."

"And the less a woman wears, the more powerful she becomes?"

I flinched, as though jolted awake from a dream, and turned my head toward the unexpected sound of Madame Purple's voice.

She stood in the center of the room, which meant she hadn't just entered. She'd been there for a while. One hand was on her hip and she was splitting her attention equally between us, smiling with her eyes but not with her lips.

"Dr. Hanover." She indicated with her chin toward the lingerie rack. "Did you see anything you like?"

I glanced to Victor and found him frowning at my boss like he was trying to make sense of her words. Or maybe he was trying to make sense of her sudden presence.

Abruptly, he released the fabric of the kimono and stiffened, taking a step back and blinking around the room as though suddenly remembering himself.

"I—sorry." He shook his head, looking dazed and maybe a little mortified. Then again, to me, "I'm sorry."

"Why are you sorry, Dr. Hanover?" Madame Purple strolled over to us, her mouth curving into a pretty smile. She stopped less than a foot from me and used the back of her hand to brush my long hair from my shoulder. She then trailed a finger down my arm and her grin widened when his eyes followed the movement. "Nothing you did was forbidden."

His eyes lifted to hers and he swallowed, the uneasiness in his gaze quickly giving way to repulsion. "Just because a thing is allowed"—his eyes flickered over me, all hint of their earlier esteem gone—"doesn't mean it should be done."

Oh.

Okay.

Well.

His words stung like rejection and smelled of pretention, a heady combination.

A new type of embarrassment—the really, really bad kind—clawed its way up my throat while waves of heat flooded my neck and cheeks.

I tore my eyes from his and lifted my chin, giving Madame Purple a tight smile. "Are we finished?"

She inspected me impassively for a quick moment, and then nodded. "Yes. Thank you, Lavender."

Holding the kimono closed at my neck, I side-stepped Professor Hanover and walked quickly to the dressing room. I thought I heard him make a strangled sound just as I hurried past, but I ignored it. I ignored him. I ignored everything.

I stomped into the dressing room, past the board of notices, past a few of my coworkers in various stages of undress, and by the time I'd made it to my own dressing area I was in a tizzy.

Because, I mean, how fucking dare he! The puritan prude. Wearing lingerie for a living meant that I should be ashamed of myself? What a dickwad. What a judgmental asshat.

He was the taint.

"Taint!" I pulled the kimono from my shoulders and threw it at my chair, forcefully tugging off the stockings next and chucking them at the pile of red silk.

"Whoa, wait. Emily." My coworker Helen jogged over from her spot, placing her hand over mine where I was tearing at the bra clasp. "Girl, this bra costs eight hundred dollars. And that's the spider silk kimono you just threw. That thing costs more than the down payment for my house. Calm down."

I growled. Then huffed. Then growled again, glancing up at the ceiling while I blinked back tears. Why the fuck did I feel like crying?

"I don't care."

"Okay, Honey Badger." She rubbed a circle on my bare back. "What happened?"

"Nothing."

"Nothing?"

"Nothing. Nothing at all. Not a damn thing. It's just, you know, a person I respected and admired looked at me like I revolted him—right after turning me on like a strand of Christmas lights—and then said something to make me feel like garbage. No big deal."

She huffed a short laugh. "What are you talking about?"

"Nothing," I ground out through clenched teeth. "Just ignore me."

"Right. Well—" Helen squeezed my shoulder, moving to my discarded stockings and kimono. "You don't want Purple to see this. Let me hang them up for you."

"It's just—" I shoved my fingers into my hair, digging them into my scalp. "Who the hell do these people think they are? Nobody held a gun to their head, to bring them here. If they find what we do to be so—"

Helen cleared her throat loudly, her eyes growing wide as they looked beyond me.

I straightened, the fine hairs on the back of my neck coming to attention just as I discerned the sound of high heels clicking on the linoleum floor.

"Crap," I sighed, closing my eyes. It had to be Madame Purple. Helen wouldn't have cut me off if it had been anyone else.

Our boss rarely entered the dressing stalls, typically only when she had big news to discuss. Or she needed to fire someone.

"Lavender."

I forced calm into my voice and pasted a smile over my mouth as I turned to face her. "Madame Purple."

Her gaze flickered over me, much like she'd done in my private showroom just a few moments ago. But this time she wore a frown instead of the smooth, impassive expression she put on for clients.

"Are you okay?"

"Yes." I nodded succinctly, forcing my smile wider. "And how are you?"

"I'm very well." She squinted at me just slightly, an almost imperceptible narrowing of the eyes. "In fact, I'm great."

"Good. That's good." I reached behind me, carefully unclasping the bra, and realizing I'd broken one of the cardinal rules. Models were never supposed to leave the showroom wearing merchandise. "I—uh—sorry about—"

"Don't let it happen again," she said, but she waved away my apology like it was unnecessary. "That's not why I'm here."

"Oh." I successfully unhooked the bra and covered my breasts with my forearm as best I could, handing the lacy item to my boss.

She accepted it, reaching for the T-shirt on my dressing table and tossing it to me. "Tell me, did your last client say or do anything I should know about? The camera didn't pick up what he said before I walked in."

I shook my head before she'd finished her question, but I also ground my teeth at the memory and the silly way I'd behaved. He'd touched me. And I liked it. I'd liked it a lot. And maybe I thought he'd liked it.

An image of him, of the revulsion in his gaze as he looked at me afterward, flashed through my mind.

Ah, jeez. So what? What the hell had I been thinking? This was work. This was my job. In the end he proved himself to be a taint and, in retrospect, I felt nothing but irritated with myself.

"No. He didn't do anything or say anything you should

know about. He didn't break the rules." I held my T-shirt to my chest and was just about to pull it on when a thought occurred to me. "Why? Did he say something about me? Because I didn't—"

"No. Not at all." Madame Purple's lips curved into a rare, genuine smile. "Actually, he said you were very 'efficient' at your job."

I didn't know how to feel about that revelation. My brain seemed to think it was insulting, but my body seemed to think it was delightful. Therefore, I said nothing and ignored them both.

"In fact," her grin grew and a light disbelieving laugh tumbled from her lips, "he's now a client."

Uh.

What?

"What?" I gripped the shirt tighter to my chest, her last statement essentially freezing me in place. "What did you just say?"

"He signed up. Paid the deposit, just now. He's a member." Madame Purple reached for the hanger Helen—who'd been off to the side, listening to our entire conversation—was holding with the kimono and the stockings. Giving me one last perfunctory smile, Madame Purple turned from us both and strolled toward the exit.

What? Why would he do that? What would make him do that? I couldn't think. Especially after his little snobby speech about—

"Oh yeah"—my boss paused just outside the door, interrupting my thoughts—"and he bought everything you wore, including the kimono." She gave me an approving head bob. "Great job today, Lavender. Keep up the good work."

CHAPTER 3

EMILY

My research methods class met every Monday and Wednesday evening, from 4:00 PM to 7:00 PM, in the chemistry building's lecture hall. The hall smelled vaguely of vinegar and baking soda. By all accounts, I should despise both smells. My mother gave me baking soda for indigestion rather than pharmaceuticals. She also used to make me drink a tablespoon of apple cider vinegar every morning before elementary school. She did this to torture me, but also because we didn't have any medical insurance.

As much as I hated my daily doses of acetic acid and intermittent servings of sodium bicarbonate, I found the aroma of both comforting, which was only one of the reasons I usually looked forward to my research methods class.

The others, as I've mentioned, were Dr. Hanover's hilariously cutting sass and the subject matter. There are few subjects more relevant to how society makes choices—and therefore lives their lives—than research methods.

But before I geek out and make an impassioned case for

understanding confidence intervals and sample bias, I need to admit that on this particular day I was emphatically *not* looking forward to my research methods class.

I'd read the two chapters we'd be reviewing many times. I'd taken notes. I'd done all the sample problems plus several others online, and yet I felt completely unprepared . . . to see Dr. Hanover.

What if he recognizes me?

Imaginary scenarios played over and over in my head, ridiculous ones where he'd stop me in the middle of answering a question about experimental design, point, and yell, "It's you! Stage three naked girl! HUZZAH!"

Why I decided he would yell *huzzah* was a bit of a mystery. I'd never heard him say the word, but in my imaginings it was what he'd say. Or maybe *EUREKA!* But not *DIOS MIO!* like those fellas would do in my mother's Spanish soaps. My mother was not Spanish, but she'd taken the language in high school and loved Spanish soaps.

I paused just outside of the lecture hall, rubbing my forehead beneath my baseball hat and grimacing.

What was I even talking about?

That's right, *acetic acid and Dr. Hanover.*

"Excuse me."

I glanced up, meeting the kind brown eyes of another student who motioned to the door, looking at me like, *Are you going in or what?*

"Sorry, yes, sorry." I grabbed the handle and swung open the door, waving my hand for the student to go in front of me.

He gave me a perplexed little smile, but eventually walked past, entering the lecture hall. He was a big, tall guy, so on the spur of the moment, I decided to walk behind him, hoping to cloak my entrance into the room. You know, just in case my dear professor was staring at the door, inspecting the gait of every female student as they entered.

"Everything will be fine," I muttered to myself, peeking around the big guy to see if Dr. Hanover was already at the front of the room.

He was. Flanked by his two TAs. Standing before the long table at the front. Head bowed over a laptop. Hair flat. Baggy and shapeless brown nerd shirt, dad jeans, and pocket protector in place.

I exhaled slowly, my nerves calming, because in my weirdo imaginings not only did Dr. Hanover shout *HUZZAH!* he was also wearing his fancy clothes and looking ten kinds of objectively man-hot.

He did not look hot today. He looked like a less severe version of Dwight Schrute, just with nicer lips and a more defined jawline, and larger eyes and thicker hair.

Okay, he still looked hot. It's like that old saying, "What has been seen can never be unseen." Pandora's box had been opened and inside was a hot version of Dr. Hanover. But he was still an asshole and, therefore, I was in no danger of crushing on the man. I had a type and that type was limited to small of stature sweet guys, shy guys, and guys with so much empathy, they were often paralyzed by it.

I de-peeked, hiding myself more fully behind the tall student, and bided my time until we arrived at my usual row. Breaking away, I hurriedly slipped past the three spots before mine and sat, reached into my bag, pulled out my laptop, and hid myself behind it.

I made it.

Good. Good and fine and good.

Seconds became minutes and I pulled up my notes, my body relaxing, and I chuckled at myself. If he didn't recognize me up close at the Pinkery, the chances of him recognizing me here—one of a hundred students, dressed in baggy cargo pants, baseball hat, and sweatshirt—were zero.

. . . Well, 3%, with a 3% margin of error, a 97% confidence interval, and a 2.17 z level.

"We're talking about qualitative data today."

I flinched, a slight quake in my belly at the sound of Dr. Hanover's deep voice slicing through the hum of chatter in the lecture hall. Just like that, the room fell silent and he had everyone's attention.

"By a show of hands, who among you read and understood the difference between qualitative data and quantitative data?"

Half of the class lifted an arm and I sensed his gaze sweep over me in a detached cataloging of the room. It was always best to answer this question honestly, because the next thing he did was call on someone with their hand raised and ask she or he to explain the concept in question.

"Mr. Jeru. Explain the difference to me in three sentences or less."

"Uh." The student's voice cracked and he cleared his throat, the sound abnormally loud, echoing around the large room. "Quantitative data is, like, numbers? And qualitative is feelings."

Dr. Hanover's brow furrowed, a sure sign that he disliked the answer given. "Ms. Jesuine, same question."

"Quantitative data can be measured, and qualitative data is about quality."

I peeked around my laptop screen and saw Dr. Hanover's head was now bent over the class roster. Which was why it made sense when the next name he called also began with a J.

"Mr. Jibbes, same question."

"I-uh-didn't understand qualitative data."

Without looking up, Dr. Hanover asked, "Did you read the chapter?"

He hesitated and I winced, because hesitation with Professor Hanover was always a mistake.

Now comes the sass.

"Did you forget whether you read the chapter? Or did you forget how to read?"

The student chuckled, it sounded nervous, but said nothing.

Our professor glanced up from the roster and stared impassively at the student, and it struck me that Dr. Hanover knew exactly where to look for Mr. Jibbes. "Are you feeling okay? Do you require medical attention? Are you suffering from a dissociative fugue? Are you having a stroke?"

"No, sir."

"Then why are you wasting my time?"

"I didn't read the chapter," Jibbes finally admitted, so low I could barely hear him.

Dr. Hanover stared at the student, his expression unreadable, and tension became a greasy kind of thickness, coating the room.

After a long—very, very long—moment, where I began to feel suffocated with anxiety on behalf of my fellow student, Dr. Hanover sighed.

He then turned his attention to the entire room. "From now on, if you didn't read the chapter, don't come to class."

"But—" Jesuine started, and then stopped herself.

It was too late. Her outburst had drawn his attention.

"Ms. Jesuine, you have something to say. Say it."

From where I was sitting, I watched as her hands tightened on a notebook she'd placed on the table in front of her. "It's just, class participation counts for ten percent of our grade. If we're not here more than three times, then we lose ten percent."

"Class *participation*, Ms. Jesuine. If you don't read the

materials, you can't participate," Dr. Hanover responded, his voice deadpan, his left eyebrow slightly raised.

"But what if we miss something important in the lecture not covered in the book?"

I winced on her behalf, because she was paddling upstream with no boat, or paddle, or stream, or legs, or arms.

"Ms. Jesuine," he began, his tone as dry as salt, and just as salty, "persistence is only admirable when it isn't based in ignorance, otherwise it's called whining."

Her back straightened, but she said no more.

His gaze came up and again he addressed the entire class, "Research design and analysis require conversation and dialogue, and often that dialogue is contentious. Do you think great science occurs in a vacuum? With politeness? With pleases and thank yous? Do you think you are allowed to hold ideas and beliefs without ever having them openly challenged? No." Dr. Hanover hit his palm against the table. "No. Great science—like all great things—begins with doubt, with questioning, with a fundamental abhorrence for the status quo. If you do not care to inform yourself for the sake of your grade, then at least do so for the sake of your mind. And if you do not care about your mind, then you are not invited to attend my lecture."

I had to swallow here, and remind myself that I was in class, because my mouth was suddenly dry, and my heart was fluttering.

Goodness.

I'd never gotten hot before from an impassioned speech about the nature of science and its debate. Quite suddenly, my sweater was entirely too warm. Turning his attention back to the roster, he seemed to scan it. The room was so quiet, you could've heard a mouse fart.

Eventually, again without looking up, he said, "Ms.

Limones, please explain the difference between qualitative and quantitative data."

I breathed a silent sigh of relief because Ms. Limones always answered correctly. Additionally, she was succinct, intelligent, and had a pleasing voice that always seemed to put Dr. Hanover in a better mood, like she was proof of intelligent life on planet earth. Sitting up and craning my neck, I turned to where she usually sat—on the far end of the third row— and had a shock.

Ms. Limones was absent.

A short period of silence followed before Dr. Hanover lifted his head and glanced around the lecture hall, as though searching for his star student. This, also, struck me. He knew where Mr. Jibbes sat—who never knew the answer—but had no idea where Ms. Limones's seat was located.

Interesting indeed.

Someone cleared their throat, drawing his attention to the third row.

"Sorry, Dr. Hanover. Kara is sick," came a female voice, scratchy with nerves.

He blinked at the student, as though he couldn't understand why she was speaking, before finally asking, "Who is Kara?"

A beat, and then the same student responded, "Kara Limones." When he continued to give her a blank stare, she added, "Ms. Limones is Kara."

He nodded faintly, the intensity of his frown increasing. "I don't suppose you could call her on the phone, put her on speaker, and have her answer the question?"

His suggestion elicited a sparse sprinkling of laughter until people realized he was serious.

The student who had spoken shook her head. "Uh, she has laryngitis."

"I see." Dr. Hanover sighed sadly, returned his gaze to the class roster, and my stomach dropped.

My throat tightened.

I could only stare in horror.

I'm the backup.

When Hanover was desperate for an answer in order to move his lecture along, it was Ms. Limones first, Von second (that's me), Qin third, and Silver fourth.

"Von," he said, right on schedule. Mercifully, he didn't look up, but he did demand, "Answer."

Gripping the baggy fabric of my pants, I opened my mouth to respond, took a breath, and . . . forgot the freaking question.

Dosh garnit!

Once more, Dr. Hanover looked up, searching the hall. "Don't tell me Ms. Von also has laryngitis."

"No," I croaked immediately, not wanting to hesitate while also sliding lower in my seat. "I'm here."

Aahhh! What the hell are we talking about? Why won't my brain work?

I felt his gaze swing up to the back of my laptop as most gazes in the hall followed suit. "Qualitative and quantitative. Answer."

Qualitative and quantitative data, that's right!

On a burst of breath, I said, "Quantitative data provides information about quantities, data that can be directly counted and measured. Qualitative data provides information about qualities, or data that can't be measured."

He paused for a moment, and I sensed his focus intensify. "Ms. Von . . ."

I waited, holding my breath. I waited for a long time. I waited so long, a new, whispery hum rose in the lecture hall and my pulse began thrumming under my tongue.

But then he said, "Give me an example for each." And his tone held a distracted edge.

"Um," I gripped my pants tighter, the thick, stiff fabric bunching beneath my hands as I searched my brain for an appropriate example, settling without thinking on the first one that popped to mind. "An example of quantitative data might be the number of threads in a garment, whereas an example of qualitative data might be the—uh . . . the uh . . ." *Oh God. Don't say it.*

"The what?"

Dammit!

"Ms. Von?"

"The soft—softness of the garment," I finished, my cheeks aflame, and my eyes closed.

Softness of the garment?

What.

The.

Hell.

Was.

I.

Thinking.

?

The last thing I should've been discussing with Dr. Victor Hanover in the middle of class was the freaking softness of freaking garments! I wanted to hide under the desk, and I might have. I might have slithered from my seat and curled into a ball if I hadn't—once again—been so entirely frozen.

CHAPTER 4

EMILY

You know that feeling? Like you're falling but you're holding perfectly still? I had that feeling. Plus a few other feelings. Plus, an inability to open my eyes. Plus, lockjaw.

Seconds ticked by. Or maybe they didn't. I couldn't be sure. All I knew in that moment was I would have given my 3000-piece Millennium Falcon Lego set to disappear from the lecture hall and reappear in my apartment. My earlier worry that I'd be recognized, the one I'd successfully batted away and decided was virtually impossible, suddenly felt not only possible, but probable thanks in huge part to my defunct brain.

Why, Em, why? Why was the only freaking example I could think of for qualitative data garment softness? I might as well have jumped from my seat, stripped, and asked him if he'd like to touch my granny panties.

Great job, Emily. Real gold star work.

The earlier hum caused by my previous stalling sustained. It became a whispering, droning backdrop to the chant in my head, *Please don't recognize me, please don't recognize me, please don't—*

"The softness of the garment?" Professor Hanover's halting, distracted question cut through my mind-chant, making me scrunch my eyes. "That is—uh, correct," he finally said, obvious confusion in his voice.

The droning buzz tapered, the sound of Hanover clearing his throat—not once, but twice—bringing silence to the lecture hall. I lifted my eyelids scant millimeters and peeked around my laptop to the front of the room, unable to help myself. There, Dr. Hanover held his fist to his mouth, a stern wrinkle between his eyebrows, his attention affixed to some point on the table, his other hand on his hip as he held perfectly still.

Abruptly, he lifted the hand on his hip, motioning to the TA at his right. "Take over. I'll be right back."

Stiffening on instinct, and half expecting Hanover to march up to my seat and drag me out of the hall, I was stunned as he instead marched past his TA and out the door at the front of the room. I wasn't the only one surprised by his abrupt departure. TA Kris also appeared to be astonished, as did the entire class. Neither of the TA's had taken over a lecture before.

Eventually, Kris recovered and stood, her stool scraping against the floor. She fidgeted while sauntering to where Dr. Hanover had been peering at the roster and pushed her glasses higher on her nose.

"Okay. Well. Let's break down a few more examples of quantitative data." Kris lifted her chin toward me. "Building on Emily's description, can anyone else give an example?"

My eyes darted between Kris and the doorway where Dr. Hanover had disappeared while I demanded that my brain calm the heck down. I needed to think. I needed to consider my next move carefully. Because, right now? My thundering pulse urged me to run, to gather my things and leave as quietly as possible. I needed space, time to ponder away from the threat of my professor's imminent reappearance.

Over the weekend, while endeavoring to work out a basic contingency plan for dealing with Hanover, I'd briefly considered not coming to class today. That idea was quickly dismissed. Perfect attendance meant a ten-point curve on the final. I've never met an extra credit assignment I didn't like.

I therefore convinced myself all would be well, that he'd never recognize me, as long as I was quiet and hid under my hat and baggy clothes. The worst-case scenario was pushed from my mind.

But now, I was forced to confront the worst-case scenario: what would I do and what would I say if Dr. Hanover recognized me?

Chewing on my bottom lip, splitting my attention between the TA and the door, I held an imaginary conversation in my head with Victor, one I probably should've entertained prior to now.

"You're Lavender. Don't try to deny it!" he'd say, probably with a judgy sneer.

I would . . . I would nod, cross my arms, and shrug. I'd play it off, try not to incinerate with embarrassment, act like it was no big deal.

Maybe I'd say, "So?"

Saying "so" worked well in third grade, seventh grade, and as recently as my senior year of high school, no reason it shouldn't work now.

"So?!" he'd ask, overcome with emotion, whipping off his glasses and reaching for me. He'd pull me to his strong chest and peer down at me, a passion-induced fever in his wickedly intelligent eyes as he confessed, "So, I can't look at you without wanting to—"

Yikes!

I stopped the imaginary conversation here and backed up, because this make-believe scenario was quickly spinning itself into a porno. *And now I'm hot again.*

Inhaling through my nose and exhaling slowly, I tried again.

"So?" he'd ask, irritated. "So, I have no respect for a woman who takes her clothes off for a living and I refuse—"

Again, I put the make-believe (but now super self-righteous instead of sexy) Dr. Hanover on pause, because this response wasn't right either. He would never say that because it was nonsensical. A professor can't refuse to teach a student because of that student's job. In fact, what could he do?

Nothing.

I'd been attracted to him and he'd touched me while I was at work, modeling lingerie. He'd seen me stage three naked. I was his student. What was the big deal? My job didn't impact my ability to be a college student or his ability to be a professor. It's not like I cared what he thought of me—as me, Emily Von, or as my pseudonym Lavender—*why am I making this a big deal?*

Taking another deep breath, I held it in my lungs, gathering all the tightness and exhaling my weirdo fears. My hands relaxed on my cargo pants and I flexed my fingers, residual jitters fading as I evened my breathing.

No big deal, it's no big deal, I repeated until I believed it. Once I almost did, I turned my attention back to TA Kris, who was now sketching a table on the touchscreen computer that fed into the projector, a pro/con list for qualitative versus quantitative data.

Reading the list, I realized TA Kris was digging deeper into the subject than was covered in the textbook, which meant I should've been taking notes.

Determined to ignore the door where Victor had disappeared, I gave my attention to the projection board and my own laptop screen. I copied Kris's list while batting away a subtle nagging in my brain. I made notations where subject matter overlapped with the book, and where my responses to practice questions could be improved. I found the discussion interesting.

And yet, the nagging persisted, now accompanied by a prickling sensation on the back of my neck. A shiver raced down my spine and I clenched my teeth, leaning forward to itch the offending spot between my shoulder blades.

I was being watched.

Just like I knew when and where men were looking while I modeled, I knew when I was the subject of someone's pointed scrutiny while in public.

Narrowing my eyes, I stared determinedly at the projection board, forbidding myself from searching for the person inspecting me even as TA Kris's voice turned into Charlie Brown-esque trombone sounds. I tried to swallow. I couldn't. The prickling sensation persisted.

Against my will, my eyes cut to the door at the front of the room and promptly collided with those of Victor Hanover. I felt the impact to my bones, jar my teeth, send the air from my lungs as a shock of awareness sliced through me and set my heart racing. He stood inside the doorframe, leaning against it, hands in his pockets, gaze unflinching.

He'd been the one watching me.

And he knew.

He knew who I was.

Fortunately or unfortunately, Victor was too far away for me to read anything more in his expression, but maybe that was a good thing. For now.

Mind once more in chaos, I steadied myself, pulled my gaze from his, and stared forward unseeingly while unable to absorb the rest of the lecture. I heard nothing, partially because I continued to feel Victor's gaze drill into my profile. But also because I was giving him, the entire matter between us, the full force of my pragmatism.

Pragmatism, I'd discovered, is an efficient inoculation against chaotic feelings. If one persists in asking oneself, "Why does it matter?" the answer always eventually becomes, "It doesn't."

Now I know what you're thinking. *Nihilism, Emily? Really?*

Yes. Nihilism. *Because last week your extremely intelligent professor who is not at all your type saw you nearly naked, and his touch was delicious, and he was ridiculously sexy, and he made you hot. And then about a half hour ago he flipped your lady switch again with an impassioned speech about statistics* of all things! As such, the only coping strategy left to me was nihilism.

Please don't recognize me, had become, *It's no big deal,* which had morphed into, *Nothing matters.* I'd never traveled such a great distance in such a short time while sitting in one place. Thus is the power of mortification avoidance.

Even though I couldn't pay attention to the lecture, I sensed my classmates' restlessness several minutes later. Movement around me, people pulling out their phones and checking the screens, one or two old-school types glancing at the watches on their wrists was a sure sign that class was over.

TA Kris soon caught the hint and glanced at the clock on the laptop, leaning away from the screen and closing it. "That's it for today. Wednesday's reading assignment is in the syllabus and there will be a test next week. Don't forget. . ."

The rest of her words were lost in the ruckus of over a hundred students packing up their belongings and gossiping about the strange events of today's lecture. Snippets of conversation bounced off my consciousness, like rain against a waterproof jacket, or subtlety and nuance against the comprehension abilities of a toddler.

Although aware of the discussions, none of my attention could be spared. I was too busy debating my options. Stay or go? Put off the inevitable, or tear off the band-aid? Shutting down my computer, I slowly closed the laptop, unhurriedly tucked it into my bag, and picked old receipts out of the front pocket of my backpack, uncertain how to proceed.

It doesn't matter, nihilism told me, *Now, later, who cares? Nothing matters.*

But it did matter, and nihilism knew it. If Victor recognized me, and I was certain that he did, discovering his real reaction, his true feelings, was infinitely better than more imaginary conversations which dissolved into either sexytimes or Scarlet-Letter level condemnation.

Although, sexytimes—

No! I should not indulge in imaginary sexytimes with my professor and—technically—my client. No. No. No.

No.

Better to save it for later.

Since I usually left along with my classmates, I was obliquely surprised by how quickly the lecture hall cleared. Coming to my feet, the door in the back closed with a *slam*. It reverberated through the large space, an echoey underline to the fact that Victor and I were now completely alone.

Stealing a glance at him, I saw that he was at the front of the room again, gathering the roster and several other papers from the table, no longer looking at me.

I hesitated. But I was only given a short few moments to second-guess myself before he said, "Please, if you don't mind, come down to the front of the room."

Nodding even though he wasn't looking at me, I carried my backpack down the stairs, allowing myself to watch him as he collected materials. He peeked at me twice, just fleeting glances, and his movements seemed agitated.

"Ms. Von," he said as soon as my foot touched the bottom

stair. He'd also stopped moving, but I got the sense that he was forcing himself to hold still. "Your answer during class today was exactly correct. Nicely done."

I stared at him, uncertain what to say, or how to respond. As far as I knew, this was the first time he'd ever issued a blatant compliment to a student in his class. Twisting the strap of my bag, I let it drop to my feet while I studied him and searched for a painless way to begin this conversation.

I must've taken too long to speak, because Victor sighed, blinked, and lifted his eyes.

"Your first name is not Lavender," he said gently, an inscrutable amalgamation of dichotomous expressions on his face. Victor's eyes were soft and searching, while his lips and jaw were firm and unhappy.

He . . . was confusing. He was confusing me.

So I cleared my throat, breathing in for courage, and said, "You recognize me."

"Yes. You've . . . been on my mind." Victor's gaze flickered over me in a way that felt like a compulsion, like his eyeballs were working toward their own agenda, causing his brain to lodge a formal protest. The impression was punctuated further when he tore his attention away, his jaw ticking, and covered his eyes with his hand while simultaneously rubbing his forehead.

He didn't seem outraged or self-righteous, like my worst-case scenario version of him. He seemed frustrated, seasoned with a heavy dash of remorse and regret.

Victor's chest expanded as he inhaled and he dropped his hand, giving me a tight smile, his gaze now markedly reserved. "Anyway. Obviously, we need to discuss how you'd like to proceed."

"Proceed?" My lungs felt weird, tight as I watched him and his confusingness. I was also experiencing something that felt like regret.

"Yes," he said, his tone businesslike with a touch of compassion and patience, "as your professor, it is my responsibility to provide a learning environment where you feel safe and comfortable. Given our unfortunate interaction this past weekend—"

"Unfortunate interaction?" My mouth dropped open and the question tumbled forth before I could catch it.

Unfortunate interaction? What the hell?

"—you must be consulted on next steps. I want you to know and believe that I respect you as my student, I fully comprehend the disparity in power between us, and I'm committed to—"

"Stop. Just, stop," I cut in, stepping forward and waving my hands around. "God, just stop speaking."

Victor's eyebrows shot up, but his mouth snapped shut. He peered at me, wide-eyed, waiting for me to speak.

I found I needed to take several calming breaths before I could. Even so, irritation pumped through my veins such that my words were blurted thoughts instead of carefully crafted sentiments. "It's like, you're determined to make me a victim. I don't feel victimized, okay?"

He blinked, straightening, shoving his hands in his pockets. "Ms. Von, I apologize. My intention was not to imply that you have been victimized. However, the facts being what they are, an inappropriate situation has occurred between a student," he lifted his chin toward me, "and a professor," he pulled his hand from his pocket and pressed it against his chest. "It cannot be ignored. It must be discussed with the appropriate levels of administration and a plan of action—for how to mitigate any discomfort or feelings of distress, or worry—"

"Why are you making this such a big deal?" I cut him off again.

"Because it is a big deal." He said this like it was obvious.

"It's not." I shook my head, my words emphatic. "It's not a big deal to me. It's my *job.* It's what I do for a living. I couldn't care less that you've seen me stage three naked, or that you touched me. So what? Lots of men have seen me naked and touched my body. At this point, I should probably just walk around naked." I huffed a laugh, shrugging.

But Victor flinched, looking startled by my words and maybe even a little . . . hurt? Before I could be certain, he quickly regained his composure and his face cleared.

"Be that as it may," he began softly, then swallowed, his gaze moving to some point over my head, growing stony. "Procedures exist to protect students. I've already alerted my, uh, department chair. As I understand it, a liaison from administration will be in contact with you about next steps."

"What? When?" I was trying to keep up while also attempting to make sense of his body language. Did he feel guilty? About what happened? It wasn't his fault, he had no idea who I was. "You didn't have to do that. I'm not upset with you, not at all. And I don't feel uncomfortable here, in class, or think of you differently. Like I said, it was—"

"No big deal," he ground out, his voice rough with some emotion I couldn't place, his heated glare slicing to mine and then away as he added on a rush, "Yes. I heard you the first time, Ms. Von. Even so, you can expect their call. Good day."

"But—" I started and never finished.

Victor—*Dr. Hanover*—had already turned and left.

An email arrived from Dr. Hanover just after 11:00 PM Monday night after class, the subject line read: *Documentation.* A confused pang made my jaw tight as I opened it and read,

. . .

Dr. Ford,

Please find attached documentation regarding the issue we discussed earlier today. I've cc'd the student. Please don't hesitate to contact me with any questions or concerns.

-VH

Dr. Ford was the Dean of the College of Arts and Sciences, and she was the only person included on the email other than me. Rubbing the spot where anxiety had settled hard and heavy in my chest, I double-clicked on the icon of the paperclip and opened the Word document Dr. Hanover had attached. And then I read. And then I laughed. Not a laugh of amusement, a laugh of mystified disbelief.

He'd "documented" all of our interactions. All of them. All. And they were all numbered. From the first day of class, to the short interlude at the Pinkery, to our brief conversation this afternoon. Where he couldn't recall details—like, whether or not I'd been present in class, or whether or not I'd participated—he'd attached attendance sheets as appendixes.

The section on the Pinkery was the longest and read like a police report, free of feeling or bias or anything that would give me insight into what or how he'd been feeling. It was sterile in a way that left me feeling dirty.

Stupid Dr. Hanover. *No one puts Lavender in a corner!*

Oh jeez. *Get a grip, Emily.* Now I was thinking about my pseudonym in the third person and as a character from *Dirty Dancing*. The real questions was, did that make Dr. Hanover Patrick Swayze?

For a half second, I indulged in a flash of an imagining, Dr. Hanover taking a watermelon from my arms and then hooking my leg over his hip. Dipping me, his eyes lazily working their way over my body . . .

Yeah. That's hot.

Crap! Focus. Focus, focus, focus!

Shaking myself from the fantasy, I forced myself to reread the last paragraph of his hackneyed "documentation." Though the section on our discussion earlier in the day described word-for-word what was said, it was also seriously short on the details I actually wanted to know, like *precisely* when had Victor realized it was me, and *exactly* why was he pushing so hard for administration to get involved.

The lack of detail didn't keep me from reading it over and over (of course), obsessing about word choice and searching for some inadvertent insight into this confounding puzzle of a man. But the more times I read it, the more frustrated I became. Eventually, I shut my laptop, stood, and paced the room, wishing I had someone I could discuss this cluster-flock with.

But who could I call?

My mother was the only person in my life who knew where I worked, what I did to pay the bills. She didn't care. But I already knew what she would say about the situation, I could almost hear her voice in my head, *"Why are you letting this get you all worked up?"*

It was a question to which I wouldn't know how to respond, so I turned it over and over in my brain and made a list of potential answers.

Answer #1 I don't want anyone at the university to know what I do for a living. Obviously, yes. This was true. Not even my good friend—my *best* friend—Anna Harris knew where I worked. I'd lied to her years ago, claiming I had a sweet job at the post office sorting mail, which was how I stayed in such good shape.

Irritatingly, my friend would have been the perfect person to talk to about this situation. Anna had gone through something not-quite-similar over the summer when she and her super-hot Russian literature professor had fallen for each other. *Hard.*

Our two situations weren't all that comparable, except for the taciturn professor plus inconvenient one-sided attraction (which didn't turn out to be the case in her situation, but still), plus mountains of contradictory feelings. Regardless, I couldn't talk to her about it without admitting everything, and I wasn't ready to do that.

So, back to answer #1 and discovering the source of my angst. As I debated with myself further, answer #1 didn't quite fit. It felt incomplete.

Answer #2 I feel like people won't take me seriously if they find out what I do for a living and getting internships or recommendations from staff will be impossible. Again, yes. Obviously. But answer #2 related to answer #1, and neither explained the restlessness I felt when I thought of Victor's antiseptic retelling of events between us.

But then a little voice in my head whispered, *Answer #3 Based on what you just read, you don't believe* Dr. Hanover *takes you seriously anymore.*

"Ugh." I rubbed the spot in my chest again and stopped pacing, a stab of unhappiness flaring in my chest. "Crap," I said to the empty apartment, because answer #3 was the clear winner.

CHAPTER 5

VICTOR

Humans are bizarre creatures. Myself included.

Frustratingly, the "how" we are each bizarre, the details of our individual peculiarities, makes coexistence for some humans incredibly difficult. Myself included.

I care about humanity—deeply, passionately—but I care about very few humans. I don't like talking to people I don't know (and the majority of people I do know). I avoid new environments and situations at all costs. If I cannot avoid them, I research extensively prior to the scheduled engagement so that I may appear completely at ease and familiar with my surroundings.

For example, before I go to a new restaurant, I find the menu online and decide what I want to order, I figure out where the bathroom is either by calling or scrolling through interior pictures of the restaurant posted online, I check out the aerial-view map of the building and its surrounding areas on Google to ascertain the parking situation.

In short, I make a plan. I follow the plan. I do not deviate from the plan. I do not ask for help or speak to anyone unnecessarily. If I'm speaking to you, it's because doing so could not be avoided. And believe me, if we're speaking, I've systematically ruled out every other option.

But this is not wholly for my comfort. Honestly, this habitual avoidance of humans is for your comfort.

Being fat makes other people uncomfortable. Not all people, but enough. I know the truth of this intimately as I've been a fat human my entire life, except: a) as a baby and b) prior to just this last year. Ironically, I was not a chubby baby. As an infant, I was diagnosed with failure to thrive. I theorize that my mother overcompensated in my youth. As an only child, she constantly fussed over me and my eating habits, worried I wasn't "getting enough."

By my adolescence, I embraced my singular interests and curiosities—mechanics and aviation, statistics, ancient civilizations, Greek and Roman philosophy, economics, the structure of governance—and I'd eschewed the banal—to me—interests of most other children my age, like all facets of sports except sports statistics.

Perhaps it was the lack of social pressure to conform due to my marked disinterest in most other kids my age, and their opinions/passions, but I was (resignedly) morbidly obese by twelve. By twenty, I was over three hundred pounds, by twenty-five I was three hundred and fifty. I didn't have any endocrine diseases or other disorders, my genetics were just fine, both of which can oftentimes be the culprit of excess weight gain.

I just really, really liked food, because food—unlike most humans I'd encountered—is fucking awesome.

Food never judges. Food is not made uncomfortable by my existence. Food does not whisper about me or make jokes about how I look. Food is necessary for survival, it is nourishing, it is comforting, it is inherently good. Food can be surprising, interesting, thought provoking in a way that humans seldom are. And aside from the rare case of food poisoning, food always, *always* makes me feel good.

Until it doesn't.

But I digress.

Presently, I glanced up, scanning the elliptical machines on the second level. Again. Finding them empty, my eyes darted to Andy, an old acquaintance turned friend, a colleague at the airfield, and—more recently—my weightlifting buddy in the mornings. He'd caught me searching the second level. This was not the first time he caught me over the last six months. But usually I only looked for her once a week or so, not compulsively. Not like today.

He smirked. "You keep looking." His attention lifted to the ellipticals. "There's no one up there yet."

I shrugged, lying on the horizontal black, padded bench and gripping the bar while he spotted me. *Bench press.* Not my favorite, but one I didn't particularly mind. At least it wasn't a leg day.

Andy grinned down at me, and then made a show of glancing up at the ellipticals again. "Is it that smokin' redhead who keeps hitting on you?"

Without meaning to, I made a face. He was teasing me. He knew I had no interest in the redhead. I didn't know the redhead, I didn't want to know the redhead, and she'd never looked at me until I'd become slim and toned. Andy knew who I was looking for.

Well, he didn't know *who* she was, but he knew I'd been distracted by the kind brunette who used the second elliptical from the left at the same time we worked out on the weight floor most mornings—except Thursdays. She was never here on Thursdays.

Interestingly—and for the record, I found it both interesting and mortifying—prior to the events of yesterday's class, Emily Von was three distinct people in my mind: First, she was the nameless but exceptionally kind brunette at the campus gym. Second, she was Emily Von, a brilliant and poised student in my Monday/Wednesday research methods lecture this fall. Third, she was Lavender, a lingerie model I'd met just last Friday at the Pinkery, my father's favorite place to waste time.

Even in retrospect, even knowing what I knew now—that the kind brunette at the gym and Emily Von were the same person—I was not at all surprised by my failure to make the connection until Lavender caught my attention.

I'd seen the kind brunette many times over the last two years, but I'd never spoken to her more than a passing "hi," and always because she'd greeted me first (when she used to greet me). During my initial six months working out, she'd made eye contact and smiled. This was significant. When I was heavy, no one else at the gym had made eye contact and no one else had ever smiled. A few people laughed. A few people took photos of me working out, although they typically endeavored to feign secrecy when doing so.

It was the photos that ultimately made me switch to a personal trainer and private workout sessions for a year. Eighteen or so months ago, some anonymous person left a printout under my office door. It was me as a meme—about fat people using the gym, calling me cookie monster, or referencing that I ate other people in the showers, or some such nonsense—therefore, the decision was made.

I didn't particularly care about being photographed. As an adult, jokes and jibes about my weight no longer fazed me, I'd come to expect them, they were an accepted part of my human existence.

But I didn't like making other people uncomfortable. Best

to avoid working out in public until my appearance inspired less attention. I didn't wish to be a distraction.

Perhaps that's why the kind brunette who'd made eye contact and smiled two years ago had made such an impact. My size hadn't appeared to be an issue for her. She seemed genuinely comfortable around me and went out of her way to be kind, make conversation, and that had been significant only because it was so rare.

The stunning irony, however, was that when I returned—one hundred and thirty pounds lighter at the time—no one recognized me. The women who'd sent me distasteful glances months ago now asked for my number. The men who'd snapped surreptitious photos and laughed at the fat man using the treadmill months ago now asked me to spot them on the weight machines. Everyone who'd sneered now made eye contact and smiled, *except* the kind brunette I now knew was named Emily Von.

To her, when I returned to my early morning workouts, I'd become invisible. She still smiled and greeted anyone who had gray hair, or anyone heavier than average, or the pregnant woman who also used the elliptical. But not me. I was just another young fit guy in an ocean of young fit guys.

So, yes. I'd noticed the kind brunette. Only because she was an outlier.

"Ha! Okay, not the redhead. It's the brunette again. The nice one who always smiles at everyone but guys like us." Andy didn't sound bitter about "the brunette's" disinterest, and he shouldn't. Unlike when we were the two "fat kids" growing up, nowadays he received plenty of positive attention.

Clearing my expression, I focused on the task at hand and glared unseeingly at the high ceiling. Once my set was finished, and as soon as Andy and I switched places, I looked to the muted TV over the weightlifting area. I checked the time in the bottom right corner of CNN's scrolling news bar. It was almost 5:45 AM.

Emily was late.

It's not that I tracked her schedule. I didn't, not consciously. But since I'd come to the same gym at the same time on and off for over two years, I now recognized the faces of all the regulars.

I glanced up at the ellipticals again while Andy stood, taking the brief window while his back was turned to search the upper level for the fifth time in fifteen minutes. I saw her immediately. She'd just arrived. She was pressing the buttons of the machine, frowning at the console. She looked tired—probably my fault due to the lengthy email I'd sent last night—and her long brown hair was in a ponytail. She was biting her bottom lip. Today she wore dark-colored yoga pants and a white tank top.

I looked away. A hot, uncomfortable thickness filled my chest cavity, like I'd been shocked with a small electrical current. I tried to ignore it. I took a deep breath. It persisted.

"Hey. Your girlfriend is finally here." Andy hit me on the shoulder in that way men do: oddly rough for the situation, yet completely normal and accepted for male interaction while working out or playing sports.

I glanced at him distractedly, feigning ignorance. Feigning ignorance was a reflex, a skill honed over two decades of overhearing people whisper about my body in disparaging terms. As I've stated, fat people's existence tends to make other people—again, not all people—mildly uncomfortable. However, if a fat person also has good hearing, it seems to make them indignant as well.

"Come on, Victor. What's going on?" Andy frowned at me. "You're not talking."

I lifted an eyebrow at that.

He rolled his eyes. "Right. I mean, you're talking even less than usual."

I scratched the back of my neck, stalling, and then resumed my place on the bench for another set. I could talk to Andy, I could trust Andy, and I'd even confided in him on occasion when the mood struck, mostly if I was drunk.

He and I had very little in common on the surface other than working out and our jobs at the airfield. But a shared lived experience is an unfathomable thing. It creates a bond, a trust, and explaining my thought process with him was seldom necessary. He just simply understood.

"The female brunette," I said, not looking at my friend as I gripped the bar, prepared to lift, "I know her."

"What? Don't tell me . . . You know her?" He sounded surprised, on alert, likely because I didn't know anyone, especially not beautiful women. "What do you mean you know her? You mean you finally talked to her?"

"She's one of my students." I grunted as I said this, pushing the weighted bar up while his hands followed my movements.

"What the?" He sounded frustrated on my behalf, disappointed. "Damn. Sorry."

My lips curled into an automatic, rueful smile. "Don't be. She's brilliant in class, interested in the material, always has great thoughts and perspectives. It's been an honor to teach her."

As a student, Ms. Von was one of my favorites. I'd spoken to Emily Von many times over the last two months—she was my student, and therefore speaking to her could not be avoided—but I'd never looked at her for any length of time. I knew Ms. Von by name. However, prior to yesterday, I wouldn't have been able to pick Emily Von out of a lineup. But such was the case with almost all my students.

As an aside, I'd emailed Ms. Von's paper on experimental

design analysis to my former thesis advisor and mentor last month. I suggested she reach out to Ms. Von about summer internships with the Epidemiology Center at the National Institutes of Health this coming summer. Ms. Von was exceptionally bright and seemed to genuinely enjoy research methods. Again, she was an outlier.

Currently, Andy seemed to be studying me. "You just figured this out? That the woman you've been eyeing for six months is one of your students?"

"I haven't been eyeing her." He made it sound so lurid. I'd noticed her because she was an outlier at the gym, that was all. And technically, it had been two years, not six months. "And yes, I just figured it out yesterday. I messaged Dr. Ford last night and asked that she consider giving Emily—Emily is her name—an advocate in my class, so I won't be her professor of record."

"You what?" His question was sharp. "Doesn't that make you look bad? What—why would you do that?"

My heart thumped wildly, likely because thinking about this next part was difficult, so saying it was going to be a challenge. "Because I'm attracted to her and I can't be objective where she's concerned."

That shut Andy up. Obviously, my statement shocked the hell out of him. Good. It shocked the hell out of me too.

He knew I'd never dated anyone seriously. I'd once explained that I'd never been attracted to anyone who'd shown interest in me, and that was mostly true. My assertion didn't stop him from trying to set me up with women all the time. This never went well. Women on dates wanted to be desired for more than their minds and good deeds, which was all I had to offer.

The therapist I'd been seeing monthly to help me with my behavior modification therapy—for the weight loss—and I had discussed this often. He said it wasn't typical, but perhaps it was just my normal. I knew myself well enough to recognize I was incapable of forcing a connection just to check a box, or gain worldly experience, or make a notch in my belt.

My father had experienced and exploited humans enough —both emotionally and physically—for the both of us.

Anyway, I'd lived without female physical attention all my life. I didn't miss it. I didn't need it. I had no problem with humans as students, respected colleagues, friends. But romance? I'd convinced myself I wasn't built that way. No big deal.

And then, there was Lavender . . .

"Well, this all sucks a big pile of cow manure, but good for you," Andy said thoughtfully as I stood, his tone tinged with confusion. "Maybe we should celebrate?"

"Celebrate?"

"Yeah. Celebrate. You just admitted that you *like* her. Out loud. You're physically attracted to someone enough to make yourself look bad to your department chair. This is a big deal. A breakthrough."

"This is not a breakthrough."

"Said the thirty-year-old virgin."

I glared at him.

"Who's never been kissed."

"Forget it. I'm not telling you anything anymore," I said flatly, glancing around at nothing. I hadn't meant to tell him those details, but we'd been drunk and, well, vodka makes me vociferous.

"It's not a big deal." I shrugged again, but my disloyal eyes strayed to the ellipticals and my body told me it was a big deal.

She—the kind brunette/Ms. Von/Lavender/Emily—was

using a towel to wipe sweat from her forehead. Wholly focused on something in front of her, a book or a magazine, her eyes were bright. Perspiration dotted her skin. She was breathing hard and suddenly so was I.

Watching her, it *felt* like a big deal. It felt transformative. I didn't like it.

My stomach tensed. I swallowed. Another shock of electrical current. I looked away, finding Andy watching me, making a face like he was experiencing secondhand discomfort on my behalf.

I gestured to the bench and cleared my throat. "Your turn." My voice was rough.

He ignored me. "You know what I think your problem is?"

"My childhood friend, who—for a former marine—likes to talk about feelings a lot?"

"Marines talk about feelings, asshole. Just listen. I've been thinking about this." He pointed to the side of his head, like I didn't know where the brain was located. In all fairness, I sometimes wondered about his. "I've been thinking about when we were kids, how everything always came so easy to you."

I scoffed. "What? What came easy?"

"Math, science, all the classes, everything in school. You're the smartest fucker I know. You're the best aviation mechanic, that's for sure. You finally decide to lose the weight—" he snapped his fingers "—it falls right off."

"Two years. It took me two years. Behavior modification therapy. That's not falling right off."

"Whatever. It's off, right? Now you look like a movie star. Your face is too fucking pretty. Anything you set your mind to, it's yours. You just have to work for it. And that's the problem." Andy claimed his position on the bench, his attention on the bar as he spoke, obviously timing his words to leave me in suspense.

I said nothing, unwilling to take the wisdom-bait. Unfortunately, he gave me his wisdom-fish for free.

"You could've dated someone before now. There were awesome girls who liked you in school. You were big, yeah. So what? Being smart and witty goes a long way. But you never wanted to *work* for it."

He and I fundamentally disagreed on this point. There was a girl I liked in middle school and high school. She was smart, funny, interesting, charismatic. She also asked me to freshman homecoming.

As a joke.

"It's just too bad you didn't talk to your brunette before the semester started. If you'd talked to her—if you'd put yourself out there instead of being a cowardly jerkoff—then maybe you'd be dating her instead of grading her."

Irritated with this entire conversation, I spoke between clenched teeth. "She wouldn't have talked to me then." I knew this for a fact.

First, plenty of guys had hit on the brunette—Emily—at the gym, and she always, *always* turned them down. I'd watched this happen for two years.

Second, what had she said to me yesterday after class?

Why are you making this such a big deal? It's not a big deal to me.

What I felt at that lingerie shop might've been important to me, but it was nothing to her. She wasn't interested. I wasn't going to bother her, and I definitely wasn't going to make her uncomfortable by asking her out when I already knew what the answer would be.

"You don't know that for sure." Now he sounded ornery. "You just didn't want to work for it. You want everything to be easy because that's what you're used to. And Victor, I hate to be the one to tell you, but we're not the same guys we used to be. We have a really good chance with all kinds of women now. You've seen the women I date. Some are even hotter than your brunette girlfriend."

There were so many things I wanted to correct about his last several statements, but I decided to focus on just one. "Student. *Student.*"

"No. Not student." His voice was strained as he lifted the bar. "You're getting her that advocate, right? So technically she's not your student. Now she's just someone you're too chicken shit to make a move on."

"She comes here to work out, not to pick up guys. I'm not going to be another douche who won't leave her alone," I said. It was a strong supporting argument. Meanwhile, a traitorous question occurred to me, *Where does Emily go to pick up guys?*

. . . Or does Lavender pick up guys?

For some reason, this thought made me grimace, which made me feel like an asshole.

I'd seen and spoken to Lavender just once, and just for a few minutes. And yet, as disconcerting as it was to admit, that single encounter had definitely made a lasting impression. Yes, Emily had been beautiful playing the part of Lavender. Stunning by objective, societal standards. But it wasn't her beauty that I'd noticed, that had sliced so efficiently through my mantle of external-facing apathy.

It was when she'd said, "Think of me as a clothes hanger," with that dry, pragmatic tone of voice, and I'd never been so charmed by anyone or anything in my life.

This gorgeous woman with her perfect limbs and torso and face, whose job was to wear overpriced lingerie, truly made me believe she considered her beautiful body to be background noise, and I wanted *that.* God, how I wanted *that,* comfort in my own skin. I wanted to feel that way about my own body. What would that be like? I had no idea.

At those words, something within me had shifted, a door had opened without my consent. I noticed her, I looked at her, I *wanted* her. And Lavender—Emily—had waltzed right in, having no way of knowing that the intensity and direction of my interest was just as novel to me as an alien abduction would've been to her (or to me).

I'd been completely out of my depth.

And so, I'd been incredulous, but also envious, surprised, confused, and charmed. I'd never been charmed by a woman before. I'd been charmed by animals—dogs mostly, and videos of otters—small children, and my grandfather's girlfriend at his assisted living facility when I visited. But never by a woman close to my age. Again, Emily as Lavender had been an outlier.

"So, are you gunna ask her out?"

"What?" I wasn't paying attention to Andy. He'd been talking the whole time, but only this last question cut through my thoughts. "No. I already told you, no."

"Why not?"

"For all the reasons I've already explained."

"For someone so smart, your reasons seem dumb," he muttered.

He could think what he liked. Over the last seventy-two hours, I'd come to appreciate the simple descriptive elegance of the phrase *being charmed.* Lavender, the memory of her, had an enigmatic hold on me, as though I'd been charmed with actual witchcraft. I'd behaved rashly, buying a membership to a lingerie shop, *buying* lingerie I couldn't afford, would never need, and—logically—I knew I shouldn't want. But I couldn't stop thinking about her, replaying the short moments over and over in my mind.

Breaking oneself out of the spell of being charmed is . . .

difficult. I thought I'd snapped out of it yesterday upon discovering that Emily Von—my student—was Lavender. But then last night I'd realized the kind brunette from the gym was also Emily. Now I was something way beyond charmed. More like beguiled.

But I would figure it out. I'd ushered her out. I would close the door. All would be right again. Eventually.

CHAPTER 6

EMILY

I wasn't 100 percent certain, but I had a sneaking suspicion Dr. Ford was picturing me naked.

"Pardon my ignorance," she said, her overwrought eyebrows pulled together, "but what exactly does a private lingerie model do?" I say her eyebrows were overwrought because they couldn't seem to decide where to settle. One moment they were up, the next down, still the next meeting together in an upside-down V over her nose.

I opened my mouth to respond, but she spoke before I could. "Dr. Hanover's account of the event is quite detailed." Dr. Ford picked up a stack of papers—typed, small font, single spaced—and her gaze scanned the front page. "But I'm afraid I lack the context necessary to understand the situation."

I'd never met Dr. Ford before. I'd seen her, from a distance, and heard rumors about how she'd ascended to the position of Dean of the College of Arts and Sciences—an iron will and cold, calculated ambition—but I'd never had an occasion to speak with her.

She was busy. Bigly busy. Why Dr. Ford was meeting with

me now instead of one of her underlings—I, a mere undergraduate of no consequence—made no sense. Yet, here we were, sitting in her immense, lavishly decorated office, her peering at me with clever hazel eyes and a slight, hovering smile. Waiting.

Frowning at the sheets she held, I cleared my throat and prepared to respond.

But again, before I could speak, Dr. Ford dropped the papers, leaned back in her burgundy leather chair, and returned her searching eyes to mine. "You're not a prostitute . . . right?"

Though her question and expression lacked any hint of judgment, embarrassed heat burned the back of my throat. I snapped my mouth shut and shook my head.

"So you model—what?—underwear? And bras and such?" She sounded both curious and confused.

I nodded.

"Privately?"

"Yes."

"In people's houses?"

"No. At a shop downtown." Was that my voice? Why did I sound so hoarse?

"Hmm . . ." Her head tilted to one side. "For men?"

"My clients are usually men, yes," I said firmly.

"Hmm . . ." Now she was nodding, and her eyes moved over me again. "Cross-dressers?" she asked, the hopeful note in her voice catching me off guard and distracting me enough to ease my embarrassment.

"Not that I know of."

"Okay," she said on an exhale that sounded disappointed. "So, Dr. Hanover came in with his father, who is a client of your shop, and you were their model, and blah blah blah"—she gestured to Dr. Hanover's dry retelling of the events—"Victor saw you in your undies."

"That's right. But being in my undies is my job." I lifted my chin.

"That's a good point." Dr. Ford moved her head from side to side in a slow, considering movement, her gaze unfocused, somewhere over my head. "For example, if you were a bartender, and Dr. Hanover walked into the bar where you worked, and you made him a drink—as per the requirements of your job—well then. . ." She tossed her hands up, leaning back in her chair and shrugging. "Do you have any concerns or changes to Dr. Hanover's version of events? Is it correct?"

I struggled with how to respond, and finally settled on, "It's factually correct."

"But?" The older woman gave me a wide, white smile.

"But." I sighed, the lingering irritation and ire since he'd left me standing alone in the lecture hall yesterday, and upon reading his dossier on our interactions last night still simmered. "But I don't understand why any of this is necessary," I said flatly, maybe with a hint of antagonism. Or more than a hint.

Dr. Ford flinched, her smile waning. "What do you mean?"

"I mean, using your analogy, if I'd been a bartender serving him drinks, would I be sitting here right now?"

She gave me a little shrug. "Maybe."

"Maybe?" I scoffed. Giving into belligerence, I rolled my eyes.

"Yes," she said, unruffled. "If a faculty member believes he or she has behaved inappropriately, even in retrospect, as Dr. Hanover clearly feels he's done, then yes. You'd be sitting here right now."

I grunted my disbelief but said nothing. I was now ready to leave. I'd been ready to leave since walking into her office.

A wave of impatience seized me, and I reached for my bag. "Are we finished?"

"No." She smiled softly at me, her gaze once more assessing. "I see what you want, what you're doing."

"What's that?"

"You want to think this"—she gestured to the stack of Dr. Hanover's words on her desk—"is about your job. You think Victor brought this to me because you try on underwear for a living."

"Isn't it?"

"No. Well . . ." She paused. "Well *mostly* no. He did see you nearly naked, and he clearly, uh—" Her gaze grew suddenly piercing. "May I speak candidly?"

A short laugh tumbled from my lips. "You haven't been speaking candidly?"

"You're right, I shouldn't speak candidly. It always gets the university sued. Let's just say, Dr. Hanover's behavior was inappropriate and leave it at that."

"But he didn't even know it was me, he did nothing wrong!"

"But now that he does know it was you, one of his students, he was right to report it. In retrospect, it was inappropriate." Her voice was patient, but a twinkle had entered her eyes, like she found something about me adorable.

"How so? He didn't do anything dozens of other men and women haven't already done. It's my *job.*"

"Maybe. But now he knows it was you, he's taking steps to protect your interests against any potential bias he might show you—good or bad—in the future."

I snorted. "Why would he do that?"

"Protect you?"

"Show bias."

"Oh Lord, give me prudence." Dr. Ford lifted her eyes heavenward, and then was quiet for a long time, glancing at the clock on her desk, straightening the papers, aligning two pencils such that they were perfectly parallel, all the while visibly biting her tongue and trying not to smile. Her movements were restless, and I got the sense she really, really wanted to speak candidly.

After folding and refolding her hands at least four times, she leveled me with a still twinkling gaze and said, "Ms. Von, why don't you ask me something I'm allowed to answer?"

Now I flinched, surprised, sitting up straighter in my seat. I decided that at some point in the future, after Dr. Ford retired, I'd find her, take her out for a beer, and force her to speak candidly. My life would remain incomplete until that day.

While I stared at her dumbfounded, her smile seemed to grow, and eventually she said, "Why don't you ask me why Victor came to me, instead of student affairs or your advisor, to triage this issue? Doesn't that strike you as odd?"

"Why did . . .?"

"Let's just pretend you asked," she whispered conspiratorially. Using her normal voice, she said, "Dr. Hanover asked me to personally oversee this matter as he wanted to protect your privacy as much as possible. He said he was concerned that small-minded folks might judge you, or hold your current job against you, or that you might miss out on future opportunities, and he didn't want that to happen. Therefore, this incident will stay out of your record completely, and will only be added to his—with your name and details redacted—should you wish it. Furthermore, I'm giving you the option of having an advocate appointed, to grade your assignments and such, should you wish it."

I was officially a swirling mess of confusion.

"He did that?" I croaked, my bag now forgotten on the floor along with any urgency I'd felt about leaving.

"Yes. He did. He told me that he thinks very highly of you and didn't want you to be distressed."

Relaxing into the cushion of my chair for the first time since sitting down, my eyes drifted to the papers on her desk.

He doesn't want me to be distressed . . .

My chest felt tight, and soft, and warm all at the same time, but her words had whipped my mind into a frenzy. Before I could settle on just one thought, she was speaking again.

"Ms. Von, I don't think this'll shock you, but folks aren't ideal. In an ideal world, a professor would never admire his students for anything other than their academic erudition. Likewise, admiration for academic erudition would never lead to attraction. Similarly, a professor would be able to go into a private lingerie shop, watch a private lingerie modeling show thing, admire the beauty of the female's form, and carry no traces of desire for that female's form after he—or she—left, such that, should that female turn out to be one of his or her students, it wouldn't cause any problems."

She paused, as though watching me for some reaction, maybe a sign of distress, but when I stared at her unflinchingly, she continued, "Though you may not be experiencing any lasting effects or troublesome thoughts after your brief encounter with Dr. Hanover at your workplace, he obviously is. I am sorry if this information is burdensome to hear, or if it makes you uncomfortable. Like I said, you will always have the option of an advocate, should you feel you are being treated unfairly. You have my word."

Sometimes, my own thoughts and feelings frustrated me. I wanted to be unaffected by this very clever woman's assessment of the situation, but I wasn't. I rolled my lips between my teeth so I wouldn't say something stupid like, "Do you really think he admires my academic erudition?!?!" and also to give my heart and brain a moment to settle down and stop throwing an impromptu *Eeeeeeeeeeeeeeeeeeeeeeee! HE LIKES ME!!* celebration.

Swallowing, I nodded to indicate my understanding, and tried to think of an intelligent question to ask, a good segue that wouldn't make me look like I'd also been lusting after Dr. Hanover's . . . academic erudition.

"Is there any downside to having an advocate appointed?"

Dr. Ford's eyes narrowed infinitesimally. "I take your question to mean that you are uncomfortable with Dr. Hanover continuing as your professor?"

"No. Not at all." I was quick to contradict, and leaned forward again, placing my hand on her desk. "Not even a little. Like I said before, I don't think Vi-uh, Dr. Hanover has done anything wrong. So, no. I don't want anything about this to be put on his record."

"Okay," she nodded slowly, her shrewd eyes now cloudy with confusion, "but you want an advocate?"

"Not necessarily, not for me. But if it would make Dr. Hanover more comfortable. I guess, let me ask you this, why do students usually have advocates? Other than in my case, where there might be some potential for bias with the professor." I stopped myself before bringing up my friend Anna Harris, the one who'd fallen for her Russian Lit professor. She'd been appointed an advocate over the summer when she and Luca, i.e. Professor Kroft, had started dating.

"Advocates are assigned exclusively for that reason, where there might be bias, negative or positive."

"Can you explain what you mean by positive bias?" Despite the continued internal squeeing between my heart and brain, I was feeling more relaxed, and this was feeling more like a conversation than an interview.

"Positive bias, as in when a professor is showing preferential treatment for a student they might have a relationship with," she said this evenly, her features unaffected, giving me the impression Dr. Ford was merely answering the questions as I asked them and suspected no ulterior motive. "An advocate may be used to give both the student and the rest of the class assurances that the grade given is the grade earned if, for example, a student is related to a professor, or is the child of a close friend."

Or a significant other.

"Hmm." I rubbed my chin thoughtfully, meeting Dr. Ford's gaze evenly, as I tried to keep my imagination from running away from me.

Too late.

I was already imagining the moment I would tell Professor Hanover that I'd opted to have an advocate. In my daydream, he would understand my reasons immediately, give me that clever grin, stalk toward me until my back was against the wall, cup my cheek with his strong hand, and then—

"Ms. Von."

"Uh, yes?" I shook myself from my musings, bringing Dr. Ford and her fancy office back into focus.

Her eyes had turned sharp and now shone with what looked like suspicion. "Ms. Von, are you officially asking for an advocate?"

I nodded. "I am."

I didn't know how it was possible, but her gaze seemed to grow even more perceptive, like she was picking through the gray matter of my brain. "Because you worry for Dr. Hanover's level of comfort?"

Pressing my lips together so I wouldn't smile, I reclaimed my bag, I stood, and I shrugged. "You could say that."

CHAPTER 7

EMILY

I was a creature of habit. One might even call me *habitual.* I wasn't a big deviator. I stayed in my lane.

As an example, over my college career, I typically took all my course hours on Mondays, Tuesdays (during the day), and Wednesdays. Tuesday nights were trivia night with BFF Anna. Wednesdays after class I usually (but not always) drove home to visit my mom, spent the night, and drove back Thursday afternoon. Thursday evenings I taught sewing and pattern making workshops at the North Side Community Center, because knowing how to make your own clothes is a) awesome and b) saves a lot of money.

I worked Fridays and Saturdays.

Sundays were my day of rest, catching up on homework and preparing for the week.

But every morning except Thursdays, I always, always, always worked out for two hours. I always arrived as soon as the campus gym opened at 5:30 AM, 5:45 AM at the latest. My current employability was dependent on what my body looked like, which meant whether or not I ate, had funds for tuition, or money for rent also depended on what my body looked like.

And yet, I dreamed of the day when I could quit my job and sleep in, because sleep was the best. Also the best? Banana splits with caramel, cashews, and more caramel. Also, fettuccine alfredo with bacon, peas, and mushrooms. Also, fried chicken.

Oh man. I could go on and on. But I wouldn't, because thinking about things that were firmly out of my reach never put me in a good mood. Since working at the Pinkery, I'd developed strategies for dealing with temptation, for distracting myself when my mind wandered to something I wanted or craved, but couldn't have.

If self-control was a muscle like all those experts claimed, mine was on steroids.

Which was why I found myself in a state of absolute befuddlement as I stared at Dr. Hanover's closed office door twenty-two days after my meeting with Dr. Ford.

Who am I?

What am I doing?

Why am I here?

I couldn't swallow, I was too nervous. I *knew* Dr. Hanvor was on the other side of the door. Alone. Here I was on this side of the door. Also alone. How convenient.

Over three weeks had passed since I'd been assigned an advocate, a graduate student named Gloria. She was nice. We'd met thrice. She'd administered my test this week and had collected my paper on mice.

Ugh. I'm rhyming. Sorry.

Anyway, all assignments went to Gloria, were graded by Gloria, but I attended Dr. Hanover's lectures as normal.

Except, no! Not normal!!!

But actually, yes. Ms. Crazy Brains, yes! Normal. So very, very normal.

And the normalcy was what made everything not normal. Dr. Hanover treated me just like he had before. He called on me every so often. He challenged me, just like he did with all students when it was warranted, or moved on swiftly when I answered correctly. Seemingly, nothing had changed for him.

Whereas, based on my conversation with Dr. Ford, I'd thought having an advocate assigned would free Dr. Hanover to do . . . whatever he wanted to do. I'd had daydreams about him asking me to stay late after the lecture. Or maybe he'd show up at my work—he was a member, after all—and ask me out. He wouldn't have to worry about bias or ramifications because I had an advocate. Voila!

More daydreams of us going out, both of us getting stage five, four, three, two, one, naked.

When nothing happened by the end of the first week, I'd assumed it was because he wanted to ensure the advocate was working out.

When nothing happened by the end of the second week, I'd assumed it was because he needed a little more time.

When nothing happened by the end of the third week, I had to face facts: Dr. Hanover wasn't going to make a move and all my fantasy imaginings were just that. Fantasy.

A big, furry, googly-eyed fantasy. My fantasies were like spiders, just with more legs and less venom.

I should have moved on. I should have let it go. But I couldn't. The door had been opened. What had been seen—namely, Dr. Hanover's possible interest in me as more than a student and his previously cloaked smarty-pants sexiness—could never be unseen!

Worse, I noticed things about him during class that I'd never noticed before. He encouraged his students to be better. He was passionate about knowledge and education, and deeply, truly wanted us to apply both to our lives. I'd already known he was smart before, but now his subtle wordplay and nerdy puns made me swoon in my seat.

I liked him. A lot. *Dammit.*

I thought about him. A lot. Even when I tried to flex my self-control muscle or try to distract myself, I still thought about him. Meanwhile, he . . . didn't think about me. At all. He didn't even have to grade my papers.

Oh the humidity!

No. Seriously. Oh the humidity. It was hot as Satan's armpit in the faculty office building. I pulled at my shirt, trying to get some air movement. The AC must've been broken. Or maybe I was just so nervous, I'd given myself a hot flash.

"What am I doing?"

Lurking like a lurking lurker in the hallway, sweating, staring at Dr. Hanover's closed door on a Wednesday night when I should have already been on the road to my mother's.

Wiping at my forehead, I sighed, feeling ridiculous yet galvanized. The debate within me was supersized. I couldn't stay, but I couldn't get my feet to carry me away. Clearly, I was cray-cray.

Oh no, I'm rhyming again!

"Just . . . leave!" I whispered to myself, pacing a few steps closer to his door. "Leave." I lifted my hand, licking my lips. "Go, go, go."

I heard movement within, and I tensed. Footsteps. A second later, the sound of two voices speaking to each other, faint murmurs, met my ears. My heart dropped. He wasn't alone.

What are you doing? Really? What's the plan here?

I sighed.

I shook my head.

I turned.

Then the sound of "Misirlou," by Dick Dale & His Del-Tones carried out of Dr. Hanover's office and I froze.

Pulp Fiction. He was listening to the *Pulp Fiction* soundtrack. The earlier voices weren't Dr. Hanover and someone else. The voices were two actors from the movie. It had been the Honey Bunny scene, right before the robbery. Which meant Dr. Hanover *was* alone.

"Oh, well," I whispered. "That changes nothing. You still need to leave."

I did need to leave. I knew it. I had no right to be here. I'd been the one to agree to the advocate. He wasn't my professor anymore. He might've (possibly) had an interest in me at some point, but clearly me being a student was a hard line for him.

Plus, my intentions were murky. I wanted *things.* Selfish things. And he'd been unselfish. He'd been honorable.

I took a step, and then another, and another. They were slow, but they were in the right direction, and I was just on the edge of being proud of myself when I heard a door opening behind me.

Oh noes!

A shock of adrenaline tightened my throat, caused my steps to falter, and then quicken.

"Emily?"

Ahhhhhhhcrap. It was too late.

I stopped. Not because I wanted to stop. Oh no. I didn't want to stop. I wanted to run. But, as usual and was my habit, I froze. Straining my ears, I waited and hoped. I hoped he'd —*oh jeez*. I didn't know what I hoped.

But what I heard was hesitation, insomuch as one can hear hesitation, and then footsteps.

"Emily," he said my name rather than asked this time. The sound of his voice saying my first name was very nice.

I listened as he came closer, saw in my peripheral vision

as he drew even and passed me. I watched helplessly as he came fully into my field of view and faced me, his movements relaxed, confident, assured. Tangentially, I noticed he'd changed. Gone were the brown pants, yellow and brown plaid button-down, and pocket protector. Instead, he was wearing dark blue jeans, gray socks, and a white undershirt.

But I didn't see his eyes move over me. I felt their path instead because I couldn't seem to lift my gaze higher than his neck.

His hands snagged my attention, they looked restless at his sides. For a split second I thought he might touch me. He didn't. He stuffed them into his jeans' pockets.

"Can I help you?" he asked, his voice dichotomously both gruff and smooth.

I stalled by taking a deep breath and glancing over his shoulder, attempting to arrange my face into something resembling calm. "Um," I said. It was higher pitched than my usual voice, which only served to fluster and tongue-tie me further.

He waited. And while he waited, I smelled him. Don't worry, I didn't sniff him or anything. It's just, I *could* smell him, so I did. He smelled great, like before, like the time we'd been alone together at the Pinkery, and he'd touched the silk of the kimono and me with his fingertips.

Abruptly and despite the heat, goose bumps rose over my skin, starting at my arms and racing toward my chest. Curiosity elbowed my anxiety out of the way and my gaze flickered to his. As expected, he was watching me. Unexpected, his eyes were hot. I sensed the same restlessness there that had been present in his hands, the way he was staring felt like a touch, and I finally understood what people meant when they said a person's gaze could smolder.

"Emily," he said my name a third time, capturing and holding my gaze. "What do you want?"

"I . . ." My lips parted as I struggled with my brain, and his eyes dropped to my mouth.

SAY SOMETHING!

I didn't. I couldn't. Because either it was my imagination, or he'd just leaned forward, his smoldering stare still on my mouth. My eyes widened, unable to look away from his handsome face as he grew closer. A big hand slid around my waist, heat seeping through my shirt as fingers pressed against the small of my back, urging me forward. "Misirlou" continued to reverberate from his office, a soundtrack to what was about to happen, what *was* happening between us.

My lashes fluttered, I held my breath, and my brain told me, *this isn't real, I'm imagining this,* just before his extremely real and soft and warm lips touched mine.

CHAPTER 8

EMILY

A simple kiss, a press of his mouth to mine, held for six beats of the heart. Cresting confusion followed by a surge of deep, lush heat. The beginnings of a melting surrender a split second before the kiss was broken, just as it ceased being simple. Its end punctuated with the barest of caresses, a brush of lips, a tantalizingly light touch, back and forth once. Our noses bumped softly. Stubble from his day beard sandpaper against my chin. His barely audible sigh. A sense of hesitation.

I felt it all, and the echoes of feeling lingered as he leaned away. His hands remained on my body, one on my hip, one curled around the side of my torso just below my ribs. His palms and fingers were hot, hotter than the hot hallway, hotter than the smoldering low in my abdomen. I waited—my eyes closed, my face angled upward—for him to return.

When he didn't move, I opened my eyes and found him there, peering at me. He didn't look pleased or displeased, more like . . . cautiously unrepentant. The stubborn angle of his chin and matching glint in his gaze—as though he *dared* me to be upset—made me smile.

"Hello," he said, the single word dry as dust, and I wondered if he was bracing himself, apprehensive of what I might do next.

"Hi." I grinned and knew I sounded moony, and yet I was incapable of caring about my mooniness.

Victor's glare narrowed by an infinitesimal amount, growing impossibly sharp, giving me lovely little heart flutters. I'd never met a person with such tangible intelligence behind their gaze. His eyes seemed to be brighter, more reactive than other people's, where both meanings of the word *brilliance* could be applied at once. It was, I decided, the sexiest thing about him (. . . so far).

You have beautiful eyes.

One of Victor's eyebrows rose suddenly, and he blinked twice, the sharpness in his gaze morphing into something softened by confusion. "I have beautiful eyes?"

OHNOES!

My mouth fell open and I flinched, leaning back on my heels. "Did I . . . did I say that out loud?"

He nodded, his expression unreadable (at least, unreadable to me), and his fingers on my hip and torso flexed for a beat before sliding away. He took a half step back.

"Yes. You said that out loud."

"Oh. Sorry."

"No reason to be sorry." Victor's tone was so steady, so entirely calm—remote even—I doubted my own memory for a millisecond.

Did we just kiss? Or did I imagine that?

I brought my fingers to my lips and nodded faintly to reassure myself. Yes, we'd kissed. Objectively, it might have been short and chaste by most standards, but nothing about it *felt* chaste to me. The aftereffects still held me in their disorienting grip.

"Emily," he said, drawing my attention. His gaze—less piercing than before, but no less brimming with arresting cleverness—conducted a quick sweep of my person, finally landing back on my face. I sensed a struggle within him. "We need to talk."

"Yes." I nodded, still in my moony daze.

He lifted his thumb and forefinger to gently tug at his bottom lip and glanced over my shoulder to the direction of his office, his eyebrows pulling low in a thoughtful line. "Not here. Are you hungry?"

I nodded. Or, more correctly, I continued nodding. "I could eat."

"Fine. Good." The words were spoken in abrupt staccato, a tone I recognized from class when someone gave the right answer. "Do you like Ethiopian food? Or we could go—"

"I love Ethiopian food."

"Do you have a car? I have some things to finish here first, but I can text you directions and we can meet later." Victor pulled out his phone from his back pocket, unlocked it, and held it out to me.

Still nodding, I snatched his phone and navigated to the contacts section, speed-entering my information using both of my thumbs. "I have a car. And yes, I'll meet you later."

I had to fight the murky moony-toon impulse to click on his messaging icon and send myself a text so I'd have his number ASAP. Instead, I returned his cell. This interaction was going well, so much more and better than I'd allowed myself to consider possible, I didn't want to do anything overeager that might send him running.

"Shall we say, eight o'clock?" Victor glanced at his phone before switching it off and returning it to his back pocket. When his gaze lifted, it moved past me again to his office.

"Yes. Eight. Sounds great. See you then." I stepped to the

side and around him, walking backward slowly so I could see him as I moved away.

I didn't dwell too much on his stern expression as he turned to watch me go. I was too busy doing an internal jig of self-congratulations and debating whether to rush forward, to steal a parting kiss. *Or would that be weird?*

Before I could decide, Victor gave me a brief farewell nod and turned to his office, his strides long and purposeful. He didn't look back at me before closing his door with a soft click.

It wasn't until I was sitting in my car in the student lot, replaying the events of the last half hour, that I realized he hadn't quite met my eyes again after I'd complimented his.

Time: 8:01 PM

Place: Front door of Queen of Sheba Ethiopian Restaurant

Mood: Cautiously optimistic

On the drive over, I couldn't help but indulge in all sorts of best-case fantasies regarding the evening, but I hadn't allowed my imagination to run away from me. No, no. That wouldn't do. My internal jig of self-congratulations had definitely waned, becoming more of a wary sway of anticipation.

On the one hand, he'd kissed me.

On the other hand, afterward he'd acted distant. Reserved.

And yet, on another hand—a third, surgically attached hand—this was the first time Victor had kissed me. Perhaps his behavior had been post-kiss typical for him?

Although, on an additional hand—a fourth, awesome gene-mutated hand—I'd kissed my fair share of menfolk, and this was the first time anyone had acted distant with me afterward. So . . .?

Just go inside!

Bringing myself back to the present, I reached for Queen of Sheba's front door and swung it open, stepping into the restaurant while taking a deep inhale of delicious spices, berbere and cardamom and cinnamon. Peering around the cozy space, I noted the walls were painted a shade of parchment, gauzy red curtains framed the windows on brass rods, and metalwork lamps hung from brown cords above each table, giving the room an intimate glow.

The place was busier than I would have expected from any restaurant on a weeknight at 8:00 PM. A few seconds of hunting to find Victor were required, and a few more seconds to calm my quaking nerves before leaving the safety of the front door alcove. He sat in a booth at the farthest corner of the restaurant, his attention on the menu he held up, apparently scanning its contents.

As I approached, I tried to take my cue from how calm he seemed to be. Gathering a deep breath, endeavoring to release uncertainty and nerves on a silent exhale, I managed a small smile just as I reached the table.

"Hi," I said. Despite my mighty exhale, my stomach was in knots.

Victor glanced up from his menu, blinked as though bringing me into focus, and then seemed to shake himself, as though he'd been lost in deep thought or my appearance had been a surprise.

"Emily. Yes. Hello." He immediately slid from the booth, standing, and motioning to the bench across from his with one hand while sliding the other into his back pocket, the movement awkward. "Please, have a seat."

I thought about stepping forward and giving him a kiss

on the cheek. He looked so much more approachable than usual, younger, human. Still dressed in his white T and jeans, his hair still unstyled but now sticking up at odd angles, as though he'd been pushing his fingers through it repeatedly.

And yet, I didn't step forward.

As I claimed my spot across from him, I realized why I hadn't made a move: as he'd stood and offered the seat, he hadn't looked directly at me. Even now, as I snuck a quick peek, his gaze was once again fastened to his menu, the wrinkle between his eyebrows giving me the impression it wasn't his lack of enthusiasm with the appetizer list so much as having difficulty meeting my eyes.

I didn't allow my stomach to sink, not yet. *Maybe he's just nervous. This is probably strange territory for him too.*

"What's good here?" I asked, attempting to sound as benign as possible while taking a much-needed moment to center myself. I couldn't allow my mind to wander, to entertain any of those best-case fantasies I'd been indulging earlier.

"Everything," he said, sounding distracted, "I've had everything and it's all good."

"Your sample size is adequately powered?" The statistics —and therefore research methods—joke slipped past my lips before checking with my brain. I fought against the urge to cringe, peeking at him again.

His gaze cut to mine, held, and I held my breath upon spotting the barest tug at the corner of his mouth. "Well, yes. But when one's N—the number of samples—is all available samples, power calculations are unnecessary."

"Is that true?"

"Yes. Power calculations are only necessary when N is some subset of the population being studied."

"Meaning, when N is all available samples, the results are definitive?"

"No. I didn't say that." Victor leaned back in his booth, his tone conversational, his shoulders seeming to relax. "It's important to be precise, especially when using such phrases as, 'the results are definitive.' One *could* make that argument, but only for the questions being asked, i.e. the specific aims, and only for the time point measured."

"Ah." *Okay, okay, I can do this. I can brain-spar with Dr. Victor Genius Stein.* "So, based on your statement that everything here is good, I assume you've sampled the entire menu just moments ago?"

His eyes narrowed, but his barely-there smile became a small one. "No. I didn't."

"Which means, everything on the menu might not be good tonight? As your findings are only valid for the time point measured, which was in the past."

His smile grew, and—if I wasn't mistaken—his sexy, smarty-pants eyes twinkled at me.

"Precisely," he said, his response and the way he said it causing a cascade of warmth to spread from my chest to the top of my head, from my stomach to my toes.

We engaged in a stare-athon, during which a galvanized current seemed to pass between us, both electric and magnetic. Goodness, he was so very attractive to me now, no use fighting it. My internal wary sway of anticipation began to resemble a happy jig once more, and I was just about to suggest we turn our examination of power calculations to other areas of study when Victor frowned abruptly.

Closing his eyes, he gave his head a quick shake and sighed. "Look, this isn't . . ." He swallowed, sighed again, his shoulders rising and falling with the breath. He seemed to brace himself before lifting his gaze to mine. I sensed a restless urgency and frustration there as well as in the set of his jaw, the slight furrow of his brow. "I'm sorry, this isn't going to happen."

"What? Dinner?"

"No." He moved his index finger between us in what could have been interpreted as a *come here* motion, but his words contradicted the movement. "I don't date. I've never dated. Anyone. And if I did, I would never date a student."

Oh.

"Oh." I leaned back in the booth and could feel my eyes blinking rapidly but could do nothing to stop them. I was too busy experiencing what an emotional sucker punch felt like. Interestingly, it felt a lot like an actual sucker punch.

I lowered my attention to my menu and stared at it. I—my brain and therefore my body—was frozen, as usual.

Meanwhile, Victor breathed out, another long sigh, followed by yet another that sounded pained. In my peripheral vision I saw him rub his forehead, shift in his seat, then spin his menu with restless fingers. His agitation and unrest were obvious.

"Emily—"

"Just . . . just give me a minute here." I held up a hand, endeavoring to free my mind from its gridlock so I could leave. *Or, leave now and think about this later, because thinking about it now will just lead to questions like—* "Then why did you kiss me?" I glanced at him.

"Because I wanted to." His answer was sudden and smacked of his usual bluntness, but also of something else I'd never noticed. Interacting with him up close made me wonder whether his honesty—both now and the various occasions during his lectures—was an impulse he couldn't contain, a compulsion he struggled with.

Regardless of this possible odd quirk of his personality, Victor's confession only served to confuse me further.

"Okay." I frowned at the tabletop, the gridlock in my brain loosening just enough for me to think and say at the same time, "So you're one of those guys who doesn't do relationships."

"It's not like that." His tone was stern, defensive, and drew my gaze back to his face. He'd crossed his arms. "It's not—not how you mean."

"Then how is it?" Once again, I was thinking and speaking in tandem.

The muscle at his jaw jumped, his eyes like a brick wall reinforced with brainiac steel. "It's not . . . not your concern."

This time, the sucker punch was worse, because I should have known better than to ask the question. Why was I still here? Hadn't he already shut me out and shut me down just seconds ago? As good old GW used to say, *"There's an old saying in Tennessee—I know it's in Texas, probably in Tennessee—that says, 'Fool me once, shame on—shame on you. Fool me—you can't get fooled again.'"*

"Right." I was blinking compulsively again, wincing at the ache that twisted in my abdomen and jarred my teeth. "Right. I guess I should just go." I reached for my bag and pulled out a bill—it might have been a one-dollar bill, it might have been a fifty—and scooched to the edge of the booth. We hadn't ordered anything yet, so why I was leaving money, I didn't know.

"You don't have to go. If you want to stay, you should stay." Victor placed his hand on the edge of the table halfway between us, sliding out of his bench seat.

"Why would I stay?" I mumbled this to myself as I stood, realizing too late that—once more—I'd spoken out loud.

"We could talk." He stood as he made this offer, sounding completely reasonable. "I'm interested in you."

"You're—what?"

"I mean, I'm interested in how things are going with Gloria and if you feel like your academic needs are being met."

Like before, his words surprised me enough to draw my attention to his face. But unlike before, he didn't look stern and defensive. His expression was open, beseeching even. He wanted me to stay, and that made no sense.

Placing the money on the table, I hooked my purse strap over my shoulder. "I don't want to stay."

His eyebrows pulled together, now he seemed confused. Stepping closer, quite close, he whispered, "Because I don't wish to pursue a romantic relationship with you?"

His question knocked the wind from my lungs and my brain wanted to freeze again, but I wouldn't let it. A frozen brain would mean standing at the edge of the table like an idiot and smelling him and losing myself in his erotically intelligent eyes for who knows how long.

I didn't have enough mental energy for a polite excuse, so I chose the Victor Hanover method: blunt honesty.

"No, not exactly. It's because talking to you is disorienting, and it seems like every time we talk, you end up hurting my feelings. My feelings are hurt, right now, and I'm not sure if that's you, or if that's me being overly sensitive or misreading something, or what. Instead of staying and allowing that to happen again, I'm just going to call it a night and avoid you from now on. So . . ."

I nodded at the logic and truth in my journey of words, watching Victor—Dr. Hanover—for any sign or response. But when I realized what I was doing, giving him an opportunity to hurt my feelings again with his reaction (or non-reaction), I closed my eyes, gave myself a physical shake, and turned for the exit.

For the record, I would have liked to keep my eyes closed the entire time, but there were tables to navigate. No reason to knock over some poor, unsuspecting couple's delicious injera.

With my eyes open, my brain mostly frozen, and my heart beating like mad, I strolled to the door, opened it, and walked out of it, certain of only one thing: tonight would most assuredly be the end of any unfortunate attraction I'd felt for Dr. Victor Hanover—magnetic, electric, or otherwise.

CHAPTER 9

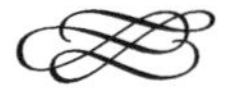

EMILY

The first thing I did upon closing the door to my car was unlock my phone, navigate to Dr. Hanover's text message with directions to Queen of Sheba, and delete the conversation. I then tapped over to my contacts and deleted the entry I'd created for him not more than an hour ago.

The next thing I did was call my best friend.

Anna answered after the third ring. "What's up?"

Fastening my attention to the steering wheel, I willed myself to not stare at the front door of the restaurant and watch for Victor. *No, Dr. Hanover. Not Victor.*

"Where are you?" My jaw hurt. I must've been clenching it. *I don't care if he comes after me. I don't care. I don't.*

Lies. All lies. Because movement in my peripheral vision had my eyes moving reflexively to the front door of the restaurant. Sure enough, there was Vict—*Dr. Hanover.* He'd just busted through the door, seemed to be scanning the parking lot, pushing one hand through his hair while anchoring the other to his waist. He looked. . . frustrated.

Or, maybe that's what I was hoping to see. *Yep. That's probably it.*

"I'm at Luca's and we're just cleaning up from dinner. Why?"

Ripping my eyes away from the entrance and swallowing around the tightness in my throat, I slid lower in my seat, hoping Dr. Hanover wouldn't see me. As far as I knew, he had no idea what kind of car I drove.

"Can I come over?" I'd never been to Anna's professor-manfriend's house, inviting myself over wasn't something I would normally do. But I needed my friend, so I offered instead, "Or could we meet somewhere?"

"Yes, come over. Absolutely. Yes." She didn't hesitate, which meant she didn't consult with Luca.

"Uh . . . Why don't we meet somewhere?"

"Come over, Emily." Luca said this, his voice clear as a bell.

"Wait, Anna!" I whisper-hissed. "Do you have me on speaker phone?"

"Yes. Sorry. Okay? My hands are in soapy water. I asked Luca to answer, put you on speaker, and be silent. Please forgive me!"

"You're forgiven." I frowned at my side mirror, trying to angle my head such that I could see the entrance to the restaurant again. But then I caught myself and shut my eyes.

"Here, you're off speaker now." Anna sounded contrite. "Speak freely. And both Luca and I insist you come over."

"I could use your help with something, but I don't want to—"

"Come over! If you don't come over now, I will never return your Le Creuset pot."

"It's a Dutch oven! And you better return it."

"Come over then."

"Fine." I rubbed my chest, it felt wonky. Achy and wonky. "Send me the address."

"Excellent. I'll text it and I'm hanging up now so you can't change your mind. Bye!" Anna clicked off.

"What's going on with you?"

"I'm . . . irritated," I admitted, glancing around the room.

I'd arrived less than a minute ago and I already wanted to leave. Luca's house was nice. It was small, but it was very adult-like. The furniture appeared to be expensive and antique. The room we were sitting in—some kind of library off the main entrance—looked like one of those old studies from the movies. Books were *everywhere,* stuffing the shelves, with several shelves positioned above the doorways. Many of the volumes looked old and the room smelled like leather furniture polish and smoke. It smelled like smoke because there was presently a wood fire burning in his very impressive fireplace-within-a-fireplace.

"I can see you're irritated." Anna poked me, bringing my attention back to her. "Do you want to talk about it?"

I shot her a look. An irritated look. A *I-want-to-nut-punch-someone* look.

"Yikes! That's your I-want-to-nut-punch-someone look."

"Exactly." The look quickly faded, as did some of my irritation and anxiety. It was so great to have a person in my life who knew all my looks (other than my mother). I reclined by the merest fraction against the leather couch, pleasantly surprised by how comfy it was.

"You don't have to talk about it." Anna leaned forward and wrapped me in a sitting hug, squeezing my shoulders tightly. She smelled good, like beef roast, rosemary, and geraniums. I inhaled deeply. "We can talk about anything you like, no pressure."

"I want to talk about it, but I don't want to talk about it." I was nuts. *Fact.*

Leaning away, reclaiming her spot on the other side of the couch, she examined me. "Is it your mom?"

I shook my head. "No. Things are great."

I understood why my mother was Anna's first guess. I loved my mother. She was awesome: funny, witty, clever, kind. But she didn't take great care of herself, and she suffered from depression. It was a vicious cycle with her: get sick, which made her depressed, which made her sicker, which made her more depressed, and so on. Also, she didn't have the best insurance—basically, they covered Pap smears and that's it—so I'd been paying her therapy bill for the last year.

I didn't mind!

I was happy to do it. Especially since, for the first time in my memory, things *were* great with my mom. She was seeing her therapist twice weekly, walking for a half hour daily, and her new meds seemed to be working. Yay money!

"Good. I'm glad things are great with your mom. Is it work? School?" Anna asked, apparently content to play twenty questions.

I love Anna. She had the patience of a saint. A SAINT!

"It's . . . both." I gritted my teeth.

"Both?"

"It's complicated."

"Okay. Got it. Complicated. How complicated?"

"Very." I hedged, working up the nerve to tell her the truth, or some version of it.

"On a scale from me and Luca now—so, one—to me and Luca before we started dating—so, eleventy thousand—how complicated?"

I laughed at the irony of her comparison. "You know, I'd say it's *exactly* as complicated as you and Luca before you got over yourselves, had an honest conversation, and started dating."

"Really?" Her tone told me she was impressed. "That complicated?"

"But also less complicated," I amended. "I don't know what to do about this guy."

"A guy? This is about a guy?" She leaned forward a little, her voice pitching higher. "Well, my goodness. A guy."

"Yes. A guy. Sorry. My visit won't pass the Bechdel test."

"Nah. I've been dying to tell you how vanilla orchids are pollinated outside of Mexico. Spoiler alert, it's cray-cray. We'll talk about it later." Anna pushed my shoulder gently with her fingertips. "But back to *the guy*. Who is he? Do I know him?"

"We should skip ahead to pollination of vanilla outside of Mexico, because this is probably pointless to talk about. Nothing is ever going to happen with me and this guy."

"Why would you say that?"

"Because he told me so, tonight, that nothing is ever going to happen between us." I sighed. It was a sad sigh.

"Then he's the king of morons," Anna said dismissively. "Let him sit on his throne of dumb bro-ness."

"He's not a moron. He's smart." I wanted to be dismissive and indifferent about Victor too, but I wasn't. I was sad. "I just really like him. He's . . ." I searched for the right word, "He's gentlemanly. Formal. Guys aren't formal these days. It's strange and wonderful. And he's so smart. *So. Smart.* It gets me hot, you know?"

Anna reached for my hand and we shared a commiserating look. "Yeah, I get that. Why don't you tell me what happened?"

I nodded, sighing again. "Okay. It's a long story."

"We have all night."

"Are you sure Luca won't mind?"

"Luca is grading papers, which was his plan for the evening whether you were here or not. Plus, he loves you."

"Bah." I rolled my eyes and chuckled, but then I told my story.

I had to fib in some parts so as not to disclose where I worked or that *the guy* was a professor, but I got the gist of our interactions across. Anna was used to me being vague with details, something I appreciated about our relationship, so she didn't ask any questions while I spoke. She just listened, something else I appreciated.

It felt good to tell her, to relive it through the retelling, to separate my hopes from reality. It helped me focus, to be honest with myself about how pointless this crush of mine was.

When I finished recounting a version of the evening's events, Anna—her elbow resting on the back of the couch, her chin resting in her hand, her eyes narrowed with confusion—released a large breath. Loudly. "Why'd he kiss you? If he doesn't do relationships, why do that?"

"He said he did it because he wanted to, but wouldn't give me any more of an explanation." I picked at invisible lint on my pants, feeling sad and frustrated all over again.

"Who *is* this guy?"

"Guess." I chuckled, shaking my head at myself for the millionth time. I was a mess.

"So, someone complicated?"

"Yes."

"Just as complicated as me and Luca?" Anna tapped her chin with her index finger.

"Exactly as complicated."

"A professor." She grinned suddenly, pushing my shoulder while wagging her eyebrows jokingly.

I stared at her, saying nothing.

Her grin waned while her eyes grew. "Emily."

I blinked.

Her expression became one of horror. "Oh no."

"Oh yes."

"Oh, honey. That's not a road you want to take. Which one? Who is he?"

"Dr. Hanover." My face fell to my hands and I peeked at her from between my fingers.

"WHAT?" she shrieked, jumping up on the couch and reeling back. "Dr. Hanover? You can't mean—"

"Yes. I do." Anna had taken Dr. Hanover's class two years ago during her sophomore year, his first year teaching, because she had figured out a lot earlier what her major would be.

"Dr. *Hanover*?" She shook her head, as though this was impossible for her to comprehend. "Wait, did he talk to you about an advocate? Because if he kissed you, then—"

"Yes. He arranged one last month. That's all settled." I let my hands drop and waved away her concern.

"Oh. Well. Okay. Good." But then she looked completely confused again. "Dr. Hanover? I'm sorry, but . . . I'm going to need a minute."

"What? I'm attracted to his brain." Tilting my head back and forth, I decided to amend this statement. "And his body."

Anna's gaze narrowed on me. "His *body*? Em, he's . . . he's not at all your type."

"I know, I know. I like my guys sweet and short and skinny, not stern and tall and athletic. But I can't help it!"

Anna's eyes became slits. "Are we talking about the same Dr. Hanover? Research methods?"

"Yes. And I blame you."

"Why do you blame me?"

"Because you told me to take his class instead of Dr. Wilson's."

"Dr. Wilson is a terrible professor. You'll find out when you take discrete structures, he's the only one who teaches it. You'll learn nothing. Dr. Hanover actually *teaches.*"

"Yes. He does . . ." I stared at the neatly built fire crackling in Luca's fireplace, my dumb heart fluttering at the memory of Victor's impassioned speech about challenging preconceived norms, about the nature of great scientific advancement.

So hot.

"I'm—sorry, but this is all very surprising." Anna shook her head, looking like she was about to sneeze. "I still can't believe it."

"Why not?" I sent her a side-eye.

"Well, he seems . . . old."

"He's a year older than Luca."

"Is he?" She made a face. "He seems a lot older."

"Because he's serious?"

"No. Luca is serious. It's just everything. He's stodgy."

"Who is stodgy?" Luca asked as he walked in, carrying two large glasses of wine. He handed the first to me, giving me a small, supportive looking smile. "Here. I thought you might need this."

"Thank you, Luca." Returning his smile with a small one of my own, I accepted the wine. I did need it, so I gulped it.

Luca handed the second glass to Anna. She accepted it with a hazy, lovesick grin while he settled in behind her, his arm coming around my friend's waist.

"Who are we talking about?" he asked, looking to me.

I made a face, a pleading face, an entreaty to my best friend not to divulge anything to her hot boyfriend while placing my glass on the table. She didn't see me as she'd turned her head to aforementioned hot boyfriend.

"Uh, so, Emily has a little thing for Dr. Hanover and he kissed her. Don't worry, he arranged for an advocate."

"Oh. Good." Luca nodded.

"Oh my God." Again, my face fell to my hands. "Thanks, Anna. Thanks."

"What?"

"BEST FRIEND CODE!" I shouted, but the shout was muffled by my hands.

Luca laughed, a deep, rumbly, man sound. He had a nice laugh.

"Emily, after that night with Anna—and everything that came after—I hate to break it to you, but you and I are friends." His voice held humor, but also affection.

I peeked at him, reaching for my wine again. "But, in this case, you're the enemy."

His mouth dropped open. "I'm the enemy?"

Gesturing to him wildly with my free hand, because it really should have been obvious, I said, "You are a *male*. You are a *professor*. Your situational resemblance to the—the—the doofus in question means you can't be trusted."

A charming little grin twinkled behind his fancy blue eyes. *Yes. Fancy.* They were the color of blue topaz, and that made them fancy. Likewise, Anna's eyes were the color of brown topaz and twinkled in a similar fashion, *so also fancy*.

"Shouldn't that make me more trustworthy? Or at least, my opinion is valid *because* of the—what did you call it?—situational resemblance?"

"Whatever, fancy eyes," I mumbled, taking another gulp of my wine. "Just let me sit here on this couch for ten minutes, finish my wine, discuss the pollination of vanilla orchids outside of Mexico, and I'll be out of your hair."

Anna sighed. "Emily—"

"Same goes for you, fancy eyes." I gave her my best

disgruntled look. "I'm not talking to you about anything but pollination."

Anna smirked suggestively, lifting one eyebrow.

"Of VANILLA!" I clarified. "Pollination of *vanilla* outside of Mexico. Perv."

She chuckled, but then stopped abruptly. "Wait, which one of us is *fancy eyes*?"

"You both are. You have that gemstone eye thing going on. Pair of fancy-eyed Benedict Arnolds." This time I sipped the wine, because it was really good and I wanted it to last. Plus, I was cozy. This house, this room was cozy. *No wonder Anna spends so much time here.*

Anna seamlessly handed her wineglass to Luca, he took a drink, and then the three of us sat in quiet contemplation for a few seconds. For my part, I strategized ways to avoid Victor over the next few weeks leading to the final exam.

Perhaps I could email both him and Gloria, and suggest I teach myself the material. No need to return to class. . .

"Dr. Hanover," Luca interrupted my silent strategizing, passing the wineglass back to Anna. "Engineering?"

"No. Math and Sciences," Anna said.

"Hmm. What does he look like?"

Anna took a sip of wine, swallowed. "He's tall, maybe your height, white skin, brown hair, I don't know what color his eyes are—"

"Dark green, like a mossy jade. So, also gemstone fancy," I said, taking another gulp of wine and changing my plan. Instead of savoring the wine, maybe if I finished it quickly, they'd give me a second glass.

"And he's a big guy, like my dad," Anna added.

I sent her another side-eye. Victor was not husky, and he looked nothing like Anna's dad. "What are you talking about? He's the same size as Luca. Sure, maybe his shoulders are a little wider, but—"

"Emily. He's big. He's got to be three hundred pounds if not three fifty." She lifted her hands before I could contradict her, adding, "No judgment, because I like a cuddly guy. You know my first boyfriend was a big teddy bear, and my dad has always been larger. To be honest, Dr. Hanover's size is why I'm so surprised you have a thing for him. You've always been attracted to short, super lanky guys. Short, anti-athletic, sweet nerds."

I was shaking my head so hard I almost spilled the remainder of my wine; thankfully, I saved it from splashing at the last minute, setting the glass on the coffee table. "Anna, you know I only prefer smaller guys because I don't enjoy feeling like someone could overpower me."

One time in high school with a football player was all it took to put me off athletic men. We'd been dating for three months (and having sex for two months and three-weeks of the three months), and he'd made me uncomfortable, telling me he wasn't going to let me leave his truck until I gave him a blow job.

When he crowded me, holding my wrists, uncomfortable turned to fear and I screamed. As soon as I screamed, he realized how scared I was and he let me go. He seemed stunned but quickly apologized, horrified and immediately remorseful that I'd taken him seriously.

It was too late. I broke up with him, and though we remained friendly until graduation, me and ripped, muscly guys were over forever.

Until Victor.

"Yes," her gaze turned sympathetic, "I know. But—"

"I would have no problem admitting Dr. Hanover was husky if he was—in fact—husky. But he's not. Nor is he—as you say—lanky like I usually go for. So, admittedly, that does make it unusual for me to be attracted to him. Victor might be strong and works out, but he's definitely not big like your sweetheart of a dad."

Luca snapped his fingers, sitting up straighter and pointing at me. "Victor! Victor Hanover!"

"Yes. Victor Hanover." I glanced between Luca and Anna, sharing a look of confusion with my BFF.

"I do know him. Or, I know of him. He raised a hundred and fifty thousand dollars last year for charity," Luca said with more outward expression than I'd ever seen from him.

Anna and I continued to swap confused stares, but she was the one who asked, "That's a lot of money. How'd he do that?"

"It was—ah—a faculty wellness challenge put on by one of the endowed chair sponsors for sports medicine, an ex-pro athlete. A number of faculty and staff created a wellness group, or a club, and the endowed chair promised to donate a thousand dollars per pound lost for whichever of the group reduced their weight the most."

I reared back. My mother had always struggled with weight issues, placing too much importance on a number rather than on how she felt.

Therefore, my immediate reaction was to be horrified. "Uh, weight is not the only determination of health. Some 'heavier' people are much healthier than some 'light' people." I used air quotes around heavier and light; yes, I was so riled up—and tipsy from one glass of wine after not drinking for the last several months—that I was using air quotes. "In fact, we went over a study that showed people who are just above the max BMI for 'healthy' are—in fact—generally healthier by nonobjective scales than those at the lower end. And, furthermore, additional research has shown that focus on weight loss is at least partially responsible for the increase in anorexia and—"

"Okay, Emily." Anna held up her hands. She was doing

this a lot tonight. Luca took advantage of her hand placement by stealing the wineglass from her. "We aren't arguing with you."

"Yes. Sorry. I know." I closed my eyes, rubbing my forehead. "Sorry. I guess I'm all worked up from *events.*"

I was overwrought. Tired. Tipsy. I didn't want to think about Victor anymore. And yet, now that his remarkable body metamorphosis had been revealed, I couldn't help but view his behavior over the last month through the lens of this new information.

Victor had lost one hundred and fifty pounds. *Last year.*

What must that be like for a person? How long had he carried the weight before he lost it? Had he been larger his whole life?

My mother had never said anything about my body growing up, but I'd listened to her talk about herself constantly, and never in a positive way. No matter how low her weight, it was never enough. I'd witnessed firsthand how weight—so much more than health—impacted a person's self-worth.

Anna's hand came to my shoulder, pulling me from my introspection, and she rubbed my arm. "Hey. Are you okay? What can I do?"

Taking a deep breath, I glanced between Luca and Anna, their concerned and supportive expressions mirrors of each other.

"Wine?" Luca offered.

I breathed a laugh, shaking my head and pushing to my feet. "Uh, no thanks. Actually, I guess I should go."

"No. Stay." Anna also stood. "If you leave now, we'll fail the Bechdel test."

"Fine. How do they pollinate vanilla outside of Mexico?" I turned, searching for my bag.

"By hand."

I stiffened, shifting just my eyes to her. "Is that supposed to be some kind of dirty botany joke?"

Anna opened her mouth, maybe to deny it, but then her gaze lost focus. I could see that she was thinking about it.

"Vanilla? Hand pollination?" I prompted. "See where I'm going with this?"

"Oh yeah. I can work with that." Her grin was immense. "There's a punch line in there somewhere."

Chuckling, I pulled her into a hug, and whispered, "God, I'm so glad you're my friend."

"Same, my love. Same."

"Wrapping up the section on psychosocial study designs, by a show of hands, who among you read—and understood—the purported purpose and use of the deception study design?" Dr. Hanover's gaze moved over the lecture hall, his eyebrow slightly quirked.

I was only half paying attention. Actually, it was more like 41 percent. I'd spent most of the last two and half hours writing my art history paper. I had 98 words done, just 6902 left. Go me.

Mr. Jibbes raised his hand. I was not surprised. He'd been trying to lift himself out of the hole he'd dug early in the semester.

Dr. Hanover ignored him. "Ms. Limones, explain what a deception study is."

That got my attention. I glanced at the clock on my laptop. The fact that he'd gone straight to Limones instead of torturing anyone else usually meant class was almost over. The time on my PC proved me right, five minutes left.

Thank. God.

Against my more cowardly judgment, I'd decided to not

send an email to Gloria and Dr. Hanover requesting to refrain from attending classes. Instead, I'd attended today's lecture, deciding that doing so would not only be good for building character, but it would also be a helpful exercise in seeing Dr. Hanover without feeling attraction for him.

Better to see him now, in a controlled environment, than run into him randomly and become a freaked-out fool.

So, there I was, in class, sharing space with Dr. Hanover, struggling to write a paper for a different class while not feeling attracted to him. I was failing at both, mostly because he kept saying the most brilliant and poignant things.

Dumb troublesome heart flutters.

Sighing silently, I saved my 98 words and closed my laptop, giving the remainder of the lecture my full attention. If I couldn't enjoy his gorgeous brain in private, at least I'd be able to enjoy it for the next five minutes.

"Correct," Dr. Hanover said in reply to whatever Ms. Limones had said. No surprise there, she was always correct, and I loved her for it. "Now," he continued, "tell me why deception studies are unethical."

I started, sitting straighter in my seat, my attention fastened to Vict—Dr. Hanover. His voice sounded funny, just a little off, like he had a bone to pick with deception studies.

"Deception studies are unethical because they involve lying to participants, and the consent process—which is supposed to be both informative and ethical—is neither. Therefore, subjects cannot give consent," Ms. Limones said plainly.

"That's also correct. Okay, for next week, we'll be reviewing for the last test. You can submit questions online to either of my TAs. Unless there's anything else."

What?

That's it? He asked why deception studies were unethical, but requested no counterpoint or opinion?

What the heck?

Riding a cresting wave of insanity, I raised my hand. But I didn't just raise it. Oh no. I sat forward in my chair and *waved* it in the air.

Dr. Hanover scanned the room and did a double take, his gaze snagging on my waving arm. Even though I was sitting some thirty feet away, and even though his eyes were mostly hidden by his glasses, his stare looked wary. He also seemed to hesitate, perhaps deciding whether or not to ignore me.

But in the end, crossing his arms and clearing his throat, he said, "Yes, Ms. Von. You have a question?"

"You asked why deception studies are unethical, but you didn't ask why—or under what circumstances—they might be ethical."

"Because they're not ethical."

"That's not true."

A split second of silent shock gripped my classmates, followed by the ripple of subtle movements and the low murmur of whispers. I sensed and heard the rustle and hum of people turning to look at me, disbelieving breaths, felt their eyes and attention on my skin as an eruption of heat.

But, oddly, I didn't care. I was irrationally aggravated that he'd neglected to discuss how deception studies could be ethical, if done appropriately. Therefore, all I really saw in the quietly chaotic moments that followed my statement was Dr. Hanover glaring at me.

"By all means," he drawled, using his dry as dust voice, "enlighten us."

"The debriefing process is meant to counter the unethical nature of deception."

"Yes." He nodded once. "And the debriefing process is wrought with its own process."

"But deception is all around us—advertising and politics as an example—why should psychological researchers be held to a higher standard than real life? Especially when it's their job to explain how we interact with real life."

"Science and scientists should always be held to—"

Holding up my hand, I said firmly, "I'm not finished," and the quiet chaos reached a crescendo. I ignored the noise. "Furthermore, how can psychological researchers determine answers related to true motivation and attitudes without deception studies? Bias in self-report data is rampant, evidenced by *both* medical and psychosocial studies. You ask a person how much they're in debt, nine times out of ten they lie. Why would anyone tell the truth about being a racist? And what if they don't know they're a racist? In some cases, deception studies are the only way to obtain accurate data."

Dr. Hanover waited a beat, glaring at me obstinately, and then asked, "Are you finished?"

"For now." I shrugged, returning his glare with aplomb even as my hands shook. I gripped my notebook to keep them still.

"For now?" Apparently, he was making no effort to hide his resentment at being challenged.

"We're having a conversation, aren't we? So, after you speak, I'll offer my counterpoints."

"No. We're not. That's not how this works, Ms. Von. You are a student, I am the professor. I decide when the conversation is over. And when students are rude, the conversation is over." Dr. Hanover turned his face from me, looking to his TA, opening his mouth with the clear intention of speaking to her.

A not so subtle sign that he was *done* with me.

But I was not done with him. "Oh? Really? Because, if that's the case, then you're a hypocrite."

Another split second of shock, and then the room buzzed. Loudly.

"Is that so?" He spoke over the buzz, his tone authoritative but not quite a shout, his eyes now lowered to the papers on the front table.

Oh man, he was really pissed.

For some reason that made me giddy.

"Yes. That is so." I lifted my voice to be heard over the commotion. "Weren't you the one who said research needs conversation and *dialogue,* and often that dialogue is contentious? You told this entire class that great science never occurs in a vacuum. Seldom with politeness, and never with pleases and thank yous. You asked all of us if we believed we were allowed to hold ideas and beliefs without ever having them openly challenged. You expect to challenge us, but balk at being challenged in return. So yes, you're being a hypocrite."

The ruckus that followed was immediately deafening and continued for several long seconds. But after this initial surge, it abruptly tapered off, with a few students shushing the others, now all eyes on Dr. Hanover at the front.

Eventually, the room fell to near silence again. The clock had run out on class, our three hours were up, but no one seemed to be in a hurry to leave. Clearly, they were waiting for his brilliant response.

And so was I. Reason and fear hadn't seen fit to visit my brain yet. My electrified sense of righteousness hadn't waned. Yet, I did feel the tiniest bit queasy in my stomach as his shoulders rose and fell with a breath. I thought I saw—though I was probably mistaken, because he was too far away and his face was angled down—the faintest of smiles curve his lips.

But then, without looking up, and sounding eerily calm, he spoke.

"Ms. Von, please stay after class. The rest of you are dismissed."

CHAPTER 10

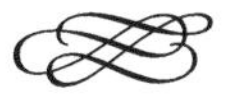

EMILY

I'd never seen the room empty so slowly. My classmates had been possessed by sloths. Excited, whispering, staring, wide-eyed sloths. Make no mistake, they were excited. And I did not doubt for one second that a contingent of them would loiter outside the lecture hall, waiting for me to emerge.

I guess I understood their curiosity. What kind of crazy person would contradict Dr. Hanover in his domain, argue the point, and then call him a hypocrite?

I mentally pointed at myself using both my thumbs. *This crazy person. This one. Right here.*

Yet, I didn't feel like a crazy person. I felt indignant and irritated. These emotions provided me sufficient wreckage upon which to cling to after my Titanic performance, a door large enough to float upon during the sluggish progress of my fellow students.

Also, for the record, there was no room for Dr. Hanover on this hypothetical floating door. He could die a cold death at the bottom of the icy sea, where all the other frigid creatures dwelt while I lounged on my spacious buoyant debris.

Eventually, my classmates did leave, the last departing footstep followed by the last reverberating slam of the door. And then we were left entirely and utterly alone.

"Please." His attention focused on the tabletop and papers scattered before him, Dr. Hanover motioned with his hand that I should come join him at the front of the class.

"No, thank you. I prefer to stay where I am," I said, tearing my eyes from his downturned head, standing, and reaching for my backpack. For some reason, the fact that he hadn't looked up yet, that he hadn't looked at me since dismissing my challenge as rude, really pissed me off. It pissed me off so much, the near constant fluttering in my chest since spotting him three hours ago finally, finally stopped.

Good riddance.

A moment later, I thought I felt the weight of his gaze, but I was too busy packing up my stuff to look, and too irritated to care. I made a mental note: hope and fear froze me, but anger and righteousness were apparently lubricants for recklessness.

"Emily, you—"

"Dr. Hanover, unless you're planning to apologize—" I shoved my laptop into my backpack with more force than necessary "—then I'm not really interested in anything you have to say."

Whoa. Go Emily. I deserve a new set of D&D dice for that.

"Apologize for what?" He didn't sound upset. He sounded curious. And closer.

I kept my attention fastened to where I was working to fit both my notebook and my textbook in the main pocket of my bag. "Apologize for insinuating that I was rude."

"I didn't insinuate. I said, quite ubiquitously, that you were rude." Footsteps on linoleum, his voice was even closer. He was climbing the stairs toward me.

But the shiver of anticipatory anxiety was chased away by a renewed burst of irritation at his words.

Pausing my efforts, I turned to face Dr. Hanover. He was still several steps away, his pace unhurried, his eyes on me.

My dumb heart twisted. I ignored it. "I wasn't rude. But if I were—being rude—you said yourself that challenging perspectives in research design, in science, was not just necessary, it was expected. So, either way, you're a hypocrite."

He nodded faintly, his gaze holding mine as he approached, reaching the step just below my row. "So, what you really want is for me to apologize for being a hypocrite?"

I huffed a laugh. "Nope. Everyone is a hypocrite. If I asked you to apologize for being one, then I'd have to apologize too. Nice try, though."

Dr. Hanover smiled. It was a very brief smile, looked completely involuntary, and it definitely wasn't my imagination.

Shoving my notebook into my bag, I zipped it, not allowing myself to think about his not-imaginary-but-definitely-involuntary smile. "So, if we're finished, then I have—"

"No. We're not finished." He now stood at the end of my row, his hands stuffed in his ugly brown pants that were too big, his intelligent eyes sparking with either irritation or humor or both, but his voice was gentle. "You can't fight with me during class because you're upset about us."

Uhhh . . . what?

He'd stunned me. I was stunned.

Therefore, I could only manage an inelegant, "What?"

"You said, the other night, that I hurt your feelings." His tone was now not only gentle, it was intimate.

"So?" Blinking uncontrollably, I crossed my arms, standing straighter. What did this have to do with anything?

He seemed to be studying me, which was a heady experience given the intellectual intensity of his gaze. "It was not—and never has been—my intention to hurt you." His words were quietly spoken, but the combination of gentleness and intimacy, affection and regret paired with the heated way he was looking at me felt considerably more forceful than when he'd all but shouted at me in front of the class ten minutes earlier.

Such tenderness. Such genuine regret! The statement felt like an assault of softness, of vulnerability. Abruptly, my skin felt too tight and my chest hurt. He had me caught in his magnetic field of boyish and sharply intelligent accidental attractiveness. *ALERT ALERT ALERT!*

Victor took a step forward. I tensed. He halted, lifting his hands, his actions reminding me of the time my mom tried to rescue a cluster of feral kittens.

"I'm sorry," he said, his voice roughened with some unknown emotion. "I don't know how to be with—or, I guess, around someone like you."

"Someone like me?" I parroted unthinkingly, turning the words over and over in my brain as I tried to make sense of them, my earlier anger eclipsed by this extraordinary turn of events and subject change.

"Someone I . . ." He breathed out, but didn't finish that thought, instead saying, "Emily, my point is, you're upset. But taking it out on me during class is not the right answer. You're better than that. If you're angry, come talk to me."

What?

Wait. . . ohhhhh!

Right.

That's right.

This is the thing we're talking about. Not the other thing. And this thing has nothing to do with the other thing.

And just like that, the wonderful web of potentially good feelings was shattered.

I chuckled, closing my eyes just briefly and shaking my head at myself, my skin relaxing, the ache in my chest easing. I shouldn't have allowed myself to be distracted from the original topic, especially because—though he was too blind or self-absorbed to admit it—our brief attraction had nothing to do with what had happened during class.

"Listen, *Dr. Hanover*—" I picked up my bag and hooked it over my shoulder "—I'm fine with teaching myself the remainder of this semester's material and finishing up my tests and assignments with Gloria. If being challenged by a student pushes you outside of your comfort zone, just say so. But don't justify your inability to engage in a debate by deluding yourself that this—" I gestured the lecture hall with a waving arm "—had anything to do with the three seconds I thought you were worth getting to know."

"That's exactly what this—" he mimicked my waving arm movement, gaining another step forward, his brilliant eyes crackling with something I refused to label "—was about, *Emily*."

Oh no he didn't!

My anger doubled-down.

"No, *professor*. It was about deception studies and—apparently—your failure and lack of willingness to engage in and foster healthy conversation. I believe deception studies have their place in the research design spectrum. Therefore, I *disagree* with you. I'm allowed to disagree with you and challenge you."

"You have no idea," Victor mumbled, an amused yet rueful grin claiming his mouth. He glanced away from me while drawing his bottom lip between his teeth.

He was now approximately two feet away and I was close enough—and the light was good enough—for me to discern the details of him. Each individual eyelash, the faint creases and lines around his eyes, the dark pointillism of his day beard, the chest hair peeking out of his shirt's collar, the sharp angle of his jaw and cheekbones.

In addition to the small details, I both saw and felt the difference in our sizes and shapes, how tall he was, how big his shoulders were, how strong. Even though I was certain he'd never rely on his strength to intimidate, I felt oddly intimidated.

I say *oddly* because it was a thrilling type of intimidation I'd never experienced before rather than the scary one that left me feeling powerless. Usually, I hated feeling intimidated. Hated it. I'd had anxiety attacks just standing next to tall, athletic men when not enough people were nearby.

So the fact that I felt thrilled by his proximity and strength was obviously odd. Or it made me odd.

Probably, it was me. *Because I am odd.*

Moving on.

What were we talking about?

Peering down at me—specifically, peering at my mouth—Victor exhaled softly. "Fine. Let's say, hypothetically, that your disruption during class—"

"Disruption?!"

"—was actually about the subject being discussed."

"Deception studies were the subject. And, for the record, my opinion on the subject is well researched because I found it fascinating when I read the materials, so I took it upon myself to read up on the subject. If dissenting opinions make you uncomfortable, nothing I can do about that. But I am ready to *discuss* the merits and appropriateness of deception studies whenever you locate your big boy pants and put them on. That is, if you own any big boy pants."

Something unexpected happened then, something I couldn't have predicted. All through my little speech, he'd been watching me with a faint smile on his lips and infuriating warmth in his eyes, like he thought I was wonderful and fascinating and special, and it reactivated my heart flutters.

But that wasn't the something unexpected (even though it certainly wasn't expected).

The something unexpected happened the moment the words *big boy pants and put them on* left my mouth. Victor flinched, his eyebrows drawing low—like he was confused, or caught unaware, or had just been slapped—and his stare flashed with clear and present hurt.

He took an immediate step back, color draining from his face, his eyes moving between mine. I watched his withdrawing reaction with confusion, especially as a flush crept up his neck, overtaking the paleness of his cheeks, leaving them and his ears red and splotchy.

Victor dropped his eyes, the muscle at his jaw ticking. "I see."

He sees? He sees what?

"What? Wait. What do you see?"

He shook his head, his eyes still fastened to the ground. "You're right, Ms. Von," his voice was rough, coldly distant, "please accept my apology."

I blinked my astonishment. He looked . . . hurt. Like I'd hurt him. Not just a little hurt, a big hurt.

Drowning in confusion, I took an automatic step forward, following his retreat. "Wait a second." I grabbed his arm—another automatic movement—keeping him from turning away from me, and studied the face angled toward the floor.

He was . . . *off.* After our handful of one-on-one run-ins and experiencing him in class three hours twice a week for the last several months, I could tell something was very, very wrong.

"Ms. Von—"

"You're acting weird. What just happened? Why are you

apologizing?" I shuffled closer, bending my knees and trying to capture his gaze, asking softly, "And why do I suddenly feel like I should be apologizing to you?"

His eyes lifted then, mossy jade, fancy, brilliant. *So sexy.* But also uncertain, questioning, cautious.

He cleared his throat, his gaze flickering like he was trying to pull it away from mine but couldn't. "I'm used to the jokes," he said quietly, it sounded like both a confession and an absolution. "It doesn't bother me."

"Jokes?" I asked, just as quietly.

"Come on." His jaw ticked again, as though he were grinding his teeth. "Big boy pants?"

I squinted at him, allowing the full force of my confusion to play out over my features.

Big boy pants . . .?

What could he—

Oh no!

I sucked in a sudden breath, my eyes growing round with abrupt understanding. He looked embarrassed. So embarrassed. And I'd embarrassed him. He thought my use of *big boy pants* had been making fun of his previous weight, or his weight loss, or something related, and that realization felt like another sucker punch.

He shook his head, his voice gravelly, tearing his eyes away to roll them.

"Victor." I invaded his space, my face and limbs hot with mortified urgency. "It's an expression I use with my friend, Anna and her cousin, Abram. It's just an expression. It wasn't a reference to . . . it's just an expression."

I watched his Adam's apple move up and down, and then he laughed lightly, self-deprecatingly, still not looking at me. "Okay. No big deal."

Ugh and blarg.

I felt so gross and I couldn't tell if he believed me or not. He absolutely *had to* believe me.

"Victor, I was not making a joke. I'm not—I don't—that would be reprehensible. And, besides, size doesn't matter."

I winced. At myself.

AAAAHHHHHHHHH!!!!

Shut up, Emily. Shut up!

Did I just say that?

God, why am I such a socially defunct doofus?

His eyes cut to mine, affection tinged with bitterness, both hinting to a lifetime of unpleasant experiences. "Now, that's something I know is absolutely false." He covered my hand on his arm and gently pried it away, swallowing thickly. "Size does matter, and no one lets you forget it."

CHAPTER 11

EMILY

I was on a carousel, but without the fiberglass horses, and the lights, and the general majesty and splendor. Okay, so, the carousel was figurative, meant to represent the cycle that held my emotions hostage this semester, ever since Dr. Hanover—*Victor*—made me feel hot and bothered while stage three naked.

One minute, I was daydreaming about Victor and his sexy intelligence. The next minute, I was hurt or confused by something he'd done or said, and then I was angry with him. And the minute after that? I was apologizing. The cycle would start again: crush, hurt, anger, apology. Repeat.

As I studied him now, and the vulnerability that served only to increase his allure, I made a conscious decision to *step off* the carousel of crazy. According to my calculations, next up was the *crush and daydream* cycle.

Instead of giving into it, instead of focusing on how delectably dreamy he was, and allowing myself to be curious about him, how I—Emily Von, strong woman, emotionally available maverick—could step in and fix this sexy, brilliant man, and find the one *thing* he so obviously needed in order for a romantic relationship between us to be possible, I decided to just be a friend.

I sighed, giving him a tight, compassionate smile, and stuck out my hand. "Hi. I'm Emily."

Victor's eyebrow arced, a movement I recognized as being entirely involuntary, something he did when faced with a surprising statement or situation. Glancing between me and my hand, he gave his head a subtle shake.

"What are you doing?"

"We're going to start over."

"Start over." He shoved his hands in his pockets, like he was holding them ransom. *Or maybe in escrow...*

I didn't drop my fingers, instead wiggling them a little. "Yes. We're starting over. I'm introducing myself. This is the part where you shake my hand and we chitchat about the weather, or traffic, or what's wrong with homeowners' associations, or why deception studies are scientifically valid."

The eyebrow dropped, his eyes narrowed, but his lips tugged to the side. "You're not going to let that go."

I made my face innocent. "Let what go? We've never spoken before. We're just meeting now."

He shook his head. "Emily—"

"Yes. That's my name. And yours?"

Breathing in and out through his nose, he took his right hand out of his pocket and shook my hand. "Fine. Victor Hanover. How do you do?" His voice was flat, like a salt field, and just as dry.

And that made me smile. Actually, it made me laugh. *He's so cute. . .*

Ah-ah-ah! No. *None of that!* No thoughts allowed about his cuteness.

"We are now friendly acquaintances, Victor Hanover," I announced, even though he'd made no move to drop my hand. Similarly, I'd made no move to drop his hand.

"Friendly acquaintances," he repeated, sounding like he didn't know whether to be amused or irritated.

"Would you like to have dinner with me? I know a great Ethiopian place. The last guy who took me there was a *real jerk*." I said this last part using my Patty and Selma voice (Marge's sisters from *The Simpsons*).

Victor laughed, his eyebrows moving down, and then up, like he still couldn't decide how to take me.

And you know what? That was fine. He didn't have to be my friendly acquaintance. He could take me or leave me and, since I'd removed the crush/daydream portion of the cycle, I was officially off the carousel. If he walked away, fine. If not, also fine.

As the kids say today, *whatevs, yo.* At least, that's what my twelve-year-old cousin says. He also does this weird thing called *dub step*. It makes me feel *soooooo oooold.*

But I digress.

"Fine." Victor's gaze dropped to my mouth, but then immediately moved beyond me. He pulled his bottom lip between his teeth, bit it, frowned, and said more determinedly, "Fine. Let's go."

"Cool, cool, cool." Now who's old, Carter? Not Cousin Emily!

I tugged on my hand. He held it for a beat, and then let it go, shoving his back into his pocket.

Still looking beyond me, he asked, "I need to take some papers to my office, and then I'll meet you there?"

"Sure. I'll go ahead and order." I hitched my backpack higher on my shoulder. "You like lentils? Or what's your favorite?"

He took a step back, clearing his throat. "I usually just get the combination platter."

"Great. Then that's what I'll get."

He nodded, his eyes coming back to mine. They were

cagey, distrustful. I grinned.

Before five minutes ago, this kind of look coming from him would've sent me into a tailspin crash-landing onto the crazy carousel. But not this time. He didn't need to trust me.

After all, we were nothing but *friendly acquaintances.*

"Good. You're here." I gestured to the seat across from me as soon as he walked up to the booth. "I need you to keep me from eating this whole thing. It's friggin' delicious."

Injera was bread from the gods, and tibbs were the food of the gods. Add the two of them together and my diet was in the corner rocking and crying and singing creepy nursery rhymes to itself. Creepily.

Victor sat down, opposite me, and glanced from where I was grabbing part of a hard-boiled egg with a shred of injera to my face.

"You already started?"

"Yes. I was hungry." I fed myself the egg and bread, and then went back for seconds, frowning at him when he remained immobile. "Hey. Friend. Do your part!" I gestured to the big platter of food with my chin. "I ordered for two."

Giving me a very small, and very wary—but clearly amused—smile, Victor ripped off a piece of bread, seemed to debate his options, and grabbed a quantity of cabbage and carrots. As he chewed, he glanced around the restaurant, a frown on his forehead when he returned his attention to the platter.

I wanted to ask, *Something wrong?* but decided friend Emily didn't care. Yet.

Instead, I got to the point. "So, Vic, tell me about yourself."

His sharp green eyes flickered to mine and I held my

breath for a second, because they were *so* sharp. I swear, sometimes, just having him look directly at me felt like being poked with a bunch of little knives.

"Don't call me Vic."

I waited for him to take another bite, and then asked, "Tor?"

A surprised laugh erupted from him and he covered his mouth with a napkin, shaking his head.

"Not Tor? That's too bad. I've always wanted to know someone named Tor." That wasn't a lie so much as a joke, I was hoping to keep the mood light. "So tell me, *Victor,* how do you spend your free time? What do you do for fun?"

He glanced to the side again, his eyes moving around the restaurant. Whatever he saw there seemed to unsettle him again. *Is he worried about being seen with me?* I shrugged off the concern.

Swallowing, he returned his attention to me. "I build and fix planes."

I reared back, my eyes expanding to their maximum. "Model ones?"

Somehow, I already knew the answer before he responded, "No. Real ones."

"No shit? Real planes?"

"That's right." He took a gulp of water, and then ripped another square of injera.

"You're going to have to tell me more about that."

"Sure," he agreed readily. "I can take you up sometime too. If you're interested. I have my pilot's license." He seemed to be relaxing into the conversation. *Good.*

"How big are these planes?"

"I build custom jets and fix antiques, Cessnas usually. My friend owns a company, I work for him."

"And you help him build them for fun?"

"Yeah. And for a paycheck," he said without shame. "Being a professor doesn't pay what it used to."

"Huh." I nodded, respecting his matter-of-fact tone about it. "So, if you could be a full-time professor or a full-time airplane builder, what would you do?"

Victor's eyes moved up and to the right, like he was giving my question serious thought. He looked so relaxed, so *into* the conversation. I had to tell the odd, giddy fluttering in my stomach to chill out.

We are friendly acquaintances, nary a crush nor a daydream in sight.

"I don't know, honestly." His sharp, sexy eyes—*no! not sexy*—intelligent eyes came back to mine. "I enjoy teaching, and research. I can't imagine *not* doing it. But I've been around planes and aeronautics my whole life. I can't imagine not doing that either."

"Huh," I said again. "So that's how you spend all your free time? Building planes? Nothing else? Not, let's say, going to upscale lingerie shops in the swanky side of town?"

His eyes dropped and, if I wasn't mistaken (which I *wasn't*) a bit of pink highlighted his cheeks. Maybe I shouldn't have brought it up, but since we were now in the friend zone end zone, I gave into my curiosity and the urge to ask.

"That's . . . my father's thing."

"Mr. Hanover?"

"Yes." Victor seemed to be gritting his teeth.

"With more wives than Henry the Eighth?"

I was pleased to see that drew a small smirk out of him. "You don't know how apt that analogy is."

I decided to let that go, for now, since I was still curious about Victor and the Pinkery. "But didn't you get a membership? If looking at lingerie is just your father's thing, why'd you do that?"

He dropped his injera on the plate and wiped his hands with a napkin, glancing over my shoulder. "I wanted . . ."

"Yeeeees?" I prompted in a cartoonish voice, still wanting to keep the mood light.

Victor's gaze became distracted, narrowing, dropping to the floor, and then lifting again to the spot behind me. Unthinkingly, I also glanced over my shoulder.

Two women. Sitting in a booth on the other end of the restaurant. Looking at him. Smiling.

When they saw me look, they quickly glanced away. It made me smile. I didn't blame them for looking. Victor Hanover was a hottie.

But when I returned my attention to Victor, he did not look pleased. He was gritting his teeth again, wiping his already clean fingers with frustrated, quick swipes.

This time, I decided to ask the question I hadn't earlier. "Hey. What's wrong?"

"Them." Without looking at *them* he lifted his chin in their direction.

"What? You don't like them looking at you?"

Victor's eyes—intensely aggravated—moved between mine, like he was searching them for the answer to a riddle that might earn him his freedom, and one of my fanciful thoughts occurred to me. Maybe he was under the spell of a wicked troll. Maybe that's what this was all about. Wicked troll magic . . .?

Stop it with the nonsense.

Eventually, after much (obvious) internal debate, he said, "I don't like it."

"What's the problem? They're not leering. They're just appreciating something beautiful."

The pink on his cheeks turned rosier and he pressed his lips together in a stern line. "Don't say that about me."

"Okay." I shrugged. "You're hideous."

He stared at me, stunned for a moment, and then he huffed a trifecta of laughs: the first sounded disbelieving, the second bitter, the third reluctantly amused.

"You have no idea what it's like."

"What it's like?"

"You don't even notice."

"Notice what?"

He glanced to his right and then tilted his head toward the bar. I looked where he indicated and found a man, on his own, drinking something with no ice. After a short moment, the man looked at me, caught me watching, and then hurriedly turned his back, rubbing the back of his neck.

"What's going on? Am I missing something?"

"Yes." He'd crossed his arms. "That guy has been looking at you since I walked in."

I waited for Victor to explain the relevance of this. When he didn't, I prompted, "So?"

"The last time we were here, men were looking at you then too."

"Okay? So what? People look at other people."

He gathered a deep breath, his stare somber, serious. "No. They don't. People don't look at *people.* People look at *beautiful people*. Everyone else is invisible. And you don't notice because you're used to it. You've always been beautiful, so it doesn't faze you. But I . . ." he swallowed, the action appeared to be a struggle.

Again, though I felt like I knew what he was going to say, I waited. I wanted to hear his perspective in his words, not fill in the blanks with my assumptions.

Victor's attention darted beyond me once more, and once more he frowned, this time leaning forward and placing his elbow on the table, his other hand right next to it, rubbing his forehead with long fingers. "If those women saw the real me, they wouldn't look."

My heart hurt at the conflicted desolation in his tone and I fought the urge to reach across the table and hold his hand.

Instead, I kept my voice low and soft and asked, "The real you?"

"Yeah." His eyes were on the table.

Grabbing another piece of injera—just to have something to hold—I twisted it between my fingers. "Am I missing something? Are you in the mafia?"

He laughed again, shaking his head. "No. Emily." His smile lingered—in his eyes and on his mouth—as he gazed at me with a blatant fondness that had my stomach doing cartwheels closer to the carousel of crazy. "You know I'm not in the mafia. I mean, the real me. None of these people would look at me twice if they saw what I looked like before."

"And that's the real you? What you looked like before?"

"Yes. I mean, no. I guess . . . it's not pretty."

"What?" I popped a rolled-up piece of bread into my mouth.

"The real me, under these clothes." He gestured to himself, to his chest, and then lifted his eyes to mine, a challenge there, like he expected me to look away. "The clothes hide the skin, but it's there. I know I could have surgery, get it removed, but I can't bring myself to do it."

I didn't look away, but my mind was racing. *Holy overshare, Batman.* I should've proposed friendship to Victor Hanover weeks ago. Jeez! I'd wasted all this time being hot for him. He didn't want another lady lusting after a body he didn't feel belonged to him. He needed . . . perspective.

"Obviously, you don't have to answer me. But are you seeing a counselor? To help you with this transition?" If he wasn't, then that would be the first thing I nagged him about from now on.

"Yes. I am." He reached for his water, twisted the glass. I noticed his fingers weren't just long, they were elegant, with elegant nails, neatly trimmed, and elegant lines at the knuckles. "Since the beginning, actually."

"Okay. Good. Then I won't nag you about that."

His lips tugged to the side. "You were going to nag me about that?"

"Absolutely. Yes. My mom's therapist has helped her a lot with her body—uh—image." I'd been about to say "body issues" but remembered *issues* was a pejorative term as well as being less accurate. "Again, you don't have to answer this question, and I'm not advocating that you do this, but I'm curious why you don't want to get the skin removed."

Victor stared at his water glass, his lips twisting to the side, his usually sharp eyes losing focus.

"You don't have to answer." I lifted my hands. "I can tell a joke instead. Have you heard the one about—"

"Right now, it feels like I'd be completely erasing who I was before," he blurted, swallowed, and then lifted his eyes to mine. They weren't so sharp. "And I liked that person, even if no one else did."

CHAPTER 12

VICTOR

"What's going on with you and the brunette? Any movement on that? You finally ask her out?"

Scowling, I debated how best to answer. Andy and I had been talking on the phone for an hour, working through all the scheduling details for the new orders, touching base on an antique Cessna rebuild. I thought I was free and clear.

No more going out for drinks with Andy after work.

"Hello? Are you there? Or are you choking on something? Should I call an ambulance?"

"We went out to dinner last week and we've decided to be friends."

"Friends." He sounded disgusted. "After all of that, after kissing her and blowing her off and regretting it for weeks, you decide to be . . . friends." He said the word *friends* like most people say the word *malignant.*

I hadn't told him about Emily's job at the Pinkery, wanting to respect her privacy, but I'd told him the rest a few weeks ago. I'd needed to tell someone. With drunken enthusiasm, he'd congratulated me on my first kiss. But then he literally *boo-ed* me—while we were still in the bar—when I told him what I'd done at the restaurant after.

"I still don't understand why you didn't just make her your girl after kissing her."

"No defensible justification exists for dating a student in my class." I chose to focus on the most obvious and logical of my reasons. I didn't expect him to inherently understand my perspective as a professor yet I had expected him to understand why—even if she hadn't been my student—dating someone like Emily would be impossible for someone like me.

"Your mind needs a tune-up. It is *always* defensible to date a woman who digs you, and who you dig in return."

I shook my head and set my jaw. Perception was nine-tenths of reality. Advocate or no, it put her in an untenable situation, one where she would be judged for our relationship in a way I wouldn't. Even if she didn't care now, one day she might care. I wouldn't do that to her. I'd witnessed enough of that kind of behavior from my father. Following in his footsteps was not an option.

"Listen. I need to go."

"You don't need to go." He sighed, grumbling, "Please tell me at least you've called her? You have plans with her now that you're *friends*? Something concrete? Hanging out with her would be good practice at least."

"Good practice?"

"Yeah. Hanging out with a lady you want to bang and not making things awkward. And don't try to deny that you want to bang her."

Ignoring his garish statement, I scratched my cheek, paying no attention to the sinking sense in my chest that I'd messed up again. "I should've called her? I don't want to bother her."

She hadn't contacted me since our dinner last week. She'd

attended the Monday review session but didn't stay after to talk. She wasn't present for the Wednesday test, but that was to be expected. Gloria had been administering all her tests for nearly a month.

I did see her at the gym, however, every morning but Thursday. She still hadn't noticed me, and I didn't know how to approach her there without making it . . . Well, without making things awkward. Or potentially making her uncomfortable.

"Not calling is okay if you already made plans."

"No plans yet."

"No plans?" He sounded indignant. "What the hell is wrong with you?"

I said nothing.

"God. You are so fucking clueless." He exhaled an obviously frustrated laugh and I was certain he was also shaking his head. "Listen, this is what you're going to do: you're going to text her, all right? Texting is no pressure, for either of you. You text her and you thank her for something. Tell her you want to get together—and don't ask *if* she wants to, just tell her *you* want to—and then you follow up next week if you get radio silence."

"What? Why would I do that? If she doesn't text me back, shouldn't I leave her alone?"

"No, *Sheldon.* You message her next week. You're the asshole. Now you got, like, the next twenty balls in your court. You have to be the one to message her first for the next few weeks. You need to be the most solicitous, most patient, most interested motherfucker in all the land. That's what you did to yourself. You want to know her? Now you have to really, really *work for* it. This is how it is: she's not going to start texting or calling you or treating you like a friend until she knows you're not going to disappear or blow her off again. Makes sense?"

I nodded, because it did make sense. Suddenly, I was winded.

"Victor?"

"Yes. It makes sense. Thanks."

"Do it now, Victor. I'm hanging up. See you in the morning for leg day. Bye."

He ended the call and my mind went blank other than the single action item: *text her now.*

I still had her number in my phone from our brief kiss in the hall over a month ago. But I wouldn't think about that. Every time I thought about it, about kissing her, having my hands on her, I got hard, flushed, dizzy. It was disorienting.

One of my friends in grad school—a female friend—had announced that I was asexual, in her opinion. I didn't agree or disagree with that label. Her opinion was merely a data point, and I understood why she'd arrived at her conclusion. I'd been attracted to one person, once, freshman year of high school. It had been a painful experience and I'd never experienced anything like it again.

Not until now.

Maybe I was asexual, or on the spectrum of asexuality. Maybe I wasn't. Unlike Andy, I didn't consider my lack of interest in physicality something to fix or cure or be distressed about. Quite the opposite. I considered it a strength.

Think about it, how much better would all manner of interactions be (for you) without instinctual sexual desire clouding perceptions?

Using the workplace as an example: no sexual harassment, no preference given to applicants or workers based on their perceived physical attractiveness. Removing physical desire would lead to more competency-based hires and promotions, controlling of course for other biases.

Anyway. Back to Emily and this inconvenient attraction.

Ultimately, whether I was attracted to her or not didn't matter. I believed Emily deserved someone experienced, sophisticated, knowledgeable, a sexual content expert. She deserved someone who could lead instead of follow. Therefore, I was not the person she deserved as a romantic partner, but I absolutely did not want to lose her as a friend.

Text her now.

I opened our short string of texts, seeing I'd been the last to text her over a month ago, directions to Queen of Sheba. My mouth dry, I began my message,

Victor: I had a really good time the other night. Thank you for coming out. Let me know when you're free to get together.

I hit send before I could think too much about it, and then promptly thought too much about it.

Did that sound okay? Was it weird? Should I add something else? Like how she was the funniest person I knew, with the best sense of humor, and that I missed her smile, and her intelligence and insight blew me away, and that she challenged me and I appreciated her, her goodness and kindness and care for other people, and that she was beautiful, that I couldn't stop thinking about—

Emily: Who is this?

I grinned.

. . .

Victor: Very funny.

Emily: How did you get this number?

I stared at her last message, frowning, uncertain if she was serious, and questioning myself. She was so funny, unexpected, witty. But had I misread things? Had I overstepped with the text and—

My phone vibrated.

Emily: I'M TEASING YOU. I can almost feel your indecision and doubt through the cell phone waves. You need to lighten up and trust, Tor. If we're going to be friends, you need to be okay with teasing, riffing, pranks, and jokes (the inside variety and the normal, everyday variety). Please confirm you consent to teasing and inside jokes. Those are dealbreakers for me.

I breathed a sigh of relief and relaxed against the back of my couch, tugging at my bottom lip and thinking how best to respond. I was also smiling. Licking my lips, I tapped out,

Victor: I will work on lightening up. Also, I consent to inside jokes and teasing, but don't call me Tor.

Emily: Why not? It's better than "Ict" which is also in your name.

I laughed. Out loud. And then I poked at the inside of my cheek with my tongue as I quickly responded,

. . .

Victor: You can call me Tor if I can call you Lavender.

I hit send, smiling, a little thrill of happiness shot through me.

But then, when I reread what I'd typed, my stomach dropped. I felt immediate remorse, whispering, "Damn," and my face flooded with heat. "That was a stupid thing to say. What the fuck is wrong with you?"

I stared at the screen, rubbing my forehead anxiously, wincing. The little three dots indicating that she was typing a message appeared and disappeared at intervals. I swallowed around the thickness of regret in my throat and began typing my apology when her message came through.

Emily: It's good you sent that, because—like you—I have some touchy topics/areas of discomfort too. And we should talk about them when I come over next week to cook dinner. Send me your address.

Victor: I apologize. I am sincerely sorry.

Emily: I don't want you to apologize anymore. And I don't want to apologize either. I want us to be friends, because you're smart and cool and I like being around you. So, let's just assume the best of each other from now on.

The area just below my ribcage ached, a gliding warmth spreading to my neck as I read her message. God, she was so great. She made me feel so many things I didn't have labels for, and many I did. Right now? Gratitude and admiration, but also something else. Something darker, deeper, rooted in the very center of me, essential and yet elusive. Thinking about it, approaching it made my hands shake and sent my mind in all directions.

I wouldn't think about it. Instead I fired off my address and thanked her again, echoing her words that I—also—liked being around her.

I set my phone on the table facedown and walked away, pacing my apartment, restless for no reason. A friendship with Emily may not have been particularly wise—she was still a student, and I was still a professor—but I thought maybe it wasn't a *terrible* idea.

Pragmatically, reasonably, logically I recognized the truth of my situation. I'd been having a particular flavor of thoughts (. . . desires) about her for weeks. I would likely have them for a while longer, no matter if we were in contact or not, friends or not.

So why not be friends? I'd had female friends my whole life. I knew how to be a good friend. I could follow that script. With time, the darker and the deeper should just fade away, but I'd still have her in my life. Having her as a friend was better than nothing at all.

Right?

My cell buzzed again a moment later, pulling me from my contemplations and causing my heart to constrict painfully, robbing me of my ability to breathe for a split second. I glanced at the phone where it lay facedown on the table.

It was probably her. My fingers twitched. I longed to pick it up. But I'd never been someone who felt it necessary to respond to texts right away. I liked my uninterrupted time to focus and concentrate, for research and writing. I usually only checked my phone once or twice a day, texting back when or if I had time.

Whatever she just texted wasn't an emergency.

Whatever it was could likely wait until tomorrow.

I shouldn't pick it up and check her message.

I'm still the same person.

Being friends with Emily isn't going to change me, I won't let it. I don't need to change. I like myself just as I am. I always have.

I walked away from the phone and into the kitchen, doing a circle around the center island before walking back out to the living room and picking up the phone because—why not? What was the big deal? I could check it now. That was fine. Checking my phone didn't mean I was becoming someone different.

Emily: Thanks for the address. I'll see you next Tuesday night for dinner if not before. I hope you like roasted beet salad with goat cheese, candies walnuts and garlic chicken!

Victor: That sounds great. I'm looking forward to it.

Emily: Oh no. That's not what I'm making. I'm bringing over frozen peas and pizza rolls. I just hope you like that other kind of stuff so you can make it for me when it's your turn to cook.

I laughed. I shook my head. I laughed again. And then I carried my phone with me into the kitchen, and then my bedroom where I changed, and then the bathroom where I brushed my teeth, and then back into my bedroom while we continued to text, back and forth, for the next three hours.

Before I knew what was happening, she'd placed a kiss on my cheek.

It momentarily stunned me. So much so, I forgot to stop the forward momentum of the hand I was extending for her to shake (also in greeting) and I ended up poking her in the stomach. She flinched back, a big smile on her face, and glanced at the hand. She laughed.

I stopped breathing, for a number of reasons: the aftershock of the kiss, her smile, the sound of her laugh, her bright eyes when they lifted back to mine and she slid her hand against my palm, giving my hand a shake.

"Hello, friend," she said, tilting her head to one side, moving our hands up and down.

"Hi," I think I said.

"Can I come in?" she asked after a moment of us standing there, holding hands at the entrance to my house. "I brought food."

"Oh, yes. Sorry. Absolutely." I tore my eyes away and stepped back, frowning at my slowness.

She bent at the waist, grabbed two bags she'd set down by the front door, and walked inside, looking around the small entrance to my house like she was searching for something. "The kitchen?"

"Here, let me help. This way." I took the bags from her and walked toward the back of the house, speaking inane nonsense, "I thought we could eat in the sunroom, even though it's not sunny—because it's nighttime, obviously—you can see the lights from the garden, but it's colder right now than the rest of the house, so let me know . . . what you think." *God. Just shut up.*

I placed her bags on the kitchen island and stepped away, shoving my hands in my pockets because I didn't know what else to do with them. *Why did I agree to this?*

"Okay, sounds good. Although, I hope this isn't a friendship dealbreaker for you, but if we're going to be friends, I insist that we call your sunroom a solarium."

I laughed, some of my nerves dissipating. "Not a dealbreaker. Now that you mention it, I think I prefer solarium over sunroom as well, and—for the record—I prefer library to den."

She made a cute face, like she was impressed. "Well, aren't you fancy. I like it. I've always wanted a tiny house—exceedingly small—and to call the rooms ridiculous names. Like have a small bedroom with one of those miniature tabletop pool tables just so I could refer to it as the billiard room."

"I'm stealing that idea."

"You can't. I own the trademark. But you can license it, for a price! Where are the knives?"

I showed her where the knives were, and then I showed her around the rest of the kitchen. She reached in cupboards and drawers for the things she needed, putting me to work cutting onions. I held my breath so I wouldn't tear up from the syn-Propanethial-S-oxide while she positioned herself at the stove and talked about her week, her car troubles, a funny joke she heard, a funny story of something that happened at trivia night last Tuesday, what movies she wanted to see when the semester was over, and plans she had with her best friend—Anna Harris, a name I recognized for some reason—for winter break.

"Why does that name sound familiar?"

"Who?"

"Anna Harris."

Emily turned to face me, wiping her hands and bringing over the bottle of wine to refill my glass. "You had her as a student two years ago."

"Oh yes, I remember Ms. Harris."

"Wow. You have a good memory."

I considered the compliment, whether to let it go or tell the truth. "Not really."

"No. Objectively speaking, remembering anyone from two years ago means you have a good memory."

I took a drink from my glass, leaning my hip against the counter. "No. I just remember her, in particular."

Emily's eyebrows lifted. "Why? Did she spit on you?"

I laughed. "No. But she always had the right answer. She was also the only black female in the class. I think she's also the only black female in her program, right?"

Emily's eyes blinked several times and she stood straighter. "Uh, I don't know. Why is that relevant?"

"Because it's unusual. She's an outlier in her cohort."

"Her *cohort*?" She reared back, like she was prepared to be upset.

"Her cohort being my classroom and the program at the university. Outliers within cohorts are special, and we should pay attention to them so we can learn how to shift trends and replicate their successes."

Her posture relaxed and she looked at me thoughtfully. "You take note of all outliers?"

"As many as I can. Some are—for all intents and purposes—free radicals and need to be discarded, they confuse the issue, like a red herring. But some are more important to a research question than how the rest of the conforming data trends."

She nodded, her pretty eyes narrowing slightly. "So, am I an outlier?"

That pulled a small smile from me and I cocked my head to the side. "In which cohort?"

Emily wrinkled her nose, giving me the impression she was a little frustrated with my—very valid—question. "I don't know. Pick one."

"Pick one?"

"Yes. Pick a cohort. In fact, do this—" she moved back to the stove, carrying the bottle of wine with her "—list a few cohorts where I'm an outlier, and I'll do the same for you." She peeked over her shoulder, giving me a grin that was both mischievous and encouraging. "I'll start. You would be an outlier at a regency role-playing and dance competition conference."

A sort of scoff/snort/laugh erupted from me, and now I was returning her grin. "That is probably true. It has never occurred to me to attend a regency role-playing and dance competition conference."

"Okay, your turn." She faced the stove, stirring the sauce and checking on the rice. "Where would I be an outlier? In which cohort?"

I rubbed my chin, my eyes moving over her back. She wore relaxed fit jeans and a long-sleeve D&D T-shirt. I'd read the front earlier and had bit back a laugh. It was the picture of a twenty-sided die with a "1" showing, and it read, "You reach out to push the orc off the bridge. But instead, lightly caress his back. He is uncomfortable."

She was a geek, a dork, a nerd. But that wasn't her only cohort, not even close. She was book-smart, but she also seemed savvy, talented at engaging people. Her emotional bravery and IQ were clearly off the charts in most areas, except—I suspected—she trusted too readily, too easily. She was friendly, kind, funny, weird, comfortable in her own skin. She gave second chances, and probably third chances, and fourth chances.

Basically—to me—she was perfect.

"Cut up the yellow pepper while you think." Her voice held a hint of teasing impatience and real irritation. "I mean, *if* you can think of a single cohort where I'm an outlier and not a conforming-to-the-trend data point."

I stopped myself from saying, *Every cohort. You are an outlier in every single cohort.*

Instead, I reached for the pepper and sliced it, beginning slowly, "You would be an outlier in . . ."

"In?"

"In a cohort of . . ."

She huffed. Setting the wooden spoon down with a *thunk* and turning to face me, an eyebrow lifted, arms crossed, "Well?"

I smiled, my attention flickering over her stance, how she'd crossed her arms, lifted her chin, liking that I was irritating her, enjoying her reaction. *Why do I like irritating her? That makes no sense.*

"Victor—"

"In a cohort of Vladimir Putin impersonators."

Her expression cleared, a soft, amused sound leaving her lips. It was obvious my response pleased her.

So I added, "And a cohort of official roundabout enthusiasts club members."

She made a face like she thought I was strange, but in a good way. "I don't know," she said slyly, grinning. "I do enjoy a good roundabout. I hear the ones in Europe are a must-see."

"Ah. Okay then. I'll tell my roundabout appreciation club you're interested in joining."

Now she laughed. Really laughed. A swelling warmth of feeling saturated each of my senses, reached the back of my throat and tightened it. And I realized, although I enjoyed and liked irritating her for some odd reason, I craved and *loved* being the cause of her smile.

CHAPTER 13

VICTOR

The subject of Emily's job didn't come up until a month later.

She didn't talk about it and neither did I, even though we saw each other at least once a week and texted each other almost daily. I reasoned she'd get around to her "touchy topics" when (or if) she was ready. Every time we were together was the highlight of my week. I didn't want to ruin that by making her uncomfortable.

It happened on a Thursday. Her car broke down on the way back into town from visiting her mom, which she did almost every Wednesday night to Thursday afternoon. Emily called me to cancel our dinner plans. Instead of canceling, I arranged to borrow one of the airfield's towing trucks and drove out to meet her.

When I spotted her car stranded on the side of the highway—her inside, holding pepper spray in one hand, her cell in the other, her teeth chattering with the cold—a strange, overwhelming, possessive anger had me grinding my teeth instead of greeting her appropriately.

She looked like she might move in for a hug, but then

extended her hand for a shake after seeing my face. I walked right past her, giving her a distracted head nod as I surveyed the piece of shit she considered transportation.

I mean, what a piece of shit. Duct tape holding up one side of the fender and more duct tape around a rusted-out portion of the wheel casing.

Duct. Tape.

"I'm sorry," she said, twisting her fingers, following me around her car as I set it up to tow. "You really didn't have to come all the way out here. My mom has roadside assistance for us, I could've called them."

"No. Always call me. No matter where it is. I'll get there faster than roadside." I could feel her eyes on my profile, but I didn't look at her as I worked. I didn't want her to see how *angry* I was.

I couldn't remember the last time I was so angry about something that was none of my business.

"I just wanted to give you a heads-up that I wouldn't be able to make it tonight, you really didn't have to drive out," she continued, like she owed me an explanation for her call.

"It's fine." It wasn't fine. Calling me was great, but her car was definitely not fine. Her car was unsafe, and she was making this drive every week. *Every week!*

Emily was quiet for a bit while I worked, tracking me with her gaze. I did my best to clear my expression. How she chose to travel wasn't my concern. She was an adult. She was responsible for herself. She made her own decisions.

But if we were together . . . Yeah. That's right. That's what I was thinking. And it made me even angrier—at her, but mostly at myself—so I bit the inside of my lip and stared at her front license plate.

She marched up to my left side while I set the crank. I perceived her take a deep breath, and then another, and then she asked, "Why are you so mad at me? I said I was sorry about calling."

"It's not about calling, Emily." I deepened my voice to keep it controlled. "I'm not mad about that, not at all. You should *always* call me. Always."

"Then why—"

Inexplicably, I exploded, "Why are you driving this piece of shit car three hours twice a week on the highway? Are you nuts? You're lucky it didn't stall out in the middle of the road! You could have been seriously hurt. Or killed!"

She reared back, her eyes wide, bouncing between mine like she didn't recognize me.

I tore my stare away, muttering under my breath, "I'm . . . dammit." I wasn't sorry, so I couldn't say it. She was making me crazy. I pushed frustrated fingers through my hair. "I shouldn't have yelled at you. But, Em, this car isn't safe."

"You're mad because my car is old?" She sounded like she didn't know how to feel about this.

"No. I am angry because your car is falling apart and you could hurt"—*yourself*—"someone. It's not safe and it's irresponsible to be driving on a highway with other cars going seventy plus miles per hour when your car shouldn't be going more than forty. It puts"—*you*—"everyone in danger."

I glanced at her. She was blinking like I'd thrown sand in her eyes, swallowing thickly, looking remorseful.

My heart squeezed punishingly. Not pausing to think, I halted the crank and pulled her into my arms. She returned the hug, albeit limply, leaning against me just slightly. I sighed against her temple, struggling under the weight of repentance.

Now I was sorry.

"I'm sorry." My voice was roughened with guilt. "I'm sorry. You don't need me getting angry at you right now. I'm sorry." I kissed her forehead and smoothed my hand down her back, more thoughtless actions. All I could think about was that stunned, mortified look on her face, and that I'd put it there.

She made a noise that sounded suspiciously like a sniffle, and I held her tighter.

"God, Em. I am sorry. You've had a shitty day, and I—I'm making everything worse."

"It's okay."

"It's not okay. Don't say it's okay."

"Fine. It's not okay. You're an asshole." Emily leaned more fully against me, finally hugging me back with feeling.

I grinned, kissing her temple now, inadvertently smelling her hair. Her hair always smelled good, sweet, like how sugar tasted.

"I mean—" she sniffled, and then huffed "—you're right about the car. It is a piece of shit." Leaning away, she captured my eyes, her eyebrows drawn together. "But it's my piece of shit. It's what I can afford. And I *have to* see my mother once a week. She . . . she needs to see me."

Chastised, I nodded. I understood her perspective. If my mom were still alive, I'd do the same, no matter what kind of car I could afford.

"So, yelling at me about it isn't going to help an impossible situation."

Biting the inside of my lip again, I examined her. "You're going to keep driving it?"

She shrugged. "I stay in the slow lane. People just go around me."

Not good enough.

Glancing over her head at the traffic moving so fast they might as well have been on a runway, I sighed. "Will you let me help you fix it?"

She stiffened immediately, pulling away. "No. You're not paying to fix my car."

"No, not pay for it. *Fix* it. I could fix it for you. I could get you a new engine and take care of this body work."

Crossing her arms, she glared at me beneath furrowed eyebrows. "You can do that?"

"Yes." I wanted to reach for her again, an instinct, the need to touch her, to assure myself she was unhurt. Instead, I restarted the crank, surveyed the stretch of highway behind us, and studied my sneakers.

"How much would it cost?" she finally asked.

EXCELLENT.

I shrugged, feigning indifference while I debated a number that wouldn't sound fake but wasn't so high that she'd turn me down. This was difficult for me. I wasn't a good liar because I didn't like to lie. However, it would cost more to fix this car—just in parts—than to buy a more reliable one.

Instead of answering directly, I hedged, "I think you'd be surprised how cheaply I could do it. Most of the cost involved in auto repair is labor, and you wouldn't have to pay for that."

"I'd want to reimburse you for your time."

I shrugged again to hide the spike of irritation at this statement.

I didn't want her money, I wanted . . . I wanted—*To take care of her.*

I couldn't say that, I could barely admit it to myself. Taking care of her wasn't my place.

No. She can take care of herself. It's no one's place but hers.

And yet, I still wanted to take care of her. "Okay. How about a trade?"

"A trade?"

"Yes. A time trade. I put in time working on your car, and you do some work for me."

She looked confused, and then suddenly her cheeks flushed. "Work for you?"

"Yes."

"D-doing what?" she stammered.

Her flustered expression perplexed me, and I examined her for a moment, wondering what she was thinking. "Something you're good at and have experience with already."

Emily sucked in a breath, her gaze dropping to the gravel at her feet, her face bright red. "You mean—you mean you want me to—to—"

"To?"

Her eyes cut to mine, wide and rimmed with several contrary emotions I couldn't decipher. Her lips parted, like she was going to fill in the blank, but then she snapped her mouth shut, crossing her arms and swallowing.

"Do literature searches? Maybe format some graphs? Make a few pivot tables?" I watched her carefully.

Her lips parted again. Now she appeared to be stunned.

"Or we could figure something else out. You could help at the airfield instead."

Abruptly, she breathed a laugh, and I couldn't tell if she looked relieved, or disappointed, or embarrassed, or what.

"Yes. Actually, that would be great. Both would be great. I'd love to help with the lit searches, and I'd also like to help at the airfield, especially when you fix my car so I can learn how."

I nodded lightly, still intensely curious why this suggestion would fluster her so completely. "Are you sure?"

"Mmm-hmm." Emily shoved her hands in her back pockets, and then withdrew them and rubbed the back of her neck, and then folded her arms again. "It's hot out here."

Locking the crank into place, I glanced at her out of the corner of my eye. "It's thirty-seven degrees."

"But it's humid, right?"

She was so cute. And nuts.

I finished securing her car into place and then I walked around to the passenger side of the truck. She followed, murmuring behind me, "Yeah, but I'm hot. I'm hot and you're not and there's got to be something that rhymes with besot."

Opening the door, I let my eyes move over her. She still seemed fidgety, embarrassed as she climbed into the truck, settled in the seat, and clicked her seatbelt into place.

"Emily."

"Victor the Victor."

"Can I ask you something?"

"Certainly." She was fiddling with the hem of her sweater, not looking at me.

"What did you think I wanted?"

Her gaze cut to mine. "What?"

"As a time trade. What did you think I was going to ask you to do?"

She tucked her lips between her teeth, her eyes wide again, and a new blush—pink, not red this time—stained her cheeks. "You don't want to know."

"I do want to know."

"No. You don't." She laughed self-deprecatingly as she said this, her attention dropping to the tops of her knees.

"I wouldn't have asked if I didn't want to know."

"It's stupid."

"I doubt that."

"Ohhh, man. You are so, so wrong." More self-deprecating laughter.

"Prove me wrong."

"I . . ." Emily lifted her chin, gazing at the visor above the windshield, visibly uncomfortable. And then she laughed again, like something was really funny. "It's actually hilarious."

"Tell me." I stepped closer to the truck, drawing her eyes

to mine, and—for some strange reason—not caring if my question or closeness made her uncomfortable. "I consented to inside jokes, remember?"

She was still laughing, but in fits and starts, like she was trying to stop. "Okay, okay. I'll tell you. But—it's so ridiculous. I'm such an idiot." Clutching her stomach, she closed her eyes, a new bout of laughter shaking her shoulders.

"You are definitely not an idiot." Now I started to chuckle because her laugh was contagious.

"So, I thought you meant—" her eyes drifted to my hairline and I got the sense she was having trouble meeting my eyes "—you wanted me to model lingerie for you."

Emily covered her face with the sleeves of her sweater as soon as the words were out, laughing hysterically.

And I was glad she couldn't see me. I was not laughing.

I thought you meant you wanted me to model lingerie for you. She had no idea. I couldn't think of anything I wanted more.

Or less.

My attention flickered over to her form in the passenger seat and I swallowed thickly, returning my eyes to the road. No matter how I struggled to focus on something, anything else, my thoughts were of a particular flavor. One that definitively suggested I was not—in fact—asexual. At least, I was not asexual where Emily was concerned.

Yes, I very much wanted Emily to model lingerie for me. Thinking about it made me dizzy with disorienting and selfish eagerness and anticipation. And I'd touch her. And I'd kiss her. And . . .

No. I very much *did not* want Emily to model lingerie for me. I had no illusions about myself. I knew a great deal about a great many things, and nothing about physical intimacy.

She deserves a content expert.

We drove in silence. I didn't have any brainpower or willpower left to dedicate to appropriate conversation. I certainly didn't trust myself to speak and not suggest or admit something foolish.

During this protracted moment, my conversation with Andy from weeks ago echoed between my ears, prophetic in retrospect.

"Hanging out with her would be good practice at least."

"Good practice?"

"Yeah. Hanging out with a lady you want to bang and not making things awkward. And don't try to deny that you want to bang her."

His assessment had been crude but accurate. And now here we were. *Say nothing. Don't make it awkward.*

Eventually, mercifully, we made it to the airfield, picked up my car, and I navigated to her place. It wasn't too late. We still had time for dinner as originally planned. I suggested conversationally that we call in an order for delivery rather than either of us cooking. I was tired, and I imagined so was she.

"Or we could eat at the restaurant," she suggested after reading off a list of possibilities from her phone.

"Delivery is better." Her attention moved over me, and I gave her a little smile. "I like your place. You have all those movies and your couch is comfortable." Emily had an impressive DVD collection, but that wasn't why I didn't want to go to a restaurant.

I didn't like the attention. I didn't like how people looked at me now, and I couldn't seem to keep myself from noticing. Being over three hundred and fifty pounds had very few advantages, but one of them—after the smattering of initial looks and comments of disgust—was being invisible. But now women especially continued to look. They continued to comment. They kept pointing. They kept talking and smiling. Sometimes they wanted to talk to me. Sometimes they insisted on it, like I owed them something because of the way I looked.

This type of attention never happened when I was heavier. Never. And I hated it.

"Couch? You mean my chaise lounge in the billiard room? Or the settee in the music room?"

We both laughed. She had a small sofa in her bedroom (billiard room) and a miniature pool table on the top of her bookshelf. The living room (music room) had a bigger couch and a kazoo next to the lamp.

"Music room, obviously."

"Okay. Delivery it is." She clicked through a few screens on her phone. "Greek okay?"

"Yeah. I'll just have their house salad."

"Chicken on top?"

"No thanks."

She was quiet for a beat. "Steak?"

"No."

Her continued examination led me to glance at her again once we stopped at a red light.

"Did you have a late lunch?" she asked, making a stern face. "Is it because you didn't want to eat my cooking?"

"What are you talking about? You're a great cook."

"Yes, but I was supposed to cook tonight. Now you just want a salad. Are you already full?"

I swallowed, not wanting to answer. In truth, other than the egg white omelet this morning, I hadn't eaten anything. I was hungry. But I'd stepped on the scale at the gym and I was three pounds heavier than the last time I'd weighed myself. I'd checked again, thinking the scale was wrong. It wasn't.

Weight gain, any weight gain, even a few pounds, made me nervous. But since Emily and I had started spending so much time together, the additional three pounds had made me panic.

Nonetheless, I wouldn't give in to the urge to lose even more weight.

The therapist I was seeing to help with behavior modification for weight loss said that I'd be tempted to go underweight as soon as I hit my goal. He'd warned me against this, saying it was a typical thought process, but that it was also a dangerous one.

A subject change was in order, one that would distract her completely from this topic. My mind grasped at possibilities.

"Victor—"

"How are you going to get to work tomorrow? Do you need a ride?"

Emily tensed. "Uh, I'll take the bus."

"I can drive you."

"No. That's okay. It's not that far. Sometimes I take the bus even when my car works. But, Victor, are you sure you don't want me to add chicken or—"

"Do you like your job?" The light turned green. I shifted my foot from the brake to the accelerator. "How long have you worked there?"

In my peripheral vision, I saw her tuck her hair behind her ears, and then place her clasped hands between her legs. "Let's see. Two years this January. I started my sophomore year."

"And you like it?"

"It's fine."

"Have you thought about doing something else?"

"Why?" Her voice held an edge, and she'd turned her face to look out the window.

"Meaning an internship. Something in your field of study," I explained conversationally.

"Sure. But internships don't pay what they used to, professor."

We glanced at each other, sharing a smile at her use of my phrase from the first time we'd gone out to dinner as friends.

"Valid point," I conceded.

Emily breathed out, turning her attention back to the window and lifting her elbow to rest on the sill. Now that the subject of my eating choices seemed to be well and truly forgotten, I was content to drive the rest of the way in silence. Just being with her was enough.

A moment later, her eyes still trained out the window, she said, "I actually don't hate it."

"Pardon?"

"Modeling lingerie for rich people. It's not terrible. I've been a cashier at a grocery store, a server at a restaurant, an "associate" at a clothing store, a barista, and it pays better than all of those. All I have to do is stand there and let people look at me. It's kinda boring."

I wanted to ask if she'd been bored that night she'd poured me a drink and encouraged me to touch her red silk robe. The words were on the tip of my tongue, but then I decided I didn't want to know.

A noncommittal "Hmm" was all I said.

She wasn't finished. "Sometimes it can be irritating, though. Like, when they want to touch me, like they think I'm there to be felt up or something."

My temper spiked, sharp and sudden, and I gripped the steering wheel forcefully, fury sticking in my throat.

Then she added, "But they're really good at putting a stop to that stuff. If Madame Purple or Madame Pink don't like the way someone looks at us, their membership is revoked. And you don't see the security team, but they're there, watching everything. I feel . . . safe. I guess. Respected in the workplace. Valued by my boss. It's nice."

"Good," I said, my blood pressure decreasing as I told myself to calm down.

The single word earned me a quick look from Emily and a tiny smile before she returned her gaze to the window. "Thank you," she said softly.

"For what?"

"For asking Dr. Ford to keep my job a secret. For not judging me for what I do."

I frowned. "Why would I judge you?" Ideally, it'd be great if she also felt fulfilled, challenged, and passionate about her work. But hearing that she was valued and felt safe, that was good.

"Because many people would." She chuckled, it sounded sad.

"Not anyone you want to know. Not anyone worth your time or worthy of your friendship."

Emily's head whipped away from the window and she stared at me like I'd surprised her. "That's a—uh—a valid point." She huffed, and then added something else under her breath.

"Pardon?"

"No one knows," she said louder. "Other than you and my mom, no one knows."

I opened and closed my hands on the steering wheel, frowning out the windshield. "Not even your friend Anna?"

"Nope."

"Why not?"

Her fidgeting intensified and she shifted in her seat, her knee bouncing. "I don't want her to look at me differently."

"Why would she?" I asked without giving the question much thought. Anna—what I remembered of her as a student—didn't seem to be the type to judge people or even care what they did for a living. But then, I only knew her as a student.

Then again, if she was truly Emily's friend, then she shouldn't care. And if she did care, if she judged Emily for it, then she wasn't truly her friend.

Turning onto her street, I felt galvanized to continue speaking my mind on the subject. "It's not something you should be ashamed of. It's just a job. I understand why you'd only want people you trust to know, but you should be able to trust your friends not to judge you."

"Calm down there, *Gail*." I heard the teasing in her tone and knew *Gail* was a reference to Oprah Winfrey's best friend. Whenever I became indignant on Emily's behalf, she called me Gail. *Inside joke.* "I guess you're right. I should tell her. I trust her. She's a lot like you, actually."

"How so?" I worked to keep my voice light but being compared to Emily's female best friend caused my tongue to taste like lemons. I liked Anna. I respected Anna. But I didn't want to be another Anna to Emily.

Then what are you doing? What is this? What do you want from her?

Friendship.

Liar.

She distracted me from the frustrated voice in my head by saying, "You're both smart. And nonjudgmental. And witty."

Okay. I liked that comparison.

"I try to avoid ignorantly judgmental people as much as possible. It would make me intensely hypocritical if I was one." I said this last part with more vehemence than I'd intended.

"Yeah. You're not intensely hypocritical. More hypocrite-lite."

I chuckled, pulling into a parking space outside her building. "Aren't we all, though?"

"Exactly." She also laughed, but the sound tapered quickly,

and her eyes turned searching. "Can I ask you a deeply personal question? You don't have to answer. But, before I ask, you should know that I understand how deeply personal it is."

I hesitated, feeling my muscles tense and brace, my mind scrambling through possibilities and contingency plans should she ask something *too* personal. And what would I do if she asked me how I felt about her? If she asked me point-blank, I wouldn't be able to lie.

Would that be such a bad thing?

"As long as you don't mind the truth." I paused to clear my throat, and then added, "You might not like my answer, and I'm sorry if it makes you uncomfortable."

"Understood." Her nod was faster than mine and she twisted to face me in her seat as I cut the engine. "Why'd you decide to lose the weight? I mean, what was the catalyst? What made you do it?"

Oh.

I relaxed and frowned, disappointed by her question for no discernable reason. Looking at her, it was easy to perceive this question, and my reaction to it had made her anxious.

Putting her at ease was my first priority. I gave her a soft smile and kept my voice light. "It's not a big mystery. I was experiencing joint pain, back pain. My doctor said I was pre-diabetes and my heart was in bad shape. That's not the case for everyone who weighs what I did, but it was the case for me. At the airfield, safety and mobility were concerns in particular. I needed my body to work consistently, reliably, so it became clear I had to work for my body."

Her nerves seemed to dissipate as I spoke. "So, it was about being healthy?"

"Yes."

"What about the charity thing? Didn't you raise money for a charity?"

My eyelids lowered by half and I swallowed an abrupt, irrepressible bitterness. "That's right," I said numbly. Just thinking about it, *the charity*, still filled me with cold rage.

I must've done a substandard job masking my feelings on the subject because Emily frowned at me, snatching my hand where it rested on my thigh and holding it with both of hers. "What? What happened? What's that? What's that look? Did I make you angry? Why do you look like that?"

I exhaled, rolling my eyes at myself. "It's a—it's not a good story."

"Tell me. Tell me the bullet points if you don't want to tell the whole thing. Just the movie version is fine."

The ice in my veins fizzled, warmed under her scrutiny, and I turned my hand to capture one of hers, bringing it back to my thigh and cradling it there. I studied her fingers as I spoke. "It was a setup."

"A—a setup?"

"Yes. My father arranged it. He orchestrated the whole thing." I'd been so stupid.

"It was fake? They didn't donate the money?"

"Oh no, he had to donate it. He promised." This was hard to explain, but for some reason I wanted to try. I wanted to tell her. "My father, he never—he didn't—he hated what I looked like. He always hated how heavy I was. When I'd go to his house, as a kid, he'd put me on a diet." And call me names, make me run behind the car, threaten to send me to *fat camp*. . . But she didn't need to hear about all that. "Anyway, I started going to the gym on campus shortly after being hired. I ran into one of his friends—Professor Wilson, he also teaches research methods—and he apparently told my father that he'd seen me working out. So my father arranged the whole thing, secretly, making it a contest for charity. Dr. Wilson was the one who told me about it and suggested I go for it, enlisting a few other people in the program to also join. I didn't find out that my father was behind the whole thing until after the check had been cut."

She looked horrified. "What? You mean he—it was all a deception? To get you to—"

"Lose the weight, yeah. Extra incentive, and it worked."

"Oh my God. I'm—I'm so sorry."

"Honestly, I don't know if I would've done it for myself. The deception definitely worked, perhaps the ends justified the means." I stared unseeingly beyond her. The sun had just set, and a hazy twilight had taken its place. "He said to me, the week after it was all over, that it was the only time he'd ever donated money to a charity. But that every dollar had been worth it, now he was no longer ashamed to call me his son."

CHAPTER 14

EMILY

"I think my coat hangers are out to destroy me."

"Not this again."

"What? I've never talked about my coat hangers before." Anna narrowed her 100 percent unperturbed eyeballs, impressing me with her ability to chop onions without crying.

"Yes. But you always think inanimate objects are out to destroy you."

"Because they are."

"Fine. How are your coat hangers plotting your doom?" I lowered the heat on our noodles and added a dash of olive oil. It was spaghetti night. We hadn't had spaghetti night in a long, long time.

"I go to pull my coat off of its hanger, right?" She popped a bit of diced onion in her mouth and chewed. "And it catches on my purple dress behind it—which was nowhere near the coat—and pulls my purple dress *off* its hanger and onto the floor of the closet, right on top of my muddy boots. Which means I have to get the dress dry-cleaned—*again* —before this weekend."

"Your wet boots? Which closet was this?"

"The front closet, by the door."

"Why wasn't your dress in your bedroom closet?"

"You're not listening. How is it possible that pulling out my coat could've caused a catastrophic clothing casualty? The coat was nowhere near the dress!"

"Maybe it's the dress, not the hangers."

"How do you mean?" Anna placed her hand on her hip, her expression far too serious for the ridiculousness of this conversation.

"Perhaps your purple dress has masochistic tendencies and it's not the hangers at all."

"Hmm. That's a thought." Now she rubbed her chin. "I'll let you know if I'm suddenly inspired to have Luca spank me when I wear it and report back."

"ANNA!"

"What?"

"Overshare," I said through my laughter.

"What? How are scientific findings overshare? And what if the purple dress *does* make me a masochist? Wouldn't you want to know? Maybe you'd like to borrow it for a hot date."

Still chuckling, I split my attention between her and my spaghetti sauce. "Yeah. Not likely anytime soon."

"Hey, so." Anna wagged her eyebrows. "You and Professor Hanover sure are spending a lot of time together."

I frowned before I could halt the tragic change in my expression and had the displeasure of watching my friend's face fall as a result.

Pasting a persevering smile on my mouth, I concentrated on stirring the tomato sauce. "Not really. I only see him once a week or so." *We text every day, but that doesn't count.*

She paused her onion chopping. "Anything you want to tell me?"

"Nah."

"Nothing?"

Unbidden, my brain conjured Victor's handsome, earnest face. Also unbidden, remembering the story he'd told me (about his father and the deception and the charity) after my car-fail. How could anyone be so unfeeling toward their own child? And how had that lifetime of cruelty shaped my beloved, sweet Victor? I couldn't shake the intermittent plagues of angry and melancholy now that I knew the whole story, they followed me around like gnats.

"As I've told you many times, Victor and I are just friends."

She gave me a small smile, openly inspecting me. "Well, there's nothing 'just' about friends. Friends are the best."

"Yes. The best." I worked to return her warm expression, but my eyes were having none of it.

"So, uh, how's your car? Is it all fixed?" Her tone sounded studiously casual.

I'd told her that my car had broken down and was presently in the shop. I hadn't told her that the shop was one of the large airplane or jet or whatever hangars where Victor built his planes. I don't know why I hadn't told her the whole story; it was definitely the kind of thing I would usually tell Anna right away, but talking about Victor these days felt personal.

Which obviously didn't make any sense since we were just friends. *Just. Friends.*

"It'll be another two weeks. They're replacing the engine."

"Oh, yikes. That sounds expensive."

"Actually, no. I got a good deal." Victor hadn't been lying when he said he could fix up my car, nor had he been stretching the truth when he'd claimed he could do it on the cheap.

"Still though." Anna looked distressed. "Do you want me to talk to the restaurant and see if they have any openings before or after your post office shifts? You were a good waitress before college, and the tips there are mighty fine. Maybe you could just replace the car?"

I stilled, my hand stopping mid-stir, and I stared at the bubbling surface of the tomato sauce. The conversation with Victor about my job had been on repeat in my brain for the last week. *It's not something you should be ashamed of. It's just a job. I understand why you'd only want people you trust to know, but you should be able to trust your friends not to judge you.*

I'd been thinking about these words constantly. He was right. He was so right. I'd withheld this part of my life from Anna and my other friends because I didn't trust them not to judge me or look at me differently. I preached about accepting other people, about being honest, about trust and bravery, but I'd been a coward.

If I wanted and expected honesty from others, a chance to prove that I practiced what I preached, then *I* had to be honest as well.

"Anna." I set the spoon down and turned off the burner for the sauce, facing my friend, my *best friend*.

"Yeah?"

"I need to tell you something." Clasping my hands in front of me, I shifted my weight from foot to foot.

Her eyes grew impossibly large. "You're pregnant."

"What? No!"

"Eh, I knew it was a long shot. But I've always wanted to be a godmother. What is it?"

I shook my head. "This is serious."

"Oh. Serious. Okay." She ceased onion chopping and wiped her hands on a towel. "You have my full attention."

My bloodstream was a river of guilt, thundering between my years. Gah. *GAH GAH GAH!* This was hard. My nose suddenly stung.

"I've been lying to you. For two years." *Why do I feel like crying?*

Her expression turned solemn. "Okay. About what?"

"My job."

"Your job."

"I'm not a postal worker. I don't sort mail."

"You don't work at the post office?"

I shook my head. "No."

"Okaaaay. Then what do you do?"

"I'm a . . . a . . ." I sucked in a breath, held it, watched her through bracing, squinted eyes. "I'm a lingerie model down at the Pinkery."

Anna reared back, just a little, and her gaze darted down and then up. "You're a what?"

"Mainly stage three naked garments."

"Stage naked three who?"

I covered my face. "I'm so sorry I didn't tell you. I'm sorry I lied!"

My friend was quiet for a moment—a long moment—during which my imagination attempted to go wild with worst-case scenarios as per usual until she said,

"I'm so confused."

I peeked through my fingers. "About what?" My words were muffled because my hands were still in front of my face.

Her nose wrinkled with plain confusion. "You model lingerie?"

I nodded, my fingers sliding from my face to twist in front of my stomach.

"Okay. But why would you keep this a secret from me? Why tell me you worked at the post office?"

"You ask that question, but I think you know the answer."

She reared back again, her mouth dropping open. "Are

you implying what I'm inferring?" I knew that face, that was her *I'm extremely offended* face.

"Maybe?" My voice was high and strained.

Anna heaved a sad sound and shuffled a few steps forward. "Emily Von. I don't even know what to say to you right now." Her hands came to her chest. "I am your best friend. Your *best friend.* Why would I possibly care what your job is? Do you really think I'm like that?"

"No," I said on an exhale, feeling abruptly tired. "No. I don't. I don't think you're like that. Not at all."

"And yet you pretended to have a job at the post office."

"I was a coward."

"Yeah. You were." Anna crossed her arms, the set of her jaw telling me she was angry. "Anything else you're not telling me? Is this really your apartment? Is your car really in the shop?"

Oh jeez. Now I had to tell her about Victor fixing my car. "Yes, this is my apartment. But . . ."

"But?" Her eyebrows jumped high on her forehead. "But what?"

"My car is in the shop, but Victor is the one doing the work. It's in one of the hangars where he works on airplanes. I'm paying for the parts and we're making a trade for his time."

She perked up, her irritation replaced by curiosity. "A trade? What does that mean?"

"He's fixing my car, body work and everything, and I'm doing lit searches for a grant he's writing."

"Huh. Well, that's cool of him."

"Yes. It is. And I'm also going to help him at the shop this Saturday morning, before work."

Now she frowned again. "You mean, before your job as a lingerie model?"

"I'm not a model."

"You model lingerie, Emily. You're a model."

"It's in a private showroom, one client at a time. It's not like I walk on a runway."

She didn't seem to be listening. "No wonder you work out all the time and won't eat my baked goods. I just thought you stopped liking my cookies."

"Oh no, I love your cookies. But garter belts and thongs don't."

"Yikes." Anna's eyes grew rounded and she grimaced, but then her gaze turned introspective and she leaned back on the counter. "You know . . . I get it."

I ceased twisting my fingers and again clasped my hands in front of me. "What do you mean?"

"I mean, I get why you didn't tell me." Her gaze flickered to mine and then away, her lips twisting to the side. "I've been known—on occasion—to make fun of Victoria Secret models, their poses, the expressions on their faces, how they *lounge* so sexily, how their bathrobes never seem to fit or stay on their shoulders."

"Yes, but I do too. If you remember, we used to make fun of those catalogs together."

"You know, I'd never considered that maybe their bathrobes have masochistic tendencies." Her lips curved into a small smile. Picking up the knife again, she poked at the chopped onions with the tip.

"It would explain a lot." Watching my friend, her unfocused gaze on the onions, my heart constricted hopefully. "I am so sorry, Anna. I should have told you."

"You shouldn't have lied," she said firmly, and then gave me her eyes. They were full of sincerity and understanding. "But maybe I should be more open-minded too. It's so easy, to split girls into sexy *or* nerdy, smart *or* pretty. One or the other. Us versus them. 'There are two kinds of women, those who do xyz, or those who do abc.' But that's not true. There are billions of types of women, infinite possible combinations, and people change over time. Why do we want to regulate ourselves into a tidy little box? Limit ourselves?"

"Because the idea of infinite possibilities can be frightening?"

"Maybe." She nodded absentmindedly.

"Do you forgive me?"

Her eyes cut to mine and she looked at me like I was crazy. "What are you talking about? Of course. Of course I do. I'm glad you told me, and I'm sorry you thought for one second that you couldn't."

"I was being stupid." I stumbled over to her—relieved, so relieved—opening my arms for a hug. "I will try to stop being so stupid."

"You're not stupid." Enfolding me in her arms, we rocked back and forth, and I felt her sigh before adding, "I love you, Em. I'll always love you. Maybe even more now that I know why you won't eat my cookies."

I gasped, my hand flying to my chest. "How dare you!"

Victor turned, his questioning gaze moving down and then up. "What? What did I say?"

"Pluto is a planet!"

His lips formed a super flat line and his eyelids drooped. When he did this, in this way, it meant he was trying not to smile. "You cannot believe that Pluto is a planet. It's not the Easter Bunny. It's not something one *believes* in. Fact, it's not a planet."

"Then why does it have a name?" I marched past him, my boots crunching on the snow, and lifted my index finger near his face. "Ah-ha! Don't have an answer for that, do you? Checkmate."

We were on a hike. Actually, not an actual hike, more like a walk. I'd shown up to help him with my car Saturday morning and—after an awkward moment where I extended my hand for a shake and he moved in for a hug—I discovered he was all finished. Not only had he fixed all the crumpled sections of metal, he'd added a new fender, bumper, tail-lights, etc. Both of my doors opened and closed without creaking, and the power windows and locks also worked. He'd also painted it red. Bright red. My car looked better than new.

"It's a safe color. Everyone will see you, so you don't have to worry about someone cutting you off," he'd said, explaining his choice.

When I said nothing, just stared at him, he added, "Or I can paint it something else."

I'd never had a car that was just one color before and not blue plus primer gray, or maroon plus primer gray, or black plus—you get the picture.

As such, I'd been overwhelmed, which I managed to explain along with offering my profuse gratitude. The gratitude made him look extremely uncomfortable. I didn't care. Let him be uncomfortable in the face of my praise. So be it. He would just have to suck it up. I WAS GRATEFUL!

Since I'd cleared my schedule for the day to work on a car that no longer needed work, he suggested we take it for a ride over to Walden Pond. I'd never been, and it was far enough away to get used to the new engine, but not so far that I'd be late for work that evening.

Which brings me to now and our hike and his sacrilegious statements about Pluto.

"No. Not checkmate. Astrophysicists name all kinds of stellar objects, not just planets."

"But Pluto has that heart." I twisted back to him as I offered this fact.

"You mean the asteroid we call Pluto has a crater that resembles the shape of a heart, which has nothing to do with whether or not it's a planet."

"I disagree. I believe there's a law that if a stellar object has the shape of a heart on its surface, it automatically gets a free pass to planet town."

"Planet town?" came his laughing question from behind me.

I liked his face when he laughed, especially how his eyes seemed to grow both sharper and softer, so I stopped and turned to watch him approach. "That's right. Planet town."

Biting his bottom lip, his gaze moving over my face like he thought I was something special, he stopped directly in front of me. "Do you have a name for this scientific law?"

I lost my breath a little when he looked at me that way, but I did manage to say, "Goofy's Theorem."

He lifted an eyebrow. "I thought you said it was a law."

"It is." I shrugged, like *whatchagunnado?* shaking off some of the aftereffects of his sharp and soft look. "But first it was a theorem, and they didn't get around to changing the name when it became a law."

Victor's grin was slow, spreading over his lips, cheeks, to his eyes, which warmed as they moved between mine. "You are . . ." His unfinished thought was spoken in a deliciously deep voice.

Oh. *Oh my.*

I did my best to hold still under the heat of his inspection and the scrumptiousness of his tone, both of which caused goose bumps to rise over my skin. But I couldn't stop my smile. "I am?"

His grin waned. He blinked. He glanced at the ground. He gave his head a little shake. "You are cold? Maybe we should head back."

"I'm not cold," I answered reflexively, studying this strange retreat. "Are you cold?"

He shook his head, lifting his eyes to some spot beyond my shoulder. "It's pretty. Here, with the snow."

"You've never been here when it snowed before?"

He continued shaking his head. "No. We lived out near Framingham. My mom would take me here in the summer sometimes for swimming, but not in the winter."

Wrapping my arms around myself, because I was truthfully a little cold, I continued our walk. "Is your mom still in Framingham?"

"Uh, no." I heard him exhale a deep breath before adding, "She died a few years ago."

"Oh. I'm so sorry." I turned, again stopping, placing a hand on his arm. This poor guy, he never caught a break. "Do you mind if I ask what happened?"

Victor's eyes were on the ground, and he shrugged. "No. It's fine. It was a car accident. She lost control of her car at night on an icy road. It could've happened to anyone."

"God. I'm so sorry." I shuffled an inch or so closer, wanting to hug him, or offer more comfort, or do something.

Again, his gaze lifted to some point in the distance, he seemed to study it. But this time, since we were so close, I was able to study his profile.

Abruptly, he said, "She wasn't a very happy person."

"What?"

"I don't think she ever got over my dad leaving her. She was his mistress first before she became his second wife. When they met, she was seventeen and he was very experienced, worldly, all the things she wasn't." His eyes returned to mine and his tone was very matter-of-fact, like he'd dissected this topic and came to a conclusion. "She'd never dated anyone before him. And he was always telling her that he loved her, even after the divorce. He'd say he missed her whenever he'd split from one of his wives. They'd get back together for a while, and then he'd eventually say he needed more than what she could give him. I think she always hoped he would come back for good."

Victor's gaze traveled from my lips to my eyes, like he was reading something there. He smiled at what he found, amused, but also a little sad. "My thoughts exactly."

I didn't want to think about what my expression was, since clearly my thoughts had been visible on my face.

"Anyway. I didn't have a bad childhood, though. Not at all. She was a great mom." He sighed, starting forward again. I fell into step next to him, and after a few paces he bumped me with his shoulder. "I'm sorry every time I talk about my family it seems so depressing. I promise I'll tell a funny anecdote next time."

"Don't be sorry." I bumped his shoulder in return. "It's like reading one of those classic Russian novels, but without having to carry it around everywhere."

He chuckled. "Yeah. That's an apt analogy. Dostoyevsky could've written my memoir."

"You should meet Anna's boyfriend, Luca. He teaches Russian literature and is one of the nicest—and yet most morose—people I know." I glanced at Victor's profile; he was frowning as though deep in thought.

After a long moment he asked, "Luca? As in Luca Kroft? The professor?"

"That's right."

Victor's wide eyes swung to mine and then away. "Anna is dating a professor?"

I nodded, studying him, his jaw clenched, and his mouth an unhappy slash on his face.

"Hey. What's wrong?" I bumped his arm again.

"It's just—" He placed his hand on my elbow, bringing me to a stop, and faced me. "How did they meet?"

"Uh—"

"Was he ever her professor?"

I shrugged. "Yes, he was. She took his class last summer. Why?"

His mouth dropped open. "And he's *dating* her?"

I nodded slowly. "Yeah."

Victor made a sound of disbelief, his eyes lifting to the sky like he was searching it for answers.

"What's the big deal?"

His attention cut to me, his gaze agitated. "What's the big deal?!"

"Victor." I placed my hands on his shoulders. "They met about a year ago, before she took his class. Months later, she took Russian lit, not knowing he was the professor. Time passed, they realized they liked each other, so now they date."

"Just like that?" The question and his face were both incredulous, his eyes a little wild with something like outrage.

"Yep. Thus is the magic of mutual attraction and respect. It sometimes leads to dating." I removed my hands from his shoulders and wiggled my fingers in front of his face. "Magic!"

Some of the agitation leached from his features, but his indignation persisted. "It's not appropriate. Professors and teachers should never cross that line."

"What? It's not appropriate? Says who?" I stood straighter, crossing my arms. "It's not illegal. There's no rule or law against it."

Shoving his gloved hands in his jacket pockets, he opened his mouth like he wanted to say something, his attention darting over my face. After a long moment, he shook his head and marched away like a man on a mission.

I heaved a sigh, and then followed at a distance, getting the sense he needed some marching time to himself. One minute became ten minutes, which then became fifteen. I lost sight of him at one point, but no matter. I wasn't worried he would leave me here, especially since I had the car keys in my pocket. Content to be in the quiet woods, the smell and taste of snow on my tongue, watching the cloud of my breath just beyond my nose, I enjoyed my peaceful stroll.

Gradually, I became aware of the crunching sound of boots that were not my own. Turning, I found Victor walking slowly toward me, his jaw set, a stubborn glint in his eyes.

Upon reaching me, he announced, "Just because a thing is allowed, doesn't mean it should be done." It sounded like a proclamation, and if he'd added *Hear ye, hear ye,* it wouldn't have been out of place.

Just because a thing is allowed, doesn't mean it should be done. Where had I heard those words before? Ah yes! The Pinkery. Months ago. From him.

I wrinkled my nose.

He lifted an eyebrow.

I shook my head.

He nodded.

I pushed at his shoulder with my fingertips. "Are you trying to be funny?"

"Funny? How is that funny?"

"Because you said something similar to me at the Pinkery, when you came in with your dad. Remember?"

His gaze lost focus, like he was pulling up the memory. I saw the precise moment he remembered because his lips parted, he looked a little shocked and immediately contrite.

"Em—"

"Another thing you said, just a week or so ago, was that you should be able to trust your friends not to judge you. Right?"

All his righteousness seemed to deflate, and that look

reappeared, the one where it was obvious he was trying not to smile. This time his cheeks turned a tad pink, like he'd been caught.

But instead of pressing his lips into a flat line, he gave into the barest of grins. "Yes. I believe I said that."

"Speaking of which—" I covered the bottom half of my face with my hands and breathed into my gloves, warming my nose. "I meant to thank you for that golden nugget of advice."

"Oh?" He seemed to sway closer.

"Yes. I told Anna about my job and we hugged it out. So, thank you."

"There's no need to thank me."

"Oh, but there is. I wouldn't have told her if you hadn't said what you did. Maybe I just needed someone to point out the obvious. Or maybe I just needed someone not to be a fraud."

"Not to be a fraud?" The side of his mouth hitched.

"Yes. I needed someone to practice what they preach."

"Ah. You needed evidence." He nodded, giving me what could only be described as a gentle look. "I get that."

"Yes! Evidence. I needed evidence. Even if it was empirical."

"And I was that someone?"

"Yes."

We stared at each other, mutual like and respect passing between us. Suddenly gripped by an urge, I couldn't help myself. I lifted to my tiptoes and placed a quick kiss on his cheek, gripping his shoulders and giving him a small shake as I leaned away.

"Victor, I needed to believe in myself, and trust my friends, and let go of thinking I can control what judgmental, small-minded people think. I can't. I can't control them."

He nodded like he understood. "It would be like herding PhD candidates."

I laughed. "PhD candidates are difficult to corral?"

He lifted an eyebrow, giving me a half-smile and looking incredibly sexy and adorable. "Honestly? Worse than cats."

That made me laugh harder, and while I did so, Victor's hands came to my waist, settling there as we laughed together. Eventually, the laughter tapered. Looking at each other while laughing abruptly became staring at each other while smiling. Then his gaze dropped to my lips and his smile faded. He blinked. He cleared his throat and I sensed he was about to pull away.

So I tugged him into a hurried hug, not ready for the moment to be over. *I just like him so darn much.*

"But seriously, though. Thank you for lending me your strength."

His strong arms came around me and he held me tightly, his voice a little rough as he said, "I didn't do anything, Emily."

"You did." I squeezed my eyes shut, smelling him and the snow, and luxuriated in the feel of him, holding him, having him hold me, even if it was through a million layers of clothes. "Thank you for your great advice. And thank you for your belief in me, so that I could believe in myself."

CHAPTER 15

VICTOR

"I booked the surgery. I'm getting it done over spring break."

Andy blinked once. Hard. And then he frowned. And then he shifted his eyes from the stubborn bolt he'd been cursing for the last three minutes to mine. "What?"

"The panniculectomy."

"To get the skin removed?"

"Yeah."

He stared at me for several seconds before he said, "I'm probably going to regret asking this, because you know I've been trying to get you to do it for months, but . . ." He took a deep breath. "Why do you want to get the surgery now when you've always been so against it? What changed?"

"Well, for one thing, it's uncomfortable. It's in the way, when we work out especially."

"But you said it wasn't *that* uncomfortable and you would deal with it."

I nodded, rearranging the toolbox next to us. "That's true. But why deal with it if I don't have to?"

"That was my argument." His attention shifted back to the bolt. "And you said, and I quote, 'It's part of—'"

"'—who I am.' Yes. I remember."

"And now it's not part of who you are?" He grunted as he asked this, trying the bolt again.

I didn't have an answer, so I organized the wrenches in size order, disliking the disordered direction of my thoughts.

"You want to know what I think? I'll tell you what I think. I think you want your brunette girlfriend more than you want to hold on to sanctimonious pride. That's what I think."

I swallowed with difficulty. "I don't . . ."

"Don't what?"

"I don't want her," I lied, but it was also the truth.

"Nah, man. You want her. You just don't *want* to want her. That's what you don't want. Motherfucker!" He tossed the three-quarters he was using to the toolbox, upsetting my arrangement, and growling at the bolt.

"Just use the power wrench."

"I don't want to strip it." He wiped his hands on a rag and glowered at the bolt.

"You won't strip it."

"These old joints, they're not built for power tools. You use a plug-in, they strip. I'm telling you." Visibly disgusted, Andy stood and paced away, leaving me on the cement.

I was about to suggest we check out the long torque wrench when he paced back and pointed at me. "Get the fucking surgery. Get all the fucking surgeries. And stop punishing yourself for other people being dicks."

"Other people being dicks," I repeated flatly, having no idea what he was talking about.

"That's right. So some ignorant assholes treated you like shit because you were big, and now they don't. But guess what? People treat other people like shit for all sorts of reasons—size, shape, color, scars, amputations, disabilities, mental illness, religion, politics, just look at what the gays have to deal with!—it fucking happens. Get over it. Stop letting other people make your decisions for you. Live your best life. Move on."

"What are you talking about? I'm not doing that."

He laughed. "You are."

"If I were letting other people make my decisions for me, I would've gotten the surgery already."

"Nooooo." He shook his head firmly.

"Yeeeessss." I nodded just as stubbornly.

"No. You didn't want to get the surgery because you wanted to show all those shallow assholes that you don't care what they think, that you might look like a Ken doll with your clothes on, but underneath they're not going to like the saggy skin, and fuck them. Right? Fuck them. Like, 'Surprise, motherfucker! You thought you wanted this? Guess what, I'm still ugly to you. You're not worthy. Now go eat shit and die.' Give me a break. You cling to your moral superiority like it's a fucking life raft."

I tested the bolt he'd been working on, trying to keep my temper. Not because he was wrong, but because he was right. Dammit, he was so right.

What had Emily said? *I needed to believe in myself, and trust my friends, and let go of thinking I can control what judgmental, small-minded people think. I can't control them.*

She was right then, and Andy was right now. I couldn't control what judgmental, small-minded people thought, but I'd been letting what they thought control me.

Andy paced back and forth, his hands on his hips. "Get the surgery. Date the girl. Be happy. It's not that hard."

My heart jumped to my throat, clogging it. "It's not about Emily."

"Like hell it isn't."

"It's not. Even if I do get the surgery, I still won't be with Emily."

"What? Why not?"

"Because she was my student." I tried the words on again as an excuse, this time they didn't fit. That wasn't the reason.

Andy seemed to read my mind because he made the "wrong buzzer" sound, "*Eeeeeerrrnt*. Survey says, bullshit. Try again."

I searched my mind for the other reasons. "Because she's very young."

"Uh, something tells me she's got more maturity and experience than you. So, again, bullshit."

"Because she's—"

"Beautiful."

Dammit.

"It's because she's beautiful." He nodded at his own statement, smirking at me. "See, I know you. I know how your mind works, because I was you. You don't think you're worthy of her."

"That's not it. It's not about worth." I glanced at my greasy hands.

"Then what's it about?"

I thought about that, really and truly thought about it, and decided to tell him the truth. "What can I offer her? As you so frequently like to remind me, I'm a thirty-year-old virgin. I have nothing to offer."

"Uh, I've seen your dick. You've got plenty to offer."

Scowling at him, I shook my head. "What difference does that make if I don't know how to use it?"

He chuckled. "You don't think it'll be fun figuring that out? For the both of you?"

"It's never going to happen," I said firmly, mostly because I needed to hear it. "We're incompatible."

"Give me one good reason, other than you being a virgin."

"She doesn't notice when people look at her."

"So?"

"She's used to being subjectively attractive. She takes it for granted."

"And you're not/you don't."

"Exactly."

"Don't you think you could? Over time?"

"I honestly don't think so." And that was the truth. I couldn't imagine ever getting used to it.

Andy seemed to contemplate me for a long time before sighing and nodding. "Okay. So. You've gone your whole life—prior to now—without anyone telling you you're attractive. Again, I say, so what? Some people go their whole life without someone telling them that they're good or smart. Or talented. Or interesting or funny. Not everyone is good, smart, or talented, or interesting or funny, and not everyone is good-looking. What's the big deal? You think fat people don't have great sex? Or stupid people? I had tons of great sex before I joined the marines. And you know I've had bigger girlfriends, and sex was never the problem. Man, you know Tasha was a—" He whistled, then sighed. "I wonder what she's up to."

"The big deal is that subjective attractiveness—more than any of those other traits—is biologically programmed to be the main factor in whether or not a human passes on their genes."

"Their jeans?" Clearly, Andy was only half-listening as he picked through the Craftsman toolbox.

"Genes. Procreation."

"Ah."

"You can be morally bankrupt, stupid, talentless, boring, and humorless, and yet still have the opportunity to procreate with very little effort if you're attractive."

He tilted his head back and forth in a considering motion.

"Okay. Fair point. But would you want to be that person? Would you want to live that life? Isn't your dad that guy? He's miserable. And attractiveness is relative. And! It doesn't matter who you are, attractiveness fades. Time stops for no person, except maybe Paul Rudd. You know that guy is fifty?"

"What? Are you serious?" Fifty?!

"Yeah, man. He's like that book you gave me, the one with the picture in the attic somewhere."

"The Picture of Dorian Gray."

"Exactly. And from the way you talk about Emily, it sounds like her inside matches the outside."

"It certainly appears to," I agreed absentmindedly. *Paul Rudd is fifty?*

"Or, and I'm just spitballing here, *maybe* you like the way the outside looks so much because of what's on the inside?"

"No."

He pulled a face, but I had to be honest.

"No, Andy. I mean, she *is* great. She's funny and smart and a good, kind person. But also, she's . . . "

"What?"

"She's so fucking hot." I blew out a breath, shaking my head at my use of the expletive, but it had to be said. "Every time I'm around her, I can't think straight. Her eyes are amazing, gorgeous, this very particular shade of brown and gold, like honey. And she has this oval face, a perfect oval, and her lips. Her top lip is larger than the bottom, with a cupid's bow—do you know what that is?"

"Na-ah." He didn't sound interested. "I guess she's pretty, but she's not my type. Not the way I order my hamburger. Therefore professor, I still think you like her outside so much because you like her inside a lot."

I scratched the back of my neck, thinking about her lips. "She's the most beautiful woman I've ever seen."

"You say it like it's a bad thing."

"It is."

"How is her being beautiful a bad thing?" Andy glared at the stubborn bolt, as though he could intimidate it into moving.

"Because . . ."

"Because?"

I'd committed to being honest thus far. "Because it means I'll never be able to date her."

Andy shifted his eyes from the bolt to me. "Are we back to this again? Why?"

Wasn't it obvious? "How do I know it's not just her outside I want? That it's not just strictly physical? I've determined it's unwise for me to date physically attractive people."

He wiped his forehead, smearing a trail of grease over his eyebrow, grumbling, "What are you going on about? That's not a thing."

"It's a thing."

"It's not. Everyone is interested in people they find physically attractive. It's *the thing,* the one misguided habit every single person on this planet has in common. It's inescapable."

"Not for me." I shook my head.

"So you're saying you'll only go out with ugly people? That's the plan?"

"No one is ever truly ugly."

"Fake news."

"Name one ugly person."

"Price Cooper is one ugly sonofabitch. Fight me."

A protest died on my lips. Price Cooper was a guy we'd gone to high school with. He'd been good-looking then, and an asshole. Now he was ugly, and still an asshole. I studied Andy thoughtfully as he crossed to where I sat, his grin stretching the closer he got.

"Ugly, right?"

I stood and shoved my hands in my pockets. "It's his personality."

"It's his face." He backed away, gesturing to his own face.

"It's both."

"Whatever. Point is, there are ugly—objectively ugly—people out there. Denying their existence is stupid. Just like there are *morally bankrupt* people, and dumb people, and humorless people. But being ugly doesn't make a person bad, just like being stupid doesn't make a person bad, or being humorless. The key thing here is that ugly people exist—fact. And you're telling me—now that your interest has *finally* been piqued—that you want to exclusively date the ugly folk?"

"No," I drawled out, trying not to laugh at how he said *the ugly folk*, like unattractive people were fairies or leprechauns. "I'm saying I don't want to spend time dating anyone who is objectively attractive, and definitely not someone beautiful." *Like Emily.*

"And yet, you still haven't told me why. Do you even know?"

"Because I want to be with someone based on who they are on the inside, not based on something illusory and meaningless like 'good looks.'"

He pulled another face, placing his hands on his hips and lifting an eyebrow. "What you're saying here is pretty darn twisted."

"How is it twisted?"

"You're assuming good-looking people have nothing going for them other than their looks, right? But take me for instance." He gestured to himself with both thumbs. "I'm one seriously handsome bastard and the funniest, coolest, smartest guy you hang out with on the weekend in a hangar, am I right?"

"You're the only guy I hang out with on the weekend in a hangar."

"Admit it, it's pretty shitty of you to assume just because a person is good-looking they're not worth your time. Good, worthy people come in all shapes and sizes and attractiveness."

I pushed a hand through my hair. "I'm not saying that. I merely hypothesize that people who aren't objectively attractive have—in general terms, as a generalization to the population at large—more going for them by all other quality measures than objectively attractive people, and are therefore more worth my time. What? Why are you shaking your head?"

Andy gave me a pitying glance, chuckling again. "You dumb, sweet, clueless man-child."

"I'm clueless? How am I clueless?"

"That's not how this works. That's not how any of this works."

"Maybe not for you, but for me—"

"Nope. Not for you, either. You are not special, Victor. Listen—" he took a step closer, placing a hand on my shoulder as though to confide in me "—you want to eat cow tongue?"

Cow tongue?

"What?"

"Do. You. Want. To. Eat. Cow. Tongue?"

"Why would I do that?"

"It's full of essential vitamins and minerals and omega-3 fatty acids. All that good shit."

"No, it's not."

"Just pretend for a minute that it is. Just pretend it's the healthiest food in the whole damn world, all right? Now, knowing it's the best thing for you, do you want to eat it? Or how about monkey ass? Or sheep's balls? The hair is the best part, full of fiber."

I glared at my friend.

"Exactly." He nodded once, definitively, as though I'd just proved a point.

"What, exactly?"

"Fucking other people is like eating food. Yeah, if you're starving, it doesn't matter all that much. You might be able to gag down a sea urchin toenail or two."

"Sea urchins don't have toenails."

He ignored me. "But usually, you want to eat something that looks and tastes and smells good—*to you*—and makes *you* feel good. One person's cow tongue is another person's filet mignon. Personal taste and texture matters, presentation matters. Choking on octopus intestines every day is going to get old real fast, unless you just love yourself some octopus intestines. Sooner or later, if you try to force it with someone you're not attracted to, you'll get tired of fucking with the lights off."

With one last squeeze of my shoulder and a tight smile, Andy turned away, strolling toward the power wrench in the corner of the shop.

Conflicted, I watched him go. What he said made sense, and I hated that it made sense, *but*—

"Do whatever you want, Victor. Pretend you worked day and night to fix her car and make it like new because you wanted to be a good friend, pretend you've got everything under control, pretend you're not in love with her." His shoulders rose and fell, calling, "But do you really think she's going to wait around forever?"

I stiffened. "What does that mean?"

"Like you said before, she gets hit on all the time. How long before she finds her own filet mignon and leaves you with an empty plate?"

Do you really think she's going to wait around forever?

Even before Andy gave voice to it, this question had been stalking me. Just the thought of Emily with someone else, a boyfriend she'd probably introduce me to, made me feel as though I might go insane. I didn't like this feeling.

I am not myself.

I'd shrugged off checking my phone constantly throughout any given day, hoping that she'd messaged, my heart jumping whenever she did. I'd explained away this new, persistent panic every time I stepped on the scale and the pressing urge to lose even more weight as a passing phase. I'd rationalized spending the majority of my free hours either with her or doing something for her as temporary. She was a new friend. So what if I prioritized our dinners over going out with my other friends?

And so what if I thought about her constantly, missed her constantly, had difficulty concentrating at home and at work, rearranged my schedule to move all my shifts at the airfield to when I knew she'd be busy?

Staring at my reflection in the mirror, my eyes moved over the loose skin on my chest. Drifting past the defined muscles of my upper stomach, I pushed the towel around my waist lower so I could see the sagging folds at my lower abdomen.

I'd told Andy the truth about why I'd decided to have the surgery. The skin was uncomfortable, especially when working out or when I was active. He was right about why I'd held off for so long, I'd allowed other people and their opinions dictate my decisions. I'd held off to spite them, because I—as he put it—clung to my moral superiority like a life raft.

But he was also right about Emily being one of the

reasons. I didn't like what that said about me. I didn't like how I'd allowed her to change me, how I'd let her influence my motivations, how I thought about her before making decisions. I didn't like that her opinion mattered so much.

And what would happen when she did find someone else?

"I'm not myself," I said on a tired sigh.

Wrapping the towel once more around my waist, I left the bathroom. She was coming over tonight. It was my turn to cook, and I'd been planning this dinner for over a week. But after my conversation with Andy this afternoon, I'd wanted to cancel.

I didn't. I wouldn't do that to her. I knew she cared about me, in her own way, and I wouldn't just disappear on her without an explanation. I owed her more than that.

When the time came for us to part ways, when our friendship ended—and I was convinced it would have to come to an end eventually—I would tell her the truth: *I love you, it hurts too much to see you with someone else, I know nothing can ever happen between us and that's fine, I wish you nothing but happiness.* That's what I'd resolved to do.

But until that day, until she introduced me to the man *she* loved, I'd want to be her friend. I'd want to support her, take care of her in my small way, and spend as much time as possible in her company.

It would be enough.

I'd picked up the lobsters from a fish market across from the university. Presently, they were still alive, crawling around a makeshift fish tank in my garage. I'd made bread earlier in the day, before my shift at the airfield, letting it rise and then baking it while I took a shower. A friend of mine near Umbria, Italy had sent me truffles, parmesan, balsamic glaze, and homemade pasta from a market near his house. I already had a few bottles of Chianti, prosecco, and olive oil from a shipment over winter break.

Tonight, we would have wine, fresh bread with olive oil and garlic, truffle carbonara, and fresh steamed lobsters. I hadn't eaten dinner yesterday or any food today, saving my calories for the planned feast.

Therefore, I was a little dizzy when I opened the door, made dizzier still by Emily's giant smile.

"Hello!" She leaned forward.

Low on food, my brain wasn't working properly. I just stood there, tense and unmoving. I couldn't decide whether to greet her with a cheek kiss, or a hug, or a handshake, or—

"Bah!" she said, grabbing me and hugging me and then huffing as she pulled away and stepped into my house. "We've got to do something about this. We're never on the same page."

"What do you mean?"

"I mean with how we greet each other. Sometimes, you extend your hand. Sometimes I do, and then you go in for the hug. Or I go in for the kiss and you're going for the shake and we sort of, you know, smash together." She laughed, pulling off her coat, her eyes bright and happy.

"I guess we do need to work on it," I agreed absentmindedly, distracted by her happy expression.

"So, which is it? Hmm? What are we doing? High five, handshake, air kiss, hug? What?" She moved her arms with each suggestion as though miming the actions as they were listed.

I shoved my hands in my pockets. "We're deciding?"

"Yes. How are we friend greeting each other from now on? I need directions. I need—"

"Kiss on the cheek."

Her eyebrows jumped. "Kiss on the cheek?"

"Yes," I said firmly, committing to it. It had slipped out, a desire spoken, but I wanted her kisses on me, even if I had to settle for the cheek. It was selfish and reckless, and I didn't fucking care.

"Okay. Kiss on the cheek." She nodded, like it was decided. "Which way are you going?"

"Going?" Did she mean the kitchen or . . .?

"Left or right? We need to work it out so we don't both go the same direction and then more smashing occurs. Oh my God, why does it smell like fresh bread in here? Did you bake bread?"

"I did bake bread, and I'll go to my le—uh, my right?"

"You're left-handed or right-handed?" She walked past me toward the kitchen, her steps hurried.

I followed behind, checking her out, as was my habit. Tonight, she wore snug black pants—maybe they were yoga pants?—and a pink T-shirt with nothing on it.

"I'm left-handed," I said, tearing my eyes away from her ass.

"Then you should go to the left, that'll be your first instinct. I can go left because I swing both ways."

I choked. "Pardon?"

"I'm ambidextrous." She glanced at me fleetingly as she entered the kitchen, her attention immediately arrested by the bread and olive oil mixture I'd placed on the counter. "I can go either way, so I'll just follow your lead. I can't believe you baked bread. I never eat bread like this." Dipping a slice into the olive oil, garlic, balsamic, and spices, she shoved the piece into her mouth, her eyes rolling back in her head as she groaned and chewed. "One piece," she moaned around a mouthful. "Only let me have one piece. Otherwise I have to spend four hours at the gym tomorrow and I hate the gym."

Her pleasure sounds struck me directly in the groin and I chased a breath, turning away from her and staring unseeingly at the stovetop. I couldn't decide if I should never feed her anything delicious again, or if I should bake bread for her daily.

"Sorry. It's just that I lust crusty bread. This is so good."

I laughed lightly, shaking myself, and opening the carton of eggs on the counter for the carbonara sauce. But then I promptly forgot what I was doing when she moaned again.

Dammit. I was not myself.

Or maybe I was finally seeing myself for who I truly was. *I'm naïve. I lack confidence because I lack knowledge and experience.*

Andy had been right about almost everything: I wanted her, badly. I was in love with her. I wasn't in control.

But he'd been wrong about one very important fact: Emily deserved so much more and better than me. And it wasn't because of the way I looked with my clothes off, and it wasn't because I'd been heavy my whole life until now, and it wasn't because I didn't think I was smart, or kind, or attractive. I knew I was intelligent, and good, and—objectively—handsome.

It was because she was just so much more, in every way, on every list. Emily was the outlier in every cohort. No amount of adding my positive traits together would ever balance the sheet between us.

I would never be enough.

CHAPTER 16

EMILY

"Admit it, it's delicious." I poked him in the side.

Anna's cousin shook his head, his lips pressed tightly together.

"Admit it, Abram! It's the best boxed wine you've ever had." Anna also poked him.

Abram caught her hand, giving her a cagey look. "It's pretty good."

"Pretty good?!" Anna and I said in unison, making him laugh.

It was one of those rare Saturdays when I didn't have to work. The day was mine to do with whatever I pleased, and so it pleased me to hang out with Anna and her cousin, drinking red wine before we went out to an art show, pretending to be sophisticated. Abram was a musician, lived in New York, and I'd known him since I was seven.

Taking another sip, he sauntered over to Anna's couch. We stared after him, stunned. He sat at one end, sniffing his glass. "I've had a lot of boxed wine in my time, and—"

Anna snorted. "Yeah. Okay, grandpa."

"*And*, this is pretty good, if you like your reds sweet with no legs. I'll give you a list of others to check out for a better balance and robust body."

I was about to tell him how pretentious he sounded when my phone rang, distracting me.

"You sound ridiculous," Anna said, following him into the living room. "Better balance and robust body.'" I couldn't see her face, but I knew she was rolling her eyes. "Oh? Really? Are you spending the summer in Napa? Fancy yourself a bit of a sommelier, do you?"

Smirking as I glanced at my phone's screen—I could always count on Anna to speak my mind—my good humor was quickly replaced with mild irritation.

Landon. Blah.

I sent the call to voicemail and joined my friends, sitting on the coffee table and sipping on my tasty wine. Abram was currently laughing as Anna took another sip of her wine, her pinkie finger straight in the air.

"Who was it?" Anna lifted her chin toward me when she finished making fun of her cousin.

"It's . . ." I made a face and shook my head. I mean, who calls anymore? Didn't he understand the rules of engagement? The only people who get a pass from the text-first rule were grandparents, parents, and best friends. That's it. "Just this guy. Nothing important."

Landon was a guy in my differential equations class this semester who'd asked for my number last week. Presently, it was the third month of the spring term and he'd said it had taken him all three months to work up the courage to ask. I thought that was awfully sweet. So, since I was unattached, and Landon checked all the boxes on my type—cute, funny, sweet, small of stature—I'd given it to him. I realized now that I'd made a mistake.

He . . . kept . . . calling, and we hadn't even gone on a date yet. *Send a text, Landon!*

"You didn't answer it?" Abram lifted an eyebrow, and the action drew my attention to his nose. He'd broken it last year and it hadn't healed right, which meant he sometimes didn't look like himself. Like now.

"I'm here with you." I waved my free hand between my friends. "I don't need to talk to him."

"Is it *him*?" Anna's eyes grew very, very large and she lowered her voice by two octaves, making me chuckle.

Abram glanced between us. "Him? Who is him?"

"Anna—"

She cut me off. "Him is Dr. Hanover, her—"

"Gynecologist?" he asked, being the doofus that he was.

"No, Abram. Not her gynecologist." Anna sighed, making Abram laugh. The three of us had this relationship: we were the eternally exasperated younger sisters and he was the older brother who enjoyed teasing us. "Her research methods professor."

Abram shook his head as he moved it back to me, blinking his eyes cartoonishly. "Wait, what? Your research methods professor is your friend?"

"Yes. He is. But that wasn't Victor on the phone. That was someone else."

"Back up." Abram rested back on the cushions, his elbow resting on the arm of the sofa. "How did you become friends with your research methods professor?"

"It's a long story."

"Oh. Good." He checked his wrist, which didn't have a watch. "That's right, it's story time."

"I didn't say I was going to tell you the story." I sipped my wine, glaring at him over the rim.

"She's hot for him, but they decided to be friends."

"Anna!" I almost choked on my wine.

"It's not that long of a story," she said to me matter-of-factly. "You just don't want to tell him."

"He friend-zoned you?" Abram was laughing, like this information thrilled him to no end.

"I hate that word." I stuck my nose in my wineglass and took a deep breath. Ah, wine, clearly my only friend in the room.

"I hate that people hate that word." Abram shrugged. "Take the word in the spirit it's intended and stop reading so much into it."

"Fine. Then, yes. In the spirit in which the word was intended, he friend-zoned me. Or, I guess it was mutual."

"But you're hot for him," Anna helpfully reminded me.

"I was." I said this between clenched teeth.

"She is." Anna mimicked my clenched teeth voice.

"But now we're friends, and it's good," I said, reminding her and myself. "I like being his friend. He's a good friend."

"How is he a good friend?" Abram asked, rubbing his bearded chin, looking genuinely curious. "I mean, I'm interested in this. How do you be friends with someone you're hot for?"

"You want me to give you a lesson? Uh, let's see. He's had me over to his place a few times. He's made me dinner, or I've made dinner. We've been to a few movies. We went hiking. He helped me with my car, getting it fixed." Talking about Victor made my chest feel tight and uncomfortable. I missed him. I hadn't seen Victor in over three weeks. He'd left town for spring break and our schedules hadn't aligned since. But! We still texted daily.

"Huh." Abram was still rubbing his chin.

"What?" I nudged his leg with my foot.

"It's just—" Abram made a face, telling me he was confused. "Is he gay?"

"Abram!" Anna sat straight up.

"What? It's a fair question. Emily is awesome. Smart,

funny. Cool." He gestured to me with his hand. "What's his deal?"

"Then what's your deal?" Anna hit her cousin lightly on the shoulder. "You've never made a move on Emily."

"We grew up together. She's like another one of you."

"Another one of me?"

"Yes. Like a little sister. It would be—" Abram made a face of revulsion "—horrifying."

"Thanks, A-man. I feel the same way about you."

He gave me a grin, and even with the bushy beard I could just make out his dimples. "But I'm judging this guy—wait, how old is he?"

I stared at the wall over Abram's shoulder and tried to think back over the last few months, realizing I'd never asked Victor for his age. "I don't know, early thirties, I guess."

"Okay, yes. I'm judging him for putting you in the friend zone. Unless he's gay."

While I appreciated Abram acting like the big brother, I felt the need to defend Victor. "He's not gay. He's—"

"What?"

"He's got a lot going on. And he's my professor."

"*Was* your professor, last semester," Anna corrected. "Plus, he had that woman appointed as your advocate."

"Oh, like you and Luca?" Abram pointed at his cousin.

"Yes. Precisely."

"Why'd he have an advocate appointed?"

"It's a long story!" I went to take a sip of my wine, hoping it would encourage them to do the same, and found my glass was empty. Standing, I offered, "More wine?"

They shook their heads, so I walked to the kitchen.

But then I heard Anna loud-whisper, "He saw her naked."

"ANNA!" *I never should have told her about my job!*

"What?" She turned over her shoulder, giving me a

disgruntled look. "You keep saying things are long stories and they're not."

"Hold up. When and how did he see you naked?"

I glared at Anna. She swallowed uncomfortably, realizing her mistake too late.

Abram glanced between us, looking like he was ready to go into overprotective mode. "Wait. Did he—"

I waved my hand in the air. "It's fine. Whatever. I've been working at a lingerie store modeling lingerie. He came in with a customer—his dad, gross, right? But his dad is gross, not Victor—and I was stage three naked when he saw me."

"Huh." He nodded, frowning mildly. "What's stage three naked?"

Of course Abram isn't fazed by me modeling lingerie. Of course.

"That *is* a long story," Anna cut in. "Just accept the fact that he saw her naked, realized she was a student, and then had the advocate appointed for her peace of mind. It was very stand-up of him."

I shrugged, filling my glass from the wine spigot, again feeling protective of Victor. "Well, he's a stand-up guy."

"Ohhhh," Abram said, like he just realized something.

"What?" Anna and I asked in unison.

"He's a stand-up guy."

My friend and I shared a look, and she asked, "So?"

"So, he thinks you're too young to date." Abram nodded, like this explained everything.

"What?" I couldn't keep the irritation from my voice. "That's preposterous."

"It's not. The age difference, he sees you as a kid, too young to date, but he enjoys your company." Abram was back to rubbing his chin. "Well, good for him. I like him already."

"You like him because he won't date me?"

"Actually, yes. I like him because he likes you enough to hang out with you *and* not date you."

"What are you talking about?" I reclaimed my seat on the coffee table. "Why is this worthy of your respect?"

"Because most men are not this way. Either a girl is to fuck, date, related, or nothing."

Anna gasped. And then she and I shared a shocked looked. And then she said, "That's super shitty."

"That's men."

"I object. What about your friend Kaitlyn? O—or Ruthie? Or—or your friend Jenny?" Anna stumbled over her words.

"I didn't say I was that way. I have a lot of female friends. I like hanging out with women, especially other musicians. I love women. But most guys I know only have male friends."

"Why is that?"

Abram shrugged. "If I had to guess, then I'd say because they have an inability to see a woman as anything other than something sexual. Marie writes about this shit all the time."

Marie was Abram's older sister and therefore Anna's cousin. She was also a journalist.

"What? Which article?" I hadn't been keeping up with her work, though I did enjoy reading her when I was a teenager. The topics made me feel scandalized even as they informed me.

"For starters, that one about men with sisters, or raised exclusively by women, and how they're more likely to have female friends, and even then it's still super low."

"Well. That's depressing." Anna took a sip of her wine as though to punctuate her opinion.

"But it makes sense, right? Look at how women are depicted in the media. Look at all the products out there for women that aren't for men. She wrote that other piece about how people are treated differently if they're overweight, but women get it much, much, *much* worse than men, and they think this is because a woman's value is still intrinsically tied to—"

"Wait. Wait a minute." I waved my hand to get his attention. "Go back. What was that? About how overweight people are treated? What did she say?"

"She didn't say anything, she just reported on results from a meta thing."

"A meta thing? You mean a meta-analysis?" I asked.

"Yep. That's it." He nodded. "Meta-analysis, where they take a bunch of studies and look at all the information together."

"That's right. What did it say?" I leaned closer.

"Just that they're ignored—particularly women—in our society. They did these tests situations, where they sent in a thin woman, to like—you know—an auto repair shop, the grocery store, or the doctor's office. Whatever, normal, everyday places. And then they dressed the same woman up to be heavier. When she was thin, people made eye contact, smiled more, spoke more, she had to wait less to be waited on. When she was heavy, she was basically ignored."

Now I gasped. "Holy shit."

"This surprises you?" Anna asked, giving me the side-eye.

"I guess I've never thought about it. Did they do it with a man?"

"Yeah. But he wasn't *as* ignored. People didn't smile as much and all that as when he was thin, but they treated him better than the woman. They still waited on him, they just weren't as friendly."

"That is so messed up." My gaze fell to the couch as I worked through my feelings. Apparently, I had a lot of feelings about this. "Why did I not know about this? I feel like an idiot." Especially considering how my mother struggled with body image.

I'd always considered her concerns to be about self-worth, not about how others treated her. *BLARG!*

I felt ashamed of my own ignorance. But also, like the clouds that had obscured Victor parted. He didn't like hanging out in public. He liked watching movies at my place or at his. When we did go out to dinner, he always seemed hyper aware of the women who looked at him—or the men—and, invariably, just like the first time when he pointed it out, he couldn't seem to relax.

What had he said?

None of these people would look at me twice if they saw what I looked like before.

And I liked that person, even if no one else did.

"It is messed up," Abram said on a sigh. "Marie was pretty enraged. She wouldn't stop talking about it for months. She still brings it up."

"No wonder," I mumbled.

"No wonder what?" Anna nudged me with her foot like I'd done to Abram earlier.

"It's just, Victor—Dr. Hanover—doesn't like going out to restaurants, so we always go to his place or my place, and it must be because he doesn't like the attention he gets."

"Am I missing something?" Abram was glancing between us again.

Anna pointed a finger at me. "Don't say it's a long story."

Rolling my eyes, I said, "Victor lost about a hundred and fifty pounds last year."

"Whoa." Abram's eyebrows shot up.

"Yes."

"And he told you he doesn't like the attention?" he asked.

"Yeah. I never pushed him on it. When we first decided to be friends he said something like, 'If they saw the real me, they wouldn't look at me.' And so I assumed it meant he had, or has, residual body image concerns or self-consciousness about how he looks. And when I say he doesn't like going out, I mean he *really* hates it. Like, he actively scowls at women who are sending him flirty looks whenever we do."

Abram was shaking his head before I finished speaking. "Dude, you should read Marie's story. I'll send it to you. She goes over this. Usually, it's not about a person's image of themselves, it's about how they're being treated by others. This guy, this Victor guy you're friends with, think about things from his perspective. He's treated one way for most of his life, right? Like, people aren't friendly with him, women don't give him attention. That's not because there's anything wrong with *him.* Marie talks about this, that's because the world we live in sees non-thin people as less valuable."

"Ugh."

"And then, he loses the weight, right? And he's not a different person, right? He's the same—same intelligence, same interests, same sense of humor, all that—but people are treating him differently. Like, *a lot* differently. Like, he's worthier of their attention, they see him, they want to know him. And why? Because he weighs less? That would piss me off too."

I tapped my nail on the lip of my wineglass. "Well, when you put it like that."

"Man, I really like this guy. He sounds awesome." Abram took a gulp of his wine and then made a face, glancing at it. "This is really sweet. Do you guys have anything else?"

I ignored his request for an alternate beverage, mostly because I was thinking about Victor. And when I thought about Victor, it was difficult to stop. "He is actually kind of awesome."

"No wonder you're hot for him." Abram set his glass on the side table.

"Yeah." I sighed.

Just then, my phone buzzed. Again. *Oh, Landon. You are clueless, grasshopper.*

Whipping my phone out, I was prepared to send it to voicemail, but then my heart gave a little leap upon spying Victor's name. Being rude, I immediately accepted the call.

"Hello?"

"Hey, Emily. It's me. Sorry, should I have texted?"

"No! No. Always call. It's so good to hear your voice." I grinned, ignoring how Anna and her cousin shared a wide-eyed look. "What's up?"

"I know it's last minute, but I remember you texted that you weren't working this weekend. I finished up early and I wondered if you wanted to come over and watch a movie. Or we could, uh, go out if you want. I have a friend who can get us tickets to that new play downtown. Like I said, I know it's last minute, so no problem if you're busy."

I scrunched my face because *DARN. IT.* We always had a good time when we hung out, the best time, and it had been so long. Three weeks without seeing his face had felt like an eternity. "Umm, tonight?"

I glanced at Anna, checking to see if there was any wiggle room there. Maybe she'd do me a solid and let me bail. . . But, no, actually. I didn't want to bail. I hardly got to see her since she had her dear professor. Plus, Abram.

Victor seemed to hesitate for a moment before asking, "You already have plans?" His voice sounded funny.

"Who is it?" Anna whispered, frowning at me.

"It's Victor," I mouthed.

She jumped up on the couch, her eyes huge, her grin even bigger. "INVITE HIM!" she loud-whispered. "You haven't seen him in weeks."

I glanced at Abram. He was nodding. "Do it," he mouthed.

"I do h—have plans." Suddenly, I was hot. Sweaty. This was not unusual when I thought about seeing Victor again, or when I knew we'd be seeing each other soon, or when we were together. It was a sensation that was both delightful and uncomfortable, but I refused to think too much about it.

We are friends. He is my friend. I am his friend. Friends. F–R–I–E–N–D–S.

"Oh. I see." He sounded stiff, a little robotic. "I see."

"Anna, her cousin, and—well, we are going to that art exhibit, the Monet thing, at The Central. Do you want to come?"

"Oh!" Now he sounded happy, maybe even relieved? "Yes. Absolutely. That sounds great. I'd love to. What time?"

My heart did a little flip thing and I ignored that too. Eventually, I'd just get used to heart flips and body sweats. No biggie. "We're heading over in an hour. Want to meet us there?"

"Sure. I'll get ready. See you then." He sounded like he was smiling, which made me smile, but I'm sure my smile was much goofier than his.

"Okay. Great. See you then. Bye."

"Bye, Emily."

He clicked off and I lowered my phone, still smiling at the screen. What a great day. *Everything is coming up Emily!*

I felt two shoes nudge my legs and looked up to find both Anna and Abram giving me meaningful looks.

"What?" My eyes bounced between the pair.

Abram fluttered his eyelashes and sighed dramatically. "Oh, Victor." Given his bushy beard, man bun, and muscly chest, he looked ridiculous. Anna giggled.

"Shut it." I crossed my arms, glaring at them both. "I do not sound like that."

"You totally do." Anna wagged her eyebrows, setting down her wineglass to rub her hands together. "And now I'm super excited. This is going to be so good!"

Abram nodded, an undeniably mischievous glint in his

eyes, and he lifted his hand for Anna to give him a high five. "Yep. This'll be good."

My face fell, my heart galloping as I surveyed my friends with growing dread. "You two better be on your best behavior. No funny business!"

"Us?" Abram pointed to himself, like he was offended. "Now, when have we ever been funny?"

Anna giggled again. It sounded evil.

Crap.

CHAPTER 17

EMILY

In retrospect, I should've done so many things differently that night.

For example, the kiss on the cheek. It had been a terrible mistake. Over three weeks ago, when Victor and I had hung out at his house, we'd discussed how friends greet each other. A high five, a handshake, an air kiss, hug, some combination. So many options. We'd decided a kiss on the cheek was what we as friends would do moving forward.

Great. Fine. Whatever. No big deal.

I thought I was prepared because I'd been thinking about and anticipating our next greeting, a cheek kiss, since we'd had the conversation. I'd been imagining it, living it over and over in my head, and it always happened the same way (in my head): He'd show up. We'd smile friend-smiles at each other. I'd say something pleasant—or he would—as I gave him a quick, benign peck. He'd do the same. We would move away from each other because it would be easy because we were friends because that's all that he wanted and that's all that I wanted and so . . . there you go.

But that's not what happened.

"How tall is he?" Abram craned his neck, his head high above the crowd, and inspected the faces coming through the main entrance.

We were standing past the large foyer, before the line for entry, next to one of the soaring columns bracketing the wide cement and stone staircase. Our spot gave us a good view of the entire area, and—as long as we were watching carefully—Victor wouldn't be able to enter without us seeing him.

I shrugged and glanced at my phone, rereading Victor's latest message for the fourth time. "I don't know. He's pretty tall, but maybe a little shorter than you. He should be here any minute. His last text said he'd found a parking spot close by."

"It's a Monet miracle," Anna muttered, and we exchanged a quick commiserating look. We'd been forced to park on campus, about three-fourths of a mile away, after circling the lot and street parking for a half hour.

Usually, the museum wasn't crowded and finding a spot or a friend among the patrons wouldn't have been a problem. But the Monet exhibit had drawn an unexpected crowd of impressionist enthusiasts. Or maybe I was just out of touch with what the artsy people found exciting.

"Do you have a picture of him?"

"Uh, no." I shook my head, my heart giving an odd thump. Victor had a picture of us, a selfie taken while we'd been hiking around Walden Pond in the snow, but I'd felt weird about asking him to send it to me.

"What about his faculty picture?" Anna pulled out her phone.

"He doesn't have one up on the website." I didn't volunteer how I knew this, which—between you and me—was because I'd been missing him a few weeks ago and convinced myself it was perfectly normal to seek out his photo on the university website.

"So then, what's his hair color? Brown? Red? Blond? What's his skin color? Eye color? Big nose or small nose? What does he look like?"

"His hair is dark brown, his skin is white, he wears black horn-rimmed glasses, and he looks like—" I sighed, feeling unaccountably flustered as I conjured Victor's handsome face and sharply intelligent eyes. Stalling, I tucked my phone away in my purse and wiped my sweaty hands on my skirt. It wasn't hot, but my hands were hot. I blamed the crowd.

"He looks a little like Captain America, but with darker hair." This statement earned Anna eyebrow raises from both Abram and me. She looked between us, also putting her phone away. "He does. I mean, he did when I had him for research methods. But"—she gestured to me—"I haven't seen him since he lost weight. So, I don't know if that's true now."

Abram glanced at me out of the corner of his eye. "Your guy looks like Captain America?"

I shook my head, my neck now hot. But Anna was right. Victor looked almost exactly like Chris Evans, but with darker hair and jade-green eyes. "He's not my guy. But, okay, maybe, yes. I guess he does kind of look like *the actor* who plays Captain America."

Anna snapped her fingers. "Chris Evans. That's the actor."

"Right. Maybe a little." *A LOT.* "Whatever." I wiped my hands on my skirt again.

Anna's cousin moved his attention back to the door, his eyes narrowing. "So, I'm looking for a dark-haired Captain America look-alike."

We were all quiet then, and I swallowed for no discernible reason, feeling extremely nervous for no discernible reason, and wishing I'd worn something else—like pants with pockets instead of this black dress with its short circle skirt and long sleeves and square neckline and pockets—for no discernible reason.

Abram's spine straightened, the sudden movement catching my attention. "What? What is it?"

"Wait," he said, lifting a hand. He leaned to one side, closer to me, and pointed toward the entryway. "Is that him?"

My heart quickening, I followed my friend's line of sight and sucked in an abridged breath. My gaze connected with Victor's. My heart lurched. He smiled. So did I.

He was wearing a suit. The last time I'd seen him in a suit had been at the Pinkery, when I'd been stage three naked attire. Furthermore, his hair was styled, and his jaw looked remarkably square, chiseled. *Why does his jaw look so chiseled? Is it the suit? Is it because I haven't seen his face in so long? What is it? Bah!*

His eyes never leaving mine, Victor's lips formed the words *Excuse me* and *Pardon* as he stepped around and between people.

Next to me, Abram said something like, "You were right, Anna. Looks just like him."

And Anna said something like, "Even more now, actually. Wow. He's really pretty."

But I wasn't paying much attention to my friends. My stomach all aflutter, I was unable to keep my feet from taking several steps forward as soon as he broke through the crowd, nor was I able to stem my grin as we both stopped, two feet separating us.

Victor's gaze swept over my face. "Hi."

"Hi." I waved. Inanely. Still smiling.

"You look . . ." He swallowed, cleared his throat, his eyebrows pulling together and then up, causing wrinkles to form on his forehead. "Thank you for inviting me. It's good to see you."

I lost myself for a split second in my admiration for his stunningly intelligent eyes, but then shook myself before my staring veered into creeper territory. "It's good to see you too. I'm glad you could make it," I said on a rush, a little too loud. And because I'm a doofus, I also added, "You look very handsome. I like your suit." I wasn't just nervous; I was extremely nervous; and I didn't have the mental wherewithal to question why I was this level of nervous or consider whether complimenting his suit and calling him handsome was prudent.

Thankfully, his forehead cleared, and he laughed lightly. "Thank you."

"You're welcome," I said earnestly, and my eyes dropped to his right cheek, reminding myself he would go left. Shifting my weight, it was now time for the cheek kiss.

Now.

Now was the time.

. . . Now.

I licked my lips, staring at the place where I should kiss him, but was distracted again by the line of his jaw. It was really just super angular tonight, almost sharp-looking. Clearly he'd just shaved because Victor's omnipresent five-o' clock shadow was absent. From where I stood, I also detected a faint hint of aftershave, which further supported my shave theory.

Up close, when I kissed his cheek, the scent would probably be stronger. . . *shoooooooooot.*

I couldn't move. My throat was dry and tight at the thought. Why hadn't I insisted on a fist bump as our friend greeting? A fist bump was a perfectly fine greeting. I must've been out of my mind agreeing to any kind of lip-to-skin contact. I mean, I'd done it before, but tonight for some reason I couldn't—

"Emily," he whispered, my name a quiet, scraping sound.

My eyes cut to his and I found Victor's focus on my cheek. Or maybe on my mouth? I couldn't be sure. Also, he wasn't smiling anymore. Probably because I was acting so weird. *Stop being a lunatic and just kiss him!*

It's what we'd agreed, right? It's what we'd decided. There was no reason not to do it. *Say something pleasant, give him a quick peck, and then lean away. It'll be so easy. It's no big deal.*

Sucking in a deep inhale for courage, I skipped the "say something pleasant" part and stepped forward, laying my hand on his coat at the shoulder, and closed my eyes. Aiming for his cheek, I realized too late that I'd gone slightly off course. I'd ventured too far, stepped too close, and my lips pressed against the hard bone of his jaw, my nose brushing his ear.

And so I loitered, frozen, debating whether I should give him an additional kiss to correct my error, this time with my eyes open so as to ensure I found the center of his cheek. But in that split second, before I could make up my mind, I felt the warmth of his palms and the firm dig of his fingers on my back just as he placed a soft, lingering kiss on my neck.

On.

My.

Neck.

My eyes flew open, aware of so, so much and all at once. Like how he'd pulled me against him, my front pressed completely to his. Like how his lips hadn't moved or lifted, but instead remained on my pulse point. Like how the scent I'd identified as aftershave was actually just shaving cream, and his skin smelled simply delicious. Like how his breath on my neck caused an involuntary reaction in me, raised goose bumps on my arms and chest, and speedily manifested as a twisting ache of desire between my legs.

Like how my brain wasn't working because my imagination had taken over, debuting a deluge of un-friend-like thoughts.

A suit? Was that all it took? A suit and the smell of shaving cream? I struggled to find the surface of my confused haze, break through to the other side where I didn't have these kinds of feelings for Victor anymore. *Ha ha, Emily. You nut. This is your friend, not a man. Clearly, you need to get laid.*

NOT BY HIM!

Oh God.

My stupid imagination, imagining all the stupid things, making me feel foolish and flustered. And yet, now, here, in this museum, surrounded by an unexpected crowd of impressionist enthusiasts, something was really happening.

Victor's lips and nose trailed lightly up my neck to my jaw, placing another lazy kiss there, and then another in the center of my cheek, all the while I stood perfectly still and my heart beat like a frightened rabbit because something was most definitely happening.

What is happening?

And then, someone cleared their throat loudly behind me —*a man . . . No. Not a man. An Abram*—and I felt Victor stiffen, his fingers at my back applying more pressure as he lifted his head.

"You must be Dr. Hanover," Abram's voice said just as Victor straightened fully, his attention skipping over my face and moving behind me. I watched Victor's eyes with rapt fascination as they narrowed slightly, presumably finding Anna's cousin.

"I'm Abram." My childhood friend was now suddenly standing next to us, and I glanced at him. Abram had extended his hand for a shake toward my . . . my . . . *my not childhood friend.*

I looked back to Victor and watched as he stood straighter, his hands falling away from me, a small frown settling between his eyebrows.

"Anna's cousin, Em's *friend*," Abram added. I didn't like how he'd said *friend* and I didn't like how his voice sounded funny, deeper, or how the massive, dazzling smile on his mouth twinkled in his eyes. "Nice to meet you."

What is happening? What is Abram doing?

Wait, wait, wait. Is he trying to make Victor jealous?

I knew Abram had a history of trying to make his friend Kaitlyn's boyfriend jealous, because he *hated* that guy. Also, he sometimes flirted with other girls in front of their boyfriends, because he liked to flirt, and girls with boyfriends were safe flirt repositories because they were already taken. But I'd never thought he'd do something like that with me.

So, what is he doing?

Victor stepped back, away from me, and seemed to hesitate for just a split second, the intensity of his frown increasing. But then his features cleared of all expression and he accepted Abram's hand, his mouth curved into not quite a smile.

"Nice to meet you." My former professor was formal and polite, and the unmistakable edge of aloofness sent something cold and hard to the base of my throat.

Theirs was a quick handshake—grasp, down, up, release—but it looked like it might've been a little painful. I noticed both men flex their fingers afterward, my unease making me breathless.

As Abram stepped back, still smiling, I shot him a warning glare. It did nothing to disarm the mischievous death ray in his eyes. In fact—the fiend!—he winked at me.

Oh no!

I looked over just in time to catch Victor's brief glance, and my heart plummeted. If I'd been a scholar of anything over the last few months, it had been as a student of the many expressions of Victor Hanover. The brilliance in his eyes had dimmed and the subtle unhappiness in the line of his jaw was unmistakable. But before I could say anything—not that I knew what to say or why I needed to say anything at all—he turned to Anna and gave her a temperate smile.

"Anna. Good to see you." Victor extended his hand to her.

She took it and returned his welcome, their shake much more leisurely than the previous one with Abram.

"Professor Hanover. I'm so glad you could join us."

"Please, call me Victor." His smile warmed and he released her hand, stuffing both of his in his pants pockets.

"Oh! Can I call you Vic?" Her smile was really big. Really. Big.

He seemed genuinely charmed and laughed, shrugging. "Only if I can call you Na."

And that made her laugh, and so I laughed. But then I stopped laughing almost immediately and swallowed because, even to my own ears, the laugh sounded a little frantic.

CALM DOWN RIGHT NOW! But I couldn't. I was too agitated. I couldn't quite think. *Something had happened between us!* Or, rather, something had almost happened. Or maybe nothing had happened.

"No deal. I guess I'll be calling you Victor. Shall we go in?" Anna twisted slightly toward the exhibit entrance, smiling at each of us in turn.

"Yes, let's!" Abram agreed with a hefty dose of cheerfulness. He then slid next to me and placed his hand on the center of my back, taking advantage of my distracted sensibilities. Before I quite understood his intent, Abram had navigated us around Victor and Anna, calling over his shoulder as he speed-walked us inside the exhibit, "Anna can give you your ticket, Victor. No need to stop by the box office. We'll meet you two inside."

"What are you—" I tried to stop.

"Shh." Abram was so much stronger than me and basically picked me up and sped us forward, cutting off my protest to whisper, "Come with me."

I sent my friend a severe frown, also whispering, "What are you doing?"

"I'm helping him."

"Helping him? Helping who?"

"Victor."

"What are you talking about? How are you helping him?" *How did I get here?*

"Em." Abram gave me a flat look, pulling me through the first room, into the second, and around a corner before finally stopping, relinquishing his hold and facing me. "Come on. The guy is *insanely* into you. He just needs a little push."

"You . . ." I licked my lips; they were suddenly dry. If I had to describe what my heart was doing, I'd call it racing on tiptoes. "You think so?"

"Yes. I know so. He's shy. Guys like him, they *need* to be pushed or they'll never move. Trust me. He will thank me one day. I am doing this out of love."

"I can't think about this." I shook my head, thinking about it. "I can't even consider it," I reminded myself.

"What? Why?" My friend was still whispering. "He seems great, and you're great. You'll be great together."

"Because we're in a really good place, okay?" I swallowed around the lump in my throat. "We're good as friends."

"Why would you settle for being friends with a great guy you so obviously have a thing for?"

Twisting my fingers, I found I had to swallow again

before I could speak. "Because being friends doesn't hurt my heart."

Abram's gaze turned sympathetic and he sighed, like he felt some of my pain. "Oh, Em—"

"No, no. I mean it." I shook my head again, closing my eyes, not wanting Abram's sympathy. "Maybe he has non-friendly feelings for me, but it doesn't matter. I'm not hoping for more." I opened my eyes again, staring unseeingly at Abram's shirt and yet seeing the situation clearly. "I like his friendship. It's valuable to me. And I'm not willing to risk it, okay?"

Maybe something had started to happen between Victor and me in the grand foyer of the museum moments ago. Maybe I'd been caught off guard by the sight of him in his sexy suit after not seeing him for so long and that's why I'd been nervous. Maybe I'd wanted something to happen. But now that I was free of Victor's hands and lips and square jaw and suit and shaving cream deliciousness and amazing eyes, I accepted—again—what I'd known to be true for months: we were never going to be anything other than friends.

More than friends with Victor meant a heartsick and confused Emily. Emily didn't want to be heartsick and confused. Emily also didn't want to keep referring to herself in the third person.

Therefore, I returned my eyes to my friend's, feeling resolute, steady, and much more capable of facing Victor's chiseled jaw now that I'd come to my senses. Meanwhile, Abram looked grim, like he was frustrated on my behalf. But he nodded.

I mirrored his nod, seeing that we understood each other. "I know you're trying to do a nice thing, but next time check with me, okay?"

"I'm sorry. I will."

"Good. Now, let's go back."

But before I could step away to find Anna and Victor, Abram caught my arm. "Listen. I get it. But do yourself a favor. If being friends with this guy means you're not giving anyone else a chance, end the friendship. Because that means you are hoping, deep down, and you deserve someone who sees and wants you—all of you—unreservedly."

Abram and I swapped stares as I absorbed his words, or tried to. My heart would have none of it. *I gave Landon the Grasshopper my number, didn't I? I'm not closing myself off to the possibility of other people. Look how great I am at navigating this. I am the captain of the friend-zone-ship! Under no circumstances will I be ending my relationship with Victor. Ever. Ever, ever, ever!*

"Em?"

"Yes. Okay." I hurried to nod again. "Agreed. Now can we go find Anna and Victor?"

"Sure," he said, sounding a little sad.

Nevertheless, we retraced our hurried steps seeking out my *friends,* and I heaved a big sigh. Now I was prepared. Now we could all have a nice, friendly evening of friendship and friendliness.

Yay friends!

Turning the corner into the first room, Abram trailing behind me, I spotted Anna standing in front of an informational banner with Claude Monet's picture at the top, her gaze intent as she was obviously reading it. Scanning the room and finding no trace of Victor, I stepped next to her and gave my friend a little nudge with my elbow.

She glanced at me, and then sighed. "There you are." She sounded irritated.

"Yeah, sorry. I had no idea Abram was going to take off with me like that. Where's Victor?"

Anna turned from the sign and leaned to one side to peer around me, her gaze becoming a glare, her voice hard as she said, "You shouldn't have done that. He left."

"What? Who? What?" I took a step back and glanced between the cousins. "Who left?"

The lines of irritation around her mouth softened as her eyes moved back to me. "I'm sorry, Emily." Her gaze turned bracing and she grabbed my hand, squeezing it. "Victor left."

CHAPTER 18

EMILY

"Do you want anything? From the vending machine? I need to pee," Anna whispered.

Glancing up from my discrete structures notes, I squinted at my friend until she came into focus. Anna stood at the other side of our study table, her thumb tossed over her shoulder, her eyes a bit hazy. She had the stupefied look of a college student studying for finals, because that's exactly what we were doing.

Stretching my arms, I surveyed the carnage strewn between us. Seven Starbucks coffee cups, two bags of raw almonds (one empty, one half full), a plethora of napkins, a gaggle of textbooks and notebooks and pens and pencils and highlighters and note cards.

I tested the fullness of the coffee cup closest to me. It wasn't empty. "Uh, no thanks," I whispered back. "I'm good."

"Okay. Be back in a second." She opened the door of our soundproof room and stepped into the elevator lobby, which was eerily silent despite being full of people.

I liked this about our campus library, quiet hours during finals. I liked how the study rooms on the seventh floor—

well, the most sought-after study rooms—opened directly onto the elevator lobby, which was also full of long study tables. The only sounds during this time of year were the ding of the elevators, the distant flush of a high-powered toilet from one of the adjacent bathrooms, the infrequent whirr and clunk of a vending machine, and the page of a textbook being turned every so often. Even the Starbucks down the hall was relatively quiet, students ordered via slips of paper.

Anna and I had booked this particular room months ago, which meant we were allowed to talk to each other when the door was closed. Despite the fact that the room was soundproof, we always ended up whispering anyway, perhaps in subconscious homage to our silent compatriots on the other side of the door.

Regardless, booking ahead meant reaping the benefits of our foresight. *Ah, foresight. Like foreskin, but inherently cleaner.*

Whereas hindsight . . .

My heart gave a wistful tug and I tracked Anna until she left, pulling out my phone as soon as the door to the study room clicked shut. I stared at the black screen. I swallowed. I took a deep breath. I unlocked my cell. I clicked on my message app, and then the conversation string with Victor. I breathed through the painful constricting in my chest and read the last several messages.

Emily: When you get a chance, send your ETA. We're already here but we had to park on Pluto (which is a planet). Presently standing inside between the columns on the staircase.

Victor: I'm here, grabbed a spot close by. I hope you know about impressionists, because I know nothing. (Pluto is not a planet)

Emily: HA! FINALLY! Something you don't know!! (in addition to Pluto being a planet)

Victor: Oh, Emily. I'm ignorant in so many ways, you have no idea. See you in 10.

Emily: Where did you go?

Emily: Are you still here? Come back.

Emily: Come back. I was really looking forward to tonight. MY DRESS HAS POCKETS.

Emily: Victor, please pick up your phone.

Emily: Pick up your phone or I'm going to leave you voice messages of me singing.

Emily: Pick up your phone or I'm going to leave you VMs of Anna singing (and her voice is worse than mine).

Emily: Hey. So, it's been over a week. Any chance you want to get together for a movie?

Emily: Long time no talk. Are you around? Want to go play trivia with Anna, Luca, and me?

Emily: I hope you're not trapped under something heavy. Maybe I should check on you...

Emily: I saw this article on scientific literacy rates and it reminded me of you.

Emily: I went to Tennessee last week and—no lie—a chicken (!!!!!) got stuck in my engine and it was STILL ALIVE when they removed it. Crazy. I have picture proof! Which I will provide for the cost of one beer.

Emily: Thinking about you today. I hope you are well.

Emily: Missing you.

Emily: As a friend. Missing you as a friend. No pressure. I hope you are well.

Emily: This is your weekly text message. If you decide to message me, great! If not, I'll be texting next week.

Emily: Weekly text message. :-)

. . .

"It's been weeks."

I started, startled, and my cheeks heated at being caught. Without looking up, I nodded at Anna's whispered remark. I hadn't heard her come in or close the door, but she'd done both.

I could feel Anna's eyes move over me, I could feel her sympathy, I could feel her frustration. She was a master silent emoter and I already knew her feelings on this subject.

Nevertheless, she repeated the same words for the tenth time this month, "If he wanted to talk to you, he would have responded to your texts."

Sighing, I began to type out a message to Victor. "I know."

"Are you texting him again?" She didn't sound judgmental, she sounded concerned. Which—for the record—was worse. So much worse.

"I haven't sent him anything in a few days. Just let me send my—"

"Why?" she whisper-implored, taking a step toward me.

I inhaled a deep breath, placed my phone facedown on the table, and covered my face.

"Why are you doing this? Em, I don't want to be harsh, but you need to leave him alone."

"I am leaving him alone." I dropped my hands and looked at my friend, bracing for her disapproving expression.

"Texting him is not leaving him alone." Anna crossed her arms, a stern—disapproving—wrinkle between her eyebrows, her smoky topaz eyes twin beams of censure. "Weren't you the one who told me that no guy was worth torturing yourself over? That if a guy liked me—really liked me—he'd make me a priority? Well, the same goes for you. And Victor isn't just 'not making you a priority,' Victor is flat-out ignoring you. He doesn't want you to text him. Leave it. He's not worth it, Em."

Ugh. I hated past-Emily. Her wisdom was super inconvenient. She was right, of course. But *I just care about him so much.*

"I know you're right, but—" I licked my lips, drawing my bottom one between my teeth. This feeling. This horrible feeling of helplessness against my worst impulses. *What is this feeling even called?*

"Let him go." Again, she whisper-implored. "Move on. You deserve so, so much better than someone who ignores you and plays immature games. He is not worth it, no one is."

I shook my head, my attention moving to the wall behind my friend, and even though I knew she was right, my dummy heart told me differently. "I can't. I can't give up on him. I feel like he needs me, or he needs to know I'll always be here for him, that he can count on me."

"Do you really think he needs you? Or do you need him?" Anna gave me a hard stare, and then snorted lightly when I said nothing. Her eyes softened, and her lips curved downward in a gloomy line. "It's not about giving up, Emily. It's about being respectful of someone's wishes. Like I said, if he wanted you to text, he would text you back. If he wanted to talk to you, he would pick up the phone."

My brain said, *Exactly.*

My heart said, *BUT HE NEEDS ME!*

"Anna—"

"Okay, think of it this way," she raised her voice, holding up a hand, "if the roles were reversed, if it were a man texting every week and a woman receiving those texts, what would you think then? That the man was romantic in his persistence? Or that he was a creepy stalker who couldn't take a hint?"

I flinched, my breath catching painfully in my throat, a stinging sensation rising behind my eyes.

Damn.

She's right.

She was so right.

What am I doing?

God, what was I doing? If a guy had done that to me, if a guy had continued texting for weeks after I'd stopped, I would've considered him a psycho, I would've blocked his number.

He probably blocked your number weeks ago, psycho.

I rubbed my chest with my fingers and tried to swallow. I could not swallow. So I released a shaky breath, my nose now stinging, and reached for my phone.

"What are you doing?" She sounded tired.

I stared at the black screen. I tried to swallow again. I still could not swallow, so I took a deep breath and rode the shame wave. I was ashamed of myself.

If he wanted you to text him, he would have responded to your texts.

"But he hasn't," I whispered softly, nodding to myself as I unlocked my cell. I clicked on my message app. I breathed through the searing, painful tightness in my chest and I deleted my conversation string with Victor.

"Are you texting him?"

I shook my head, now numbly clicking through to his contact information. "No."

I felt her hesitation before she prompted, "Em?"

I cleared my throat, thick and strained, and finally managed a swallow. My thumb hovered over the "delete contact" button. "You're right. I've been acting crazy. I'm deleting his contact information and our text messages." I touched the button, and then the prompt afterward asking me if I was sure I wished to delete Victor Hanover from my contacts.

It was done.

Placing the phone back on the table, I stood, my legs

struggling under the heavy weight of resignation and finality. *It's done.*

"Oh, Em." Anna shot forward, pulling me into a hug. "I'm sorry. I know it's hard, and I know my cousin is an ass for what he did. But if it hadn't happened that night at the museum, it's clear Victor would've ghosted you eventually. You deserve so much more than this. You are so awesome." Her arms tightened.

I pulled away, not meeting her gaze as I stepped around her. She was right. I knew she was right. What I'd just done was the right thing to do. But I didn't want to talk about *right.*

The band-aid had just been ripped off my denial. I needed a moment to lick my wounds. And maybe a drink. Or seven. Except I couldn't drink because I still had to study for my last final exam.

"I think I'll go for a walk," I whispered, moving past her to the door. "I'll get some more coffee. Do you want coffee?" Turning briefly, I didn't quite meet her eyes, but I perceived her head shake.

Without another word, I opened the door and stepped into the lobby, the hefty burden of irrevocability making my shoulders slump and my legs unsteady. It was over.

Wise Emily reminded me, *It's been over for weeks, hun. You've just been too crazy-stalker-desperate to accept it.* And as my feet carried me . . . someplace, wise Emily also pointed out, *Plus, it never actually started. You two were friends, and that's it.*

Just friends. *That's it.*

I'd been content to be just friends with Victor, and I would've been friends with Victor indefinitely. I'd told Abram the truth about that.

However, I'd come to realize I'd also lied to Abram. I did have hopes for more. When Victor had initially stopped returning my messages, hope sprang anew. Perhaps he also wanted more? Perhaps he'd left so suddenly after seeing me with Abram because witnessing me with someone else (even if it had been fake) made him realize how much he wanted to be with me . . . ?

I breathed a silent, slightly hysterical laugh, smiling at my idiocy. I had a lot to think about, to unpack and figure out and mourn. However, right now, I needed to compartmentalize. I needed to get through this last test, and then I could wallow.

And I will wallow like the Olympic champion of wallowing. Companies will want me to be the face of their wallowing products. Box o' Wine will come calling and I will sell a special wallowing edition with my puffy face on the side of it.

Study now, wallow tomorrow.

I don't know how long I paced around the seventh floor, doing laps between the stacks, going back over every moment Victor and I had spent together and trying to understand myself. Why and when had I decided to elevate him in my esteem such that I was willing to prioritize being near Victor over being respectful of Victor as a human? At what point had I crossed the crazy line? Was it the third text or the fifth? And what had possessed me?

"So stupid," I muttered just as I glanced up and realized I was in line for coffee.

The guy in front of me gave me the side-eye, likely because I'd broken the near silence that surrounded us. I gave him a flat, hint of a smile in contrition and then turned my attention to the list of coffee drinks. I already knew what I wanted to order, but I needed something on which to focus as I berated myself for my absurdity.

But at least it was done. At least I wasn't dwelling in limbo anymore, wondering with each text whether it would be the one he answered. Wondering whether—

"Emily?"

My head whipped to the side at the sound of my name in Victor's voice. And there he was.

Just standing there.

So close.

Looking so handsome.

In line.

For coffee.

His lips parted.

Staring at me with surprise and some other unidentifiable emotion in his eyes.

It took a long moment for my brain to reengage, and when it did my first thought was, *Maybe he's afraid. I am his stalker, after all.*

No longer stunned by his sudden appearance, a sharp, aching tightness in my chest stole my breath and a shock of heat flooded my neck and cheeks. On instinct—because I was so very, very uncomfortable and flustered—I turned away, freezing, facing the guy in front of me. He was now giving Victor the side-eye.

A moment passed during which every sound of silence became a deafening roar. My mind and heart raced. I couldn't quite catch my breath and the sharp, aching tightness kept ebbing just to return sharper, more painful, more unbearable.

Ahhhh. Why now? Do something!

I felt him shift behind me, move. *Maybe he's leaving.* I closed my eyes, balling my hands into fists so as not to give into the urge to turn and check, or watch him walk away.

But then a second later, I almost jumped out of my skin as I felt his chest brush against my back and his breath against my neck as he whispered next to my ear, "Do you have a minute to talk?"

My heart leapt, but then was quickly yanked back into

place by the heavy burden of truth: *If he wanted to text you, he would have responded to your texts. If he wanted to talk to you, he would pick up the phone.*

A fissure of anger had me straightening my back and thawing the freezing instinct. He wanted to talk? Now? Why? To tell me he didn't want to talk to me? Hadn't his silence said enough? I rolled my lips between my teeth, fighting a new urge (to tell him to return any one of my hundred phone calls if he wanted to talk) and shook my head.

"Emily . . ." He breathed my name. It was said with the same cadence as a *please.*

And for some reason, that pissed me off, likely because I felt myself melting. I didn't want to melt. I melted entirely too much with Victor Hanover. Meanwhile, he melted never.

As it's been established, when I'm pissed off, I don't freeze. I boil. Stepping out of line, I made a beeline for the elevator lobby, no longer feeling heavy or burdened by the end of our non-relationship. Instead, I felt the lightness of rageful gratitude for my friend Anna, that she'd stopped me from texting him earlier. Because, if I had, it would've just been another text he didn't answer. And then, when I ran into him just now, I would've been falling all over myself to make him like me, to take me back as whatever he wanted, in whatever form suited him, *just-please-please-please-talk-to-me-again!!*

Pathetic *and* psycho.

I was marching with purpose, single-mindedly focused on getting as far away from Victor as possible, when I heard Victor say, "Emily." It wasn't whispered.

I turned the corner for the lobby when I heard him shout, "Emily! Stop!" He sounded closer than before.

Someone *shh-ed* harshly and I didn't blame them. He had broken the most sacred of rules on campus, shouting during finals week at the library. THE HORROR.

I'd almost made it to the study room when I felt a hand close around my elbow and spin me around. Victor's gorgeous and brilliant eyes darted between mine, he seemed out of breath, and he didn't release my arm when I tried to shake him off.

"Would you listen?" His eyebrows pulled into a V, and he took a step closer, using his hold on me as leverage.

I sealed my mouth shut and glared at him, crossing my arms. He still didn't let go.

"Em," he said through heavy breaths, his gaze pleading. "I'm sorry. I'm so sorry. I just—I don't know how to do this."

A bolt of agonizing sad-mad sliced through me and I shrugged to hide how close I was to crying. Part of me wanted to tell him it was okay, I'd accepted his rejection, I wouldn't be texting him anymore. He didn't need to figure out how to let me down gently or whatever he planned to do.

But then Victor tugged me closer, his eyes dropping to my lips. "I don't know how to do this," he repeated, softer.

"Do what? Be quiet?" a girl asked from somewhere in the lobby.

My gaze flickered away from Victor and caught her dirty look. Though why I'd earned the dirty look I had no idea. I hadn't said a word.

Gritting my teeth, I returned my glare to Victor, determined to persist in my apathy. But when I faced him, he caught my other arm, pulled me against him, and kissed me.

I should be forgiven for not immediately responding to the urgent press of his hot, delicious, firm and coaxing lips. I was, after all, gritting my teeth when his mouth landed on mine. And let the record show, *he* was the one who'd told me that nothing was ever going to happen between us. *He* was the one who'd ghosted me after Abram's high-handed stunt. And now *he* was . . . kissing me?

My palms flattened against his chest to push him away,

obviously. But then his arms encircled me, crushed my body to his, his fingers threading into my hair at the nape of my neck and urging me closer, his tongue moving between my stunned lips. And that's when a bit of the fog cleared. My brain told my flailing heart that Victor didn't know how to kiss.

I mean, we were kissing, and he wasn't terrible—obviously he wasn't terrible because my toes were curling in my shoes and my body wanted to climb his—but he was clumsy. All hunger and no savor, all desperation and no technique.

Huh.

I slid my hands up his shoulders to cup his angular jaw and nudged him back a little without breaking the kiss, angling my head so that our fit was more natural. Sliding my tongue against his with languid strokes, slowing his feverish kiss, I encouraged him to echo my gentleness.

He did. And he groaned. Loudly. Clearly liking this turn of events.

His digging fingers at the back of my head relaxed. Likewise, I felt his body relax while his hands slid covetously down my sides, stopping on my hips as he also angled his head, his tongue chasing mine, tasting divine.

Meanwhile, someone cleared their throat. Less than a second later (or maybe it was several days later, who can say?), someone tapped me on the shoulder.

"Emily!"

That was Anna. Why was Anna here?

Wait. Where is here?

THE LIBRARY!

Alarm speared me and I shoved Victor away, sucking in a sharp breath. He let me go, but then he followed as I stepped back. The determined, greedy glint in his eyes sent my heart to my throat, my brain already in mass disarray. Therefore, I allowed Anna to wordlessly grab my arm, lead me to the study room, and gently but firmly push me inside.

So confused, I'm so confused. I touched my lips with disbelieving fingers. *Is this a dream?*

Spinning as soon as I heard the door shut, I was only slightly surprised to discover that Victor—not Anna—stood at the other end of the room, and that Anna had disappeared.

A laugh tumbled from my lips and I covered my mouth with my hand. I honestly didn't know how to feel or what to think or . . . *WHAT THE HELL IS HAPPENING?*

All I knew was: a) I was tired, b) I was confused, and c) Victor was looking at me like I was a snack.

"Emily."

I dropped my hand, gripping the back of the chair I'd been sitting in earlier. "What do you—what is happening?"

"I don't know how to do this. I can't do this anymore." His voice was thick with some emotion as his eyes darted all over me, as though hungry for the sight of me.

"Do what?"

Victor didn't stall, he didn't hesitate.

He looked me straight in the eyes and he said, "Act like I'm not in love with you."

CHAPTER 19

EMILY

"I—I—I—what?" It finally happened. My brain was broken.

"I love you, Emily. I'm in love with you."

He . . . loves . . .?

Frowning, my eyes traveled over this Victor imposter. Perhaps because of my aforementioned brain brokenness, my attention became absorbed by his clothes. He was wearing baggy dad jeans paired with a super ugly yellow and brown checked shirt, which was also way too big. His hair was flat, longer than I remembered, and must've been obscuring his vision. The glasses on his face were the unflattering, black and thick ones.

This was real-Victor's lecture outfit. The one he wore to be invisible to his students (and everyone else). It hid his body and physical handsomeness and the brilliance of his gaze.

He's always hiding.

This Victor's chest rose and fell like he couldn't catch his breath and he pulled off the glasses with obvious reluctance, making me flinch as the full brunt of his unobstructed stare landed on me. It felt like an unveiling, like a revelation of himself. I stopped myself before I swayed too far forward.

He held the frames between his fingers, his hand suspended at chest level, giving me the impression he would fit them back in place at the slightest hint of resistance or challenge or rejection.

If you give him a reason to leave, he'll bolt.

His gorgeous eyes seemed conflicted, determined and yet panicked, and I watched his lips firm, his jaw flex, his hand that gripped his glasses tighten into a fist.

"Emily, I miss you and I love you." His voice was deep and loud and sure. "But seeing you—" He licked his lips, swallowing the rest of the thought. "I've made peace with it and I wish you nothing but happiness. If you want me to, I'll leave you alone."

"You would like that, wouldn't you?" I muttered, the words slipping out unplanned, a thought voiced.

His eyes widened, clearly confused. "Pardon?"

I crossed my arms, snapping my mouth shut, my broken mind besieged, occupied with duct-taping itself back together while also working through too many reveals at once.

He didn't think of me as a stalker. He hadn't blocked my texts. He chased me through the library, yelling my name during the sacred ritual of finals week quiet time. He kissed me—our second. He didn't push me away after—yet.

If you want me to, I'll leave you alone.

You would like that, wouldn't you?

I wasn't sorry I'd said the stream-of-consciousness words. He'd set me up to fail. If I forgave him immediately, then I had no self-respect. If I didn't forgive him, then he'd disappear. Again.

I gave him my attention but said nothing, struggling to untangle this snarled clusterfu. . . knot. The Victor who claimed to love me continued to stare. He swallowed. His breathing evened. His hand holding the frames, however, didn't move. It didn't lift to place the glasses back in place, nor did it lower to discard them or tuck them away.

But when his eyes dimmed and he shifted his weight toward the door, I panicked and blurted, "You are not forgiven! And you're not allowed to leave."

He seemed to rear back a fraction of an inch; his gaze watchful. "O—okay."

"I mean it." A spike of alarm, of distrust, had me darting forward to the door and standing in front of it, heedless that this brought me within a few feet of where he stood. Gripping the doorknob as extra insurance, I tilted my chin up and glared at him. "You are not allowed to leave me *ever again*. No more leaving. No more ghosting!"

Victor's eyes narrowed—just slightly—as they moved over me, and finally his hand lowered to tuck the ugly glasses in his pants pocket. "You don't forgive me, but you don't want me to leave you alone?"

"Yes." I nodded, ardently, and admitted on a burst of feelings, "I don't know how to talk to you. I don't know what will set you off, send you running. And I never know what you're thinking."

He swallowed again, finally pushing his hair off his forehead and out of his eyes, looking completely bewildered. "Emily, I just told you I love you."

He loves me. Weeeeeeee!

So why did he ghost me? Grrrrrrrrrr!

"Yes. You also told me months ago that nothing would ever happen between us. And then we developed this awesome friendship, and I loved our friendship. But then you disappeared like it—like I—meant nothing to you."

He eyed me warily. "You love our friendship, but not me? You want us to be friends?"

A spike of fury had me stepping away from the door and gesturing to him wildly. "See? This is what I'm talking about. I feel like you're trying to trick me into saying something to make you leave again. If I say, 'Yes, Victor. I love our friendship and I want to be friends,' you'll go silent on me, because you'll take that as a rejection. But if I say, 'No, Victor. I love *you*,' then it's like I'm giving you a free pass to stomp all over my heart, and there's plenty of your footprints there already."

"I am so sorry." He shifted forward; the movement restrained like he was trying to hold himself back. "I know I screwed up. I should've messaged you back, but I couldn't."

"Why not?"

"Because if I did, it would mean the end of our friendship."

"That makes no sense. You ended the friendship by not texting me back."

"I didn't."

"You did!"

He looked pained, uncertain, torn. But he said nothing.

I shook my head tiredly. "I don't know what to do with you. I—"

"I thought I could walk away, when the time came. But I couldn't. When I saw you with him, with Anna's cousin, I couldn't walk away like I'd planned."

"First of all, I wasn't *with* Abram. He's like a brother. Secondly, you *literally* walked away." I lifted my hand and made a sweeping motion.

His eyes seemed to grow brighter. "You're not with Abram?"

"No. Of course not." I scrunched my face, but then a thought occurred to me. "Wait a minute. You just kissed me. Are you telling me you kissed me thinking I might be with someone else?"

"Yes," he said, not hesitating, his eyes clear. "Yes. I kissed you thinking you were with someone else. And I'm not sorry I did it."

What?

"How can you—" My hands flew up. "Okay. Okay. We need to stay focused! One thing at a time. You walked out of the museum, got in your car, and left. *You* walked away."

"No, that's not—I left the museum, yes. But I didn't walk away. I couldn't. I want a chance with you," he blurted, shoving his fingers into his hair and turning away.

That had me standing straighter. "If you wanted to be with me, why not just tell me?"

Victor placed his hands on his hips. His stood in profile, but he'd turned his head as his eyes moved over my body, growing impossibly wistful as they finally came back to mine. "You—your intelligence, your sweetness, your humor, your fearlessness and courage and heart, and even your beautiful body—are a 97% confidence interval with a 3% margin of error and a Z score of 2.17009. You, every part of you, are as close to perfection as is reasonably scientifically possible." He said this like it caused him no end of torment, like it was a listing of charges against me. "And I'm—"

"Brilliant? Funny? Generous? Wonderful? Sexy?" I tossed each descriptor at him with the full force of my vehemence. "Or were you going to say distant and unfeeling? Because those also apply."

The side of his mouth hitched, but the smile was not echoed in his eyes. "I'm untested," came his quiet response.

I waited for him to clarify. When he didn't, I glanced at the ceiling, huffed, and didn't try to hide the irritation from my voice as I parroted, "Untested."

Facing me fully, he dropped his hands from his hips, and he showed me his palms, as though surrendering. "I'm inexperienced and unsure. I lack confidence because I have no track record of success because I've never tried. I've never wanted to try. I've spent my life actively avoiding needing or wanting this, and now I'm doing everything wrong." The words sounded like they were torn from him. "I'm in love with you."

Oh. That's right. He said he was in love with me. By the way, has it *for sure* been established that I wasn't currently daydreaming?

"But I'm so afraid," he added quietly, and the way he said it—pure, honest, raw vulnerability—awakened my reflexive protectiveness.

Show me where it hurts! I'll kiss it!! Yikes. I couldn't say that even though it was true. I needed to think. I needed a plan. I needed more of this, more of him talking, more bravery, but I couldn't enable his jerkish behavior by capitulating the first time he was *finally* honest.

Clearing my throat, I ordered myself to stand firm and asked, "What are you afraid of?" My feet, however, shuffled forward as though pulled until mere inches separated us. I couldn't look away from the mesmerizing mixture of intelligence and fear and determination, all swirling together behind his dazzling eyes.

"Everything. You. Me. Everything," he confessed on a whisper. Even so, his voice cracked, and his shoulders hunched, and his gaze seemed to oscillate between resentful and hopeful.

"Can you be more specific?" My head was spinning.

He cleared his throat, his attention dropping to my hands. I followed his gaze and realized I'd lifted them to chest level and had pressed my palms together, as though praying.

Staring at my fingers, he said, "The month before spring break, w—when we were spending all that time together, I stopped eating." He cleared his throat again, took another deep breath, and his voice was sturdier when he spoke next. "I was afraid to eat. And when I did, I started weighing food again, second-guessing every serving. I saved meals for when we were together. I stopped going to the airfield. Instead, I went to the gym whenever I had a free second."

I tried to follow, but it was like we were having two different conversations. He . . . *stopped eating?* "Why? Why would you do that?"

He seemed to steady himself for a second before lifting his eyes to mine. "This is not me. And I'm afraid that you see me, and you think *this* is me"—Victor gestured to his body—"but when you finally see the real me—naïve, inexperienced, messy—you'll know I'm not enough. You won't want that person."

His words were a bucket of flaming, hot coals to my brain. Quite suddenly, I was no longer overwhelmed by the feels. *Oh yeah, that's right. I'm mad at him!*

"*That person*? Victor, you won't let me close enough to know *any* version of you. You haven't kept me at arm's distance, you've kept me at a football field's distance, leaving tiny pellets of personal anecdotes outside the gate." Now I held my hands wide to emphasize just how much distance. I hurried to add as my arms dropped, "And if you think I'm perfect, you are sadly mistaken. This"—I gestured to my body—"isn't me. It's a part of me, but my exterior will never tell the entirety of my story or of my value. Don't you think I have the same kind of fears as you? Don't you think everyone does?"

His eyebrows flickered together. "*You* do?"

"Of course. Of course, I do!" I turned away from him, pacing to the other end of the table and ranting, "You're afraid of being rejected? Not being wanted for yourself? Hilarious. Welcome to the Emily and Victor show, where Emily takes whatever Victor is willing to give until he gives her absolutely nothing."

Something like panic seized his expression and he licked

his lips, charging forward. "I was wrong. But I'm trying to fix myself so that I'll be worthy of—"

I lifted my hand to halt his forward momentum, meeting his gaze squarely. "People aren't plumbing, Victor! There is no fixing people. And if you mention worthiness again, I will punch you in the throat."

Despite everything, his mouth tugged to the side. "There is some fixing, Em. I am working on myself, figuring things out. But you're absolutely correct. I should've been honest, I shouldn't have been afraid to tell you the truth, I should've trusted you. But every time I picked up the phone—"

"Instead, you rejected me."

"I didn't reject you!"

"You've rejected me *a lot*. You've told me that nothing will happen between us, you stopped returning my calls and messages." I was unable to keep the emotion out of my voice.

My words seemed to torture him, and he was already shaking his head before I finished, "But that was because—"

"If someone you were in love with ghosted you, how would that make you feel?"

Suddenly, he was standing straighter, his eyes burning with an unholy brightness. "You're in love with me?"

Dammit! I hadn't meant to admit that.

"Stop changing the subject. We're talking about you ghosting me."

"Me, the person you're in love with, ghosting you, the person who's in love with me."

"Victor!"

"Sorry. Yes. You were saying." He was grinning now. Or rather, he was trying not to grin.

Meanwhile, I was flustered, and abruptly hot, and struggling to make my point. "How am I supposed to interpret ghosting? How would you interpret it if it happened to you?

Would it scream, 'I love you!' Or would it make you feel like the other person didn't care about you at all?"

He snapped his mouth shut, his eyes narrowing, and the muscle at his jaw jumped.

Ah ha! I got him. I had him. My logic > his logic.

It was my turn to give him a small smile that I felt certain didn't reach my eyes. "Victor. Come on. I have all the evidence in the world that you don't care about me."

"I do care about you. I'm in love with you," he said firmly, his eyes flashing little hot frustration fires, his square jaw lifting stubbornly.

"So you keep saying." I gave my head a little shake even as my heart fluttered happily at his words. Inspecting him, I reminded myself of how it felt each time he rejected me. My heart ceased fluttering. "But your actions spell out indifference, or confusion at best. Cruel game playing and manipulation at worst."

His eyes a shade of petulant green, sharp and calculating, obviously he was no longer afraid. Clearly, the accidental admission of my feelings had calmed and reassured the most frantic, fearful part of himself. And presently, he looked only wickedly determined, much to my chagrin. This single-minded, scheming expression effectively shoved aside my good sense and melancholy, it caused a thrill to race along my spine and set off flares of anticipatory heat low in my stomach.

Goodness, this man's cutting intellect—even just the hint of it—got me so damn hot.

I braced myself for some kind of sexy logic assault as he peered down at me, tilting his head to one side as though considering a puzzle. "Or, do my actions spell out concern?" His voice was so different now. It was his professor voice—confident, firm, exacting—and it also got me hot.

"For who?" I squinted at him, not wanting him to see how he affected me.

"For you."

"For me?"

"Yes. For you."

I squared my shoulders and crossed my arms. BAH! I just wanted to-to-to . . . smack him and kiss him and scream and take off his pants.

"You stop returning my messages because you're concerned about me? How does that work? Please. Explain it to me like I'm a two-year-old who hasn't taken a nap, because that's about where my patience is right now."

A hint of amusement and appreciation lit behind his eyes, but they quickly dissolved into a hazy stare of solemnity. "I told myself, when the time came, when you fell for someone else, I would tell you the truth. I promised myself I would wish you well and end things in person. I would be upfront and honest, not ask anything of you, and let you go."

I stared at him, struggling *hard* to make sense of his words. "End our friendship? Are you saying you planned to stop talking to me as soon as I had a boyfriend?"

"Yes."

"Why?!" He was so frickin confusing!

"Because I'm in love with you and—"

"Ah! You're making me crazy!" I shook my fists in the air.

"—seeing you with someone else would be—*was*—too painful. I convinced myself I would never be enough for you. When I saw you with Anna's cousin, and how he touched you and led you away, I assumed you were together."

"We aren't, we weren't—"

"Yes, I know that now. But at the time I thought you were with him, and that meant the next time we spoke I would have to end things."

"So you . . . what? Stopped talking to me instead?"

"No. Yes-no-I mean, I didn't know what to do. I couldn't call and follow through with my plan. I couldn't just walk away and wish you well. I thought maybe I could still be your friend, but every time I thought about you with someone else, it felt like—" He cut himself off, turning away, breathing out roughly.

"So instead of picking up the phone to either end things or tell me how you feel, you instead wait until we run into each other, and then proceed to chase me around the library and kiss me, all the while thinking I was with Abram?" I asked, completely incredulous.

And yet, also a little thrilled. *So, yes. I'm a weirdo.*

He nodded, eying me again. "Yes."

"Were you ever going to call me?" Irritatingly, my voice cracked. "If we hadn't run into each other? Did you ever think how hurt I would be? Did it ever occur to you that leaving me without a word would *hurt me*?"

Victor's eyes grew glassy, his features pained, remorseful as I spoke, and she shifted restlessly on his feet. "Honestly? No. I thought you would just. . ."

"What? Not care that I'd lost a really, really good friend?" My stupid voice cracked again. "You hurt me, Victor. *Again.*"

Rushing forward like he couldn't help himself, he gently fit my cheeks in his palms and stole a slow, sweet kiss. Not the with-tongue kind. The soft, searching press of lips kind, like our first kiss all those months ago, the one I'd been daydreaming about—and then feeling guilty for daydreaming about—since.

My arms unfolded and I gripped his wrists, needing the solid strength of him to keep my balance. Giving the seam of my mouth a single, light, teasing lick that made my stomach clench and my breath catch, but that I'm pretty sure he didn't realize was teasing, he rested his forehead against mine.

"Emily, you are right. I was thoughtless and selfish. I'm so incredibly sorry I hurt you. I never want to hurt you. Please, let me make it up to you. Please, let me make this right."

"Be honest with me. Stop hiding. Stop walking away."

"I will. God, I promise I will. But this baggage I carry, it's my own, and you don't deserve to be burdened with it."

"But if we both carry it, it'll be lighter. And you haven't seen my baggage yet. I might have a matching set." It was official. I'd melted. I'd already forgiven him. Dosh garnit! When had it happened? I was doomed. DOOMED!

He breathed a little laugh, the sexy sound distracting me. "You deserve someone experienced, who can lead instead of follow. Someone certain, someone tested, someone proven." Victor swallowed, cleared his throat, and yet his voice was still raspy when he added, "Someone who isn't afraid."

I shook my head, careful to maintain the connection between our foreheads. "I don't care if you're inexperienced, unproven, untested. I don't care about that. And I don't care if you're afraid, because—God—I'm so afraid. I'm terrified." I swallowed, feeling the welling of tears and knowing there was nothing I could do to stop them. Allowing my chin to wobble, I took a deep breath, hating how I knew my voice would sound but needing to say the words. "The only thing I care about is whether or not you have enough courage to trust me, to have faith in me, that you can share every part of yourself, this person you keep locked up and hidden, and I won't turn into a Jane Eyre."

A surprised laugh erupted from his chest as he leaned away, his thumbs gently catching and wiping away my tears like they were precious to him, his gaze cherishing. "Jane Eyre?"

I shifted my grip to his shoulders, still not trusting him to stay, and sniffled, swallowing, gaining enough control over my vocal cords to choke out, "I mean, you can't really blame Jane. However, for the record, if you have a pyromaniac wife locked up in your tower and she wants to murder me, I'd still be willing to give things a try between us."

His lips were pressed together but he was laughing for real now, albeit quietly. His shoulders shook beneath my hands.

I sniffled again. "Maybe that makes me a terrible person, but I'm just saying it wouldn't be a dealbreaker."

"You are hilarious." Victor kissed my forehead and wrapped me in his arms, my cheek pressed against his chest. He waited a beat, his laughter dissipating, before whispering urgently, "Please. Please give me one more chance. Please."

Two fat tears rolled down my cheeks and I heaved a sad sigh. "Please, don't break my heart."

"I won't. I promise." He said the words like an oath, adding roughly, "Not even if you break mine."

CHAPTER 20

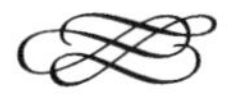

EMILY

"So you just forgave him? That's it?" Anna sounded completely horrified.

I shook my head. "No. No, no, no. There will be groveling. Mark my words." That was a lie. I was lying and that was a lie. There would be no groveling. I'd already forgiven him and now I was lying to my best friend because I *really* wanted her to like Victor again, and the only way she would do that is if she thought I was making him work for it.

Anna nodded her approval, her eyebrow slightly raised. "Good. For the record, I expect begging."

"Yes. Of course."

"And many reparations."

"Indeed. Me too."

"I'm talking wine."

"Absolutely. That's what I was thinking."

"And doing all the dishes for the rest of your natural lives."

"Yes. Yes."

"Foot massages."

"Wait. I need to write these down. Let me find a pen."

She turned to her left, grabbed a pen from the jar by my toaster and an old receipt. "Here. Use this. And many thoughtful gifts that reflect he knows and cares about your interests and passions."

I made a show of writing on the back of the receipt, but the pen didn't work. Tossing it in the trash, I walked out of the kitchen toward my room. "I know I have a pen in my bag."

"Emily."

"Yeah?"

"I'm serious." She was close behind, trailing me.

"So am I."

"If he doesn't recognize your worth, I will stab him."

"You're so violent." I glanced at her over my shoulder. "I like that about you."

Inside my room, she leaned against the doorjamb, her arms crossed. "Do. Not. Forgive. Him. Again. Got it? After this, no more chances."

I lifted an eyebrow at her demand but said nothing as I searched my purse. We both knew I was a serial forgiver.

After a few minutes of searching, I made a face at the gaping darkness of my purse. "How can I not have a pen in my bag?"

"You have more in the jar by the toaster. I'll go get one. This list is important!" She turned and darted out of my room just as the interior of my bag lit up.

My phone was ringing.

A thrill shot through me, anticipation cinching my throat. I fumbled for my cell. I hadn't called or initiated any text conversations with Victor since the scene in the library two days ago, but he'd messaged me plenty. After an extended hug and another kiss that was just on the precipice of getting wild, Anna had come back in and brought reality with her. As much as I wanted to go hide somewhere with Victor for the rest of my life, I still had a final to study for.

He'd excused himself with a promise to call me later, which he did. And then he brought over dinner for both Anna and me that night so we could keep studying. He texted me several times yesterday—to check in, to see if I needed anything, to invite me to dinner after my test, to tell me he was thinking about me—and each time I felt my heart and head relax a little, cautiously trusting his words from the library a little more.

Anna didn't ask about what happened between us until just this afternoon, now that my last test was over. As soon as I walked into my apartment, she appeared out of thin air. Obviously, she'd let herself in, and felt it necessary to scare a fart out of me as she jumped into my path in the kitchen.

"Now that your exam is over, TELL ME WHAT HAPPENED WITH VICTOR!" she'd demanded.

Presently, I struggled to get a good grip on my phone and extract it from the alternate dimension that was the interior of my bag—where space and matter cease to function according to the laws of physics—bringing it to my ear and answering breathlessly, "Hello?"

"Emily."

"Victor." I said his name on a sigh. A happy sigh. A super happy sigh.

"How are you? Your test is over, right?"

"Yes. All done." I tossed my bag to the bed and didn't even care when I missed and it hit the floor. An irrepressible smile claimed my mouth, one that felt like it originated within the mitochondria of every cell in my body.

He was calling to check on me and it felt so natural and right. *This is what I want.*

"Do you still want—" He seemed to stop himself, pause, like he was reconsidering what he'd been about to say. I heard a chair or something creak in the background. When he spoke again, his voice was deeper, firmer. "What time should I pick you up tonight?"

"About tonight, I've been thinking." I sat on the edge of my bed, working to arrange my thoughts in an order that was sensical. "Do you want to stay in?" We were supposed to go out to dinner—our first official date—but I knew he didn't like public places.

"No. I don't. I want to take you out."

I debated how to best get my point across, that I wanted him to be comfortable.

But then he said, "You're hesitating, wanting to say the right thing, not wanting to upset me. Don't do that. Just say what you're thinking."

"Fine." He asked for it. "You don't like restaurants. I don't want you uncomfortable during our first date."

"I appreciate that." He sounded like he was smiling. "But I've been thinking, maybe a little discomfort would be good for me. Without experimentation, there is no data."

"Well, there's data, but it's a retrospective study rather than prospective."

"However, you can never establish causation—with any confidence—utilizing a retrospective cohort. Causation can only be established using a prospective study design."

"And double-blind randomization," I added, another thought occurring to me as I said these words. I wondered if I should push the flirt envelope . . . *Why not?* I needed to be allowed to be myself with him. I couldn't always be second-guessing every word. If this was going to work, he was going to have to accept me for who I was. Period.

So, I just said it. "Are you saying you want me to blindfold you?"

He made a choking sound and I heard something thump

and then clatter in the background, like an object had been dropped.

"Victor?"

"Yes," he rasped. "Sorry. Coffee went down the wrong pipe."

I grinned. And then I laughed. "Okay. How about you pick me up at seven?"

"Sounds good." His voice was still rough, strained. "See you then."

"I'll bring the blindfolds."

A beat. A breath. And then, "Emily."

My name was a plea.

I giggled. Evilly.

What? He said he wanted discomfort.

Being on a date with Victor turned out to be just like hanging out with Victor except for a few details.

First, he wore a suit. He wore a sexy, sexy suit. I know clothes are just wrapping paper when you get right down to it, but a suit on Victor was some Martha Stewart, unobtainable, handstamped, gold leaf and crepe paper gift wrapping majesty.

Second, he looked at me with unveiled desire, and it made me realize how much of himself he'd been hiding. Always looking away, always stepping away, always masking his thoughts. I liked this new look from him.

Third, we greeted each other at my door with a kiss on the cheek. But then, as we slowly pulled away, and by some tacit agreement, our lips met on the retreat. Like the last time in the library, his kisses felt hungry, and things quickly began to spiral toward wild—him backing me up against my open door, me grabbing fistfuls of his hair and working through the logistics of climbing him.

But unlike last time at the library, his tongue and lips were more skillful, purposeful, making it easy for hormones to eclipse my good sense.

He was the first to pull away, tearing his mouth from mine and lowering it to my shoulder. "We need to go."

It took me a moment to decipher the puzzle of his words, during which I kissed his jaw, his neck. We were both breathing heavy.

He wants to go? No, no, no. That wouldn't do. "Or . . ."

"I made reservations."

My hands slid under his coat and his body bowed, jumped beneath my searching fingers. "Or . . ."

I sensed him swallow, stiffen. "Emily, you're the only woman I've kissed."

I tensed, my eyes flying open, my jaw growing lax.

Shocked.

I was SHOCKED!

"When I said I'm inexperienced, I meant it." He leaned away, his gaze searching, wary and yet determined as it held mine. "But, this is me. This is who I am. And if this is something you—"

I grabbed his arms before he could retreat. "It's fine. It's great. I'm just surprised. No leaving!"

Victor cracked a small smile, it looked relieved. "I'm not going to leave, I meant what I said in the library. And you didn't let me finish. I was going to say, if this is something you're concerned about, I respectfully request an opportunity to discuss how we—both of us—can reach a level of comfort with my lack of experience. Things might be awkward or difficult for a while, but I'm a fast learner, and I have every confidence I'll be able to come up to speed with enough time."

I couldn't help it, I also cracked a smile. His tone was so official. His speech sounded practiced, like he'd given this some thought and had developed a protocol.

It was cute.

It was also really damn sexy.

"You seem to have it all figured out." I slid my hands down his shoulders to the lapels of his suit jacket.

"I have a plan, and I'm an excellent researcher. But theory can only take me so far," he said, his voice still serious, which was also cute. Victor enveloped my hands in his larger ones and brought my knuckles to his lips. I watched him feather kisses on the backs of my fingers for a moment. Eventually, his fiercely intelligent eyes lifted, ensnaring mine. "I want you. But I also want to excel at everything you like to do."

"I want to play a game."

"A game?" Victor split his attention between me and his plate, his expression open and interested.

He was smiling, relaxed, and he hadn't sent any death glares to the women at the bar who'd been checking him out since we'd walked in. Our dinners had just arrived, we'd already consumed cocktails and a bottle of wine between us, and conversation had been flowing as easily as the drinks. Then again, conversation had never been a problem for us.

Thus far, excellent date. Best I'd ever had. And yet, I kept expecting Victor to pull the rug out from under me and leave me alone with my salmon and renewed sadness. Forgetting history, starting fresh, giving him another chance, it was both easy and difficult.

Therefore, I had an urge to push the envelope.

What? Therefore? What do you mean "therefore"? Why do you want to push the envelope?

Shhh. . . *Just go with it.*

"Yes. A game." I cut into my salmon with my fork and took a small bite. "One I've just made up. It's called, Ask Uncomfortable Questions That The Other Person Has To Answer Game, trademark pending. I'll start. Victor, how many women have you dated?"

His eyebrows lifted even as his eyelids lowered. "Including you, one."

My eyes widened before I could stop them, and I breathed out, "One." *One.* "Not even dates? Like this?"

He shrugged, his attention lowering to his plate. "I've been on first dates, but never second ones."

"Why?"

He seemed to take his time considering, and I took it as a good sign that his expression remained open. "Some of them remain friendly acquaintances. I guess, there's just never been any depth of interest beyond friendship with anyone."

"Until me?"

"Yes." His lips pulled to the side, and his gaze flickered to mine and then back to his plate. "Until you."

"Huh. So fascinating."

"How about you? How many men have you dated?"

"Uh, dated? Well, I've had seven boyfriends, five in high school, two in college, but I've been on *a lot* of first dates." I scooped a heap of spinach and salmon onto my fork and shoveled the bite into my mouth. The chef had used exactly the right amount of garlic.

Victor seemed to be absorbing this information, his features abstracted, like he was doing long division in his head.

Eventually, sounding honestly curious, he asked, "Why didn't it work out with any of them?"

I shrugged, thinking back over my "failed" relationships. Except they hadn't really failed, they'd just changed. "I think, honestly, they did work out. I mean, in high school it was all trying to figure out what liking a person meant, you know? I think all of my relationships worked out to be what they were meant to be, if that makes sense."

"Friends?"

Now it was my turn to consider the question. "Yes, mostly. I'm somewhat friendly with most of them. We're all friends on Instagram and they're all nice guys. But I never felt . . ." I sighed. *What is this feeling?*

Although, my last ex claimed that I'd broken his heart. I'd never set out to break anyone's heart, but I wasn't going to force what I didn't feel.

That said, I'd been his first.

"What?"

I blinked, coming back to myself. "I'm sorry, what?"

He was studying me. "You were frowning, and you looked like you were deep in thought."

"Oh." I cut off another piece of my salmon. "It's nothing."

Victor's eyes narrowed. "What was the name of this game again?"

I sighed, grumbling. "Okay, fine. My last boyfriend was convinced he was in love with me, and our breakup wasn't good. He had trouble moving on."

"When was this?"

"Two years ago."

"So you would have been—"

"Nineteen."

"How long did you date?"

"Three months." I set my fork down, feeling oddly restless, and leaned my elbows on the table. "Let's play another game."

He shook his head, his eyes growing sharp, like he had a hunch. "Why do you think he believed he was in love with you?"

Glaring at him, I wanted to lie, or deflect, but this game had been my idea. "Ugh, fine." I leaned back in my chair, crossing my arms. "I was his first—you know—and I think he confused how good the physical stuff felt with love."

"And you're sure he wasn't in love with you?"

"Yes. One hundred percent certain, in fact." I picked up my fork again, spearing a carrot.

"How can you be sure?"

Munching on the carrot, I shrugged. "You just know."

Again, that calculating look entered his eyes. "How can you be sure I love you? And that I'm not confusing the 'physical stuff' with love?"

"That's easy. First of all"—I pointed to him with my fork —"we haven't done any physical stuff, not really, not *yet*." I made sure to pause here for an eyebrow wiggle. "And secondly, you like me. You laugh at my jokes. You're genuinely interested in what I have to say."

"And he wasn't? Your last boyfriend?" Something seemed to shift in Victor's gaze, his shoulders visibly relaxed, like I'd given him the right answer.

"Exactly. First, he hated jigsaw puzzles and wouldn't stop complaining whenever we'd go over to Anna's for pints and puzzles night. He hated trivia night. He *pretended* to like D&D, but then it turned out that he'd never played."

"For the record, I was a DM in high school," Victor interjected. "Sorry. Please continue."

I sat up straighter, a fissure of excitement racing down my spine. "You're a DM?"

He nodded, like it was no big deal, chewing his steak.

"That's good to know!"

Victor's eyes seemed to dance as they watched me over the rim of his wineglass. "You like me better because I'm a DM?"

"No! Of course not." I took another bite of my dinner,

relishing in the dramatic/comedic pause before adding, "I'd never *say* that. Out loud. To your face."

He laughed, setting his glass down and shaking his head. "It's fine, because I liked you better knowing you play D&D."

Gesturing to him with my open palm, I nodded. "See? Exactly. We share interests. Carter and I shared no interests."

"Then why'd you date him?"

"He was cute and told good dad jokes. I'm a sucker for dad jokes. Okay, my turn again."

"Maybe we should stop playing this game," he said, but he also grinned slyly, which meant he was teasing.

"Nah-ah. We're just getting started. I have several more questions, in fact." And this next one was fairly serious. Unthinkingly, I glanced at his plate. He wasn't actively eating, and he'd left more than half his steak. Lifting my chin to his meal, I asked, "You said at the library that you 'stopped eating' when we were hanging out. What did you mean by that?"

I studied him carefully, watching a battle within him. It was the first time during our meal that he looked like he was on the edge of closing up again.

Finally, taking a deep breath, he bit the corner of his lip and nodded lightly. "You know I see a counselor? I have for years, specifically to help me with the weight loss, to help me keep it off and focus on the right things."

"Yes. I remember."

"He said it's not unusual for someone like me, for someone who's gone through a dramatic weight loss, to fear gaining it back. To panic if the scale moves, even a little. I thought I had it under control, and maybe I did for a while. But when we started spending so much time together, I think a part of me wondered if you would still want to know me if I were heavier again."

What?

"Victor, I—"

He lifted a hand to stop me. "Nothing you say will be the right answer, because it isn't a question for you. It's a question for me. I have to like who I am and be comfortable in my skin, no matter what you or anyone else thinks, even if I gain five pounds, even if I gain a hundred."

My skin felt like it was covered in pinpricks as we traded stares, and I fought the urge to reassure him that it didn't matter to me if he gained five pounds or one hundred.

"Anyway." His gaze drifted to his wineglass. "It's not something that will ever go away for me, it's something I'll probably live with forever. Sometimes, there is no resolution, no answer. There is only doing my best."

He said this last part like he was reminding himself rather than talking to me, and so I gave him a moment with his own thoughts. But I found I also needed a moment with my thoughts as well.

There is only doing my best.

I frickin' loved this man. I'd never been in love before, and I loved him, and he was here. With me. Doing his best. Maybe one day he'd pull the rug out from under me and leave me alone with salmon and sadness. Maybe he wouldn't. I could spend our time together waiting for him to leave, bracing for it, protecting myself.

Or I could trust. I could enjoy each moment.

Those were my options.

I want to trust him.

Victor took a deep breath, a warm little smile on his lips, and gave me back his eyes. "Any more questions?"

"Yes."

He waited a beat. When I didn't say anything, he prompted, "Yes?"

"Victor, I want to trust you."

"Okaaaay."

Straightening my back, I frowned at him. "How do I know you're not going to change your mind again and disappear?"

Something around his eyes seemed to soften and he reached across the table for my hand, curling his long fingers around mine. "Emily"—his startlingly intelligent eyes focused on mine, grew fierce—"I surrender. I'm not convinced you want me, or that I deserve you, but I surrender. I'm making this up as I go, and I can only do that because of *who you are.* I trust you to be kind. If you don't want me, I trust you to be honest. But living without you—without doing my utmost to make you happy, whatever you ultimately decide about us—is not an option."

Ignoring my fluttering heart, I tried to force steadiness into my voice. "Whatever I decide?"

"Whatever you decide." He nodded once.

I twisted my lips to the side to hide the massive grin threatening to break through. "What if I decide to be friends again?"

Victor gathered a deep inhale. "Then we will be friends again. But you should know, I will be having dirty dreams and fantasies about my friend."

I breathed a stunned laugh, drawing a grin out of him. "These are just words, but they're all I have. I will earn your trust. But please know—" he swallowed, his gorgeous eyes clear and bright "—I have no escape plan. I'm holding nothing back. The terms of this surrender are complete, because there is no alternative for me other than to give you, and this beautiful thing between us, everything I have."

CHAPTER 21

EMILY

"How is it possible that I'm the first woman you've kissed?" I asked between kisses.

We were in his car, and I was straddling his lap as he nipped and bit my neck, sending spikes of hot, liquid loveliness to the lowest part of my abdomen. We were supposed to be going to a movie. Instead, we made it as far as the theater parking lot and were presently making out. In his car. Again.

This wasn't atypical. In the weeks since our first date, we often started the evening with the best of intentions and ended it never leaving his car. Our marathon make-out sessions were why, through some unspoken arrangement, neither of us had stepped foot inside each other's house/apartment since, like we couldn't trust ourselves within easy access of a bed, or a couch, or a counter.

Also, I'd never taken so many cold showers in my life. AND WHY WOULD I???

AHHH!! *THIS IS TORTURE!*

"I've never been interested in anyone else, that way," he spoke against my neck, licking the spot beneath my ear, his fingers digging into my sides as he shifted his hips restlessly beneath me. He was hard. This was also not unusual. (See above, reference: torture).

"Ever?" I didn't know if I was trying to ruffle his composure, or if I actually wanted to know, or if the wanting him 24/7—specifically, his penis in my vagina and us stage one, bare-buck naked—but never having him was addling my brain.

Whatever. I couldn't seem to let this subject drop. He was such a truly excellent kisser.

His mouth stopped moving and his hands ceased roaming. Sensing his hesitation, I leaned away, and his fingers curled into the bare skin of my upper thighs. I was wearing a short circle skirt and lace undies because I wanted to get laid. *Just keeping it real.*

I could barely breathe with how much I wanted this man. My overactive imagination was having a field day with sexy daydreams. And I know I agreed to give him time and have patience, but—FOR THE LOVE OF GOD—how much longer?

His gaze moved over my shoulder, his breathing growing even. "There was one girl, in high school." He spoke haltingly.

"What happened?" I twisted my arms around his neck, telling myself not to wriggle on his lap. Or, you know, reach inside his pants.

He shrugged, but the movement looked stiff, and seeing his tension sobered me.

"She knew I liked her, so she asked me to homecoming as a joke. I said yes. I showed up to her house and her mother told me she'd already left with her real date."

"Ugh." *I WILL CUT HER.*

"It was stupid kid stuff." He drummed his fingers on my thigh, his thumb moving in an absentminded circle. I felt everything.

"And you've never tried with anyone else?"

"Like I said, I've never wanted to." Victor's gaze returned to me, his eyes positively burning with interest. And maybe a little bit of lust.

Okay. A lot of lust. SO MUCH LUST! I swooned a little.

"Are we playing your game again?" He settled back in his seat, his palms sliding to my knees, his eyes on my lips.

"Which game?" *Please say the sex game.* He wouldn't say the sex game because we'd only played the necking game.

Yes, I know. I was such a horndog. In my defense, and though I'd always enjoyed sex for the most part, I'd never been this insanely *needy* for another person before. Like, just thinking about him and his eyes and his smile made me pant. No lie! Last night, getting ready for bed, I was thinking about the hazy quality to his eyes and expression when he looked at my lips, and then I panted. And then I got myself off in my bed in record time, a self-O that barely scratched the surface of my agony.

"The trademark pending game," he said, his words sounding far away for some reason.

I had to super concentrate to make sense of the phrase, but eventually realization dawned. "Ah, yes." We'd shortened the title of the original game—*Ask Uncomfortable Questions That The Other Person Has To Answer Game*—to the trademark pending game. "I guess we are playing the trademark pending game."

"Good. Then I have a question." His eyes lowered to my chin, neck, the front of my shirt. I'd noticed the last time we were together that he'd seemed preoccupied by the front of my shirt. He'd kept scowling at it like the fabric posed a problem. That's why today's shirt was a button-down, for easy access, should things *progress*. "How much does it bother you that I've never dated anyone?"

"What? No! It doesn't bother me. It doesn't bother me at

all." After the words were out, I knew I'd doth protested too much.

"But?" His eyes were back on mine, searching, *penetrating.*

AH! DON'T THINK ABOUT PENETRATION!

Flustered, I leaned back, accidentally hitting the car horn, which only made me more flustered. "Sorry!"

"It's okay." He grinned, kissing my chin and holding my body tighter when I made to move back to my seat. "No. Stay. It's okay. You were saying?"

Huffing, I glanced around at the dim parking lot; the sun was setting; we didn't have a ton of privacy, but there weren't many cars nearby, and all of them were empty. "Uh, it doesn't bother me. A few weeks ago, it bothered me a little, but only because being your first everything felt like a lot of pressure. But it doesn't bother me now."

Now he grimaced, so I cupped his face and placed a kiss on his delectable lips. "Let me rephrase that. I put pressure on myself, you did not put pressure on me. I mean, you avoided this for months, right? You avoided telling me the truth for months?"

He nodded, looking resigned and a shade amused, like he was either inwardly laughing at himself or the situation. "I was very stupid."

"Why did you do that?"

"So many reasons. Many of which we've already talked about." He blew out a breath, his lips curving into a rueful-looking grin.

"But I'm guessing part of it, or one of the reasons, was because you've never dated anyone. Right?"

Victor looped a long strand of my hair around his finger while he spoke. "That was one of the reasons, but not really. It was more about what I've already said. I believed you deserved someone experienced, who already knew what to do, and wouldn't require so much direction, patience, and help."

I scoffed, pulling a face. "The truth is, I've never met a guy who didn't need direction, patience, and help."

He quirked an eyebrow at that, looking less resigned and more diverted. "Really?"

"Oh yeah. And my boyfriends have been all over the spectrum of guy-types: jocks, nerds, jock-nerds, bossy guys, timid guys, and everything in between. Every single one has needed help with his technique. Or he wanted to do stuff that was a huge turnoff for me. I almost wonder—" I stopped myself, clamping my mouth shut.

His gaze cut to mine. "What?"

I swallowed, examining him. The thing was, old habits are hard to break. I'd just almost asked him if I could be honest.

But I shouldn't have to ask him if I could be honest. I should just, you know, *be honest.*

"I wonder if it's ultimately better, easier, you know? Even with my last boyfriend, he'd done things with other girls. He just hadn't gone all the way with anyone. I wonder if it's better that we started with you having zero experience. It's like, most guys get into these bad habits. But you're a blank slate. You didn't know what you liked, or what you thought you liked. And I've been helping you figure it out, and it's been wonderful."

He gave me a smirk, albeit a warm smirk. "I think you're just trying to look on the bright side of this situation."

"I'm honestly not." I laughed, shaking my head. "The more I think about it, the more of a relief it is."

"It's a relief that I'm a virgin." His tone was flat-tire flat.

I wanted to say, *We can change that. Anytime. Like how about now?*

Instead, I said, "Yeeeeeah. It's a relief." My voice was higher than I'd intended, and I had to clear my throat before continuing, "The pressure is off for me. I don't have to worry about living up to anyone from your past, or—"

"But I do."

"No. Don't you see?" I rewound my arms around his neck, scratching my nails into the short hairs at the back of his head, and speaking my mind. "That's the best part. I shall form you into my own ideal sex toy."

He flushed and he laughed, his eyes cutting away like I'd embarrassed him. But upon further inspection, I realized that I'd pleased him. This was a flush of pleasure.

He cleared his throat, swallowed, his eyes returning to mine, bright and hot and hungry. "I'd like that."

"Me too." We shared a smile for a moment before a thought occurred to me. "Hey, do you mind homework?"

"Pardon?"

"Homework? If I gave you some books to read on the subject? For us to discuss and try out when we're together? Think of it like an independent study with a lab component."

"Not at all. Actually, I'd appreciate it." He was drumming his fingers on my thigh again and the color on his cheeks was now a deeper red. "Can we start with nomenclature?"

"With what?"

"What to call certain things. Can we come up with a list of names you prefer?"

"Names?" I cocked my head to the side, wrinkling my nose slightly. "You mean like names for our private parts?"

Victor laughed again, looking at me like I was wonderful. Later, I'd probably think back to this moment and *pant*.

"No, not necessarily. I meant names for things that we want to do."

I still wasn't getting it. "Uh, can you give me an example?"

"Sure." He licked his lips, his fingers flexing on my legs. "For example, 'fingering.' Does that term work? Or I've also seen 'finger banging' used, the equivalent of 'hand job' for men. Another way we could refer to it is using a sports analogy, which seems to be popular based on its search ranking as a synonym to the original concept, i.e. 'second base.' Musical terms have also been adopted and referenced, such as 'strumming' or 'playing.'"

And now I was panting.

This was because, when he'd spoken, his voice had grown deep, authoritative. It was his professor-splain voice, and it caused a giant sexy shock to race down my spine to the apex of my thighs, a hot, heavy, aching, thirsting, desperate emptiness.

I needed...

I need . . .

"I think we should go see the movie," I said weakly, my voice cracking, moving to unstraddle his lap before he could feel the abrupt dampness between my legs.

Once again, his hands stayed me, holding me in place. "Wait, wait. What did I say? Did I upset you?"

He was trying to catch my gaze, but I couldn't look at him, so I closed my eyes and covered my face. "No. I'm not upset."

I'm just really, really horny.

This was the longest I'd gone without sex in a relationship. My very first boyfriend—the jock who'd inadvertently scared me and then apologized later when he realized how terrified I was—had been extremely experienced for a seventeen-year-old. I'd been fifteen and my hormones had been off the chain insane. We'd had sex one week after dating and then every chance we got for three months, until I broke up with him over the freak-out incident.

With Victor, it had been three and a half weeks of just necking. No boobs had been touched—over or under the clothes—and every day without him jumping my bones wound me a little tighter.

"If you're not upset, why are you covering your face?"

"Because I want you to touch me, but I also know we need to go slow."

"Touch you? I am touching you." His hands near my knees squeezed, as though to prove his point.

"No, 'touching' as a synonym for 'fingering.'"

He was quiet, and I knew he was staring at the back of my hands obscuring my face, but I couldn't seem to drop them. It's not that I was embarrassed.

Okay, it's not that I was *only* embarrassed, I was also running low on self-control. Looking at him now, at his gorgeous jaw and lips and nose, but mostly his eyes, would only make me do something rash, like make a seduction attempt.

But then, his hands moved. They slid from my knees higher, his fingertips whispering over the inside of my thighs, and before I comprehended what was happening, he rubbed me through my underwear with the pad of his thumb.

I experienced a jolt and I stiffened, but I also moaned, my hands falling from my face and seeking his shoulders as he continued to stroke me through the fabric.

Damn.

Damn.

I didn't care that he could feel the wetness there, I didn't care that we were in his car and it wasn't fully dark and we both had all our clothes on. All I cared about was that he was touching me, and I couldn't decide if it felt like heavenly-bliss or hellish-torment.

And then, he slipped his thumb *inside* the fabric.

A hot, hitching breath escaped me, and my eyes flew open. He was watching, his eyes dark, darting all over, as though greedy for every reaction. His erection pressed insistently against the inside of my thigh and his hips moved, again restless as his stare landed on the front of my shirt.

Maybe he sent me a mental directive, maybe I'd lost my mind, who can say for certain? But the next minute, I was unbuttoning my shirt with shaking fingers and unclasping the front of my bra, exposing myself to him.

Victor released a ragged breath and abruptly surged forward, his mouth hungrily licking and biting and tasting my breast. I dug my nails into the back of his head and rocked against his thumb, wanting more, wanting him inside me.

"Please," I said, but the single word was all I could manage. So, I repeated it. "Please."

He made a sound like a groan and a growl, moving to my left breast with teeth and tongue, and cupping the other in his palm, massaging me reverently, groaning again. He was an excellent multitasker.

"Emily. I need you. I need. . ."

This was the farthest we'd gone by a huge margin, and the edges of reality were suddenly a blur. His thumb rubbing circles over my slick center, his tongue swirling around my nipple, catching my other nipple between his fingers and rolling, pinching, tugging.

"Fuck me," I breathed.

His hands left my body, and I whimpered. The little sound a pathetic protest on its own, but I followed it with, "No. Please. Don't stop," just in case he thought I might be above begging.

For the record, I was not above begging in that moment. Everything he'd done had felt so good, so incredibly essential, I wondered if I might die if he didn't continue. And then I remembered what I'd just said.

Fuck me.

Ah.

Shit!

Daaaaaaaaammmmiiiiiiiitttttttt!!!!

The words had been meant as an exclamation, but he'd probably thought I'd meant them as a suggestion, and now he was pulling away and putting the brakes on, and I'd been so close, *so* close, but then I'd ruined it and—

The sound of a zipper being undone pulled me out of my self-recrimination, that and Victor pulling the lever on his seat and reclining the back. I looked at him through the fog of my own lust, watched as he encouraged me to lift myself higher so he could push down his pants, his erection springing free.

My eyes bulged, my mouth suddenly watering.

Daaaaaaaaammmnn. . . girl. Yes! *Now that's a dick.*

Excitement and anticipation pumped through my veins, good intentions and all thought of regret completely eclipsed by the promise of having him, inside me, touching me, watching him come. I wanted it, him, so badly, and I could not distinguish between *need* and *want*.

His hand gripped his shaft and I pulled it away, wrapping my fingers in their place and moaning like a sex fiend when I felt the smooth, silky heat of him. He hissed. Our eyes met.

In the next second, his fingers were frantically digging into my underwear at my hips, trying to tug it down. My position meant that wasn't going to work, which left my crazy mind with two options, neither of which was to stop: either I could move the crotch to one side and mount him with it semi in the way, or I could tear off my underwear.

Releasing his magnificent member—and tangentially deciding *magnificent member* was what I would call it henceforth—I reached under my skirt, dug my nails into the mesh netting at my stomach, and tore the fabric wide open.

"Em—!"

I gripped him again and, not wasting another second, I

lowered myself, releasing a heady, forceful breath as my body tensed and bowed at the marvelous invasion. Victor also breathed out, pressing his head back against the headrest and releasing a string of curses that were so filthy, they both shocked and delighted me.

And then I moved.

The tightness within me coiling and releasing, easing and twisting as I rocked, pushing deeper, wanting—needing—every perfect inch of him.

"Fuck, Emily. Fuck." His fingers were punishing where they gripped my legs, his attention affixed to my breasts as I moved over him, his face flush, his eyes unnaturally bright.

I was covered in sweat. The inside of the car had fogged. I tasted salt and smelled sex and my knee was digging painfully into the center console and my hair was wild, sticking to my face and neck and breasts.

But Victor . . . *Damn.* He was so damn beautiful. And he felt so good. And he made me feel so, so good. I shifted, instead of moving up and down, I pivoted my pelvis back and forth, insatiable, wanting to feel every stroke of his length against my clitoris and the head of his cock deep, deep within me.

"Oh God," he said, his eyes starting to roll back.

"Not yet!" I grabbed his hand and placed his thumb at my center. "Touch me."

He immediately complied, lifting onto his other elbow, his teeth clenched together, his eyes on mine.

It was his eyes that sent me over the edge. Well, it was his eyes and everything else. They'd gone wild. He did not look like he was in his right mind. He looked possessed. And I loved it.

Every muscle in my body tensed, stars burst behind my eyes, and I made sounds. So many sounds. *Oh! The sounds that I made!!*

Obliquely, I felt him move beneath me, his hips rolling in an inelegant, needful rhythm, wringing another orgasm from me, my moans and sighs despairing, begging, pleading as his arms came around my body, his labored exhales falling between the valley of my breasts.

And then he fell backward, bringing me with him, his hands in my hair to move it out of my face. His lips followed, trailing over my face until they found mine, kissing me deeply as though he wished to sip the life from my body with the perfection of his tongue.

We lay like that for some indeterminate time, kissing, his hands moving over me, stroking my back, grabbing and kneading my ass, slipping between us to palm my breast.

"Emily," he whispered, an edge in his voice pulling me from my foggy euphoria and brainlessness.

"Hmm? What's wrong?" I tried to lift myself off his chest, but he held me to him.

"Nothing. Nothing is wrong. It's just . . ."

"What?" When I attempted to lift myself this time, he let me, and I found his stare searching, urgent, still tinged with wildness. "What is it?"

"I need you."

"You—"

"Again. Now."

My eyes widened. "Now?"

He nodded, his hand moving from my breast to where we were still joined, touching me, making me chase my breath and my toes curl in my shoes.

"Yes. Right now."

Wait a minute . . . was I still wearing my shoes?

Ah. What the heck. I didn't need to be naked, or shoeless, or in a bed. Clearly, I'd lost my mind over this man.

Equally as obvious, he'd also lost his mind over me.

CHAPTER 22

VICTOR

More than anything, I hadn't expected the voraciousness. But in biological terms, for bonding and mating and longevity, the insatiability made complete sense.

For instance, when you're hungry, you tend to care slightly less about everything and everyone except what (or who) you're craving. Or maybe you care more. Either way, the net total was the same.

When we finally made it out of the car and into my apartment, Emily suggested a shower. I immediately agreed and unthinkingly followed her into the bathroom, smiled at her as she smiled at me, undressed her as she undressed me, caressed her skin as she caressed mine, until—

"Victor! Oh my—these scars." Her stare was fastened to my chest and she divided her focus between my eyes and the two incisions. "What happened?"

I closed my eyes, only for a moment, as the momentum of the last hour finally caught up with me and it was like coming awake from the most miraculous dream. I hadn't meant for her to see them, not yet. I'd wanted to tell her about the surgery, and why I'd decided to have it, and when, and what it meant.

But, unthinkingly—or rather, perhaps more accurately, incapable of thought—I'd allowed her to remove my shirt, because I saw only her.

"Victor?"

"These are incisions, where the doctor cut to remove the excess skin. I have another"—I gestured to my stomach —"just beneath the waistband of my boxers."

She frowned at me, then blinked as though startled, but on a delay. "You—" she shook her head "—you had the skin removed? When? I thought—I thought—"

"Over spring break." Grasping her hands in both of mine, I placed her palms on my chest, flat over the lines. They'd healed, but they were still sensitive to the touch.

She shuffled closer, her eyes searching and troubled. "But why?"

"It was uncomfortable," I said, speaking the easiest half of the truth first before adding, "And because I decided I didn't care what anyone thought. Except you."

"Me?"

"Yes. You."

"But—but you didn't have to do this for me. I wouldn't have cared one way or the other." Her hands slid from my chest to my sides and she placed two tender kisses on the lines, her forehead wrinkled with worry. "You have to know, it's not just your skin that I love, but all of you."

"Em, I kno—"

"I mean, now that I've seen and felt your penis, I might love that part of you most of all."

I tried to stop the wry smile and failed. She sounded completely serious.

"But your body is always going to be beautiful to me," she continued, her fingers curling into my torso. "Because it's where *you* are. It houses that massive brain of yours, which is responsible for my second and third favorite parts of you."

"Second and third?"

"Your sass and your sweetness."

"I have sass?"

She rolled her eyes. "Come. On. You know what I mean. And stop trying to change the subject. Please tell me that you had the surgery for yourself, because you truly wanted it, and not because of me."

I slid my hands down her arms to her hips. "It was uncomfortable for me, especially when I was active. And I was allowing my disdain for the fickleness of physical attraction to keep me in a state of discomfort. When I realized what I was doing, giving other people power over my decisions, as though I could spite them by making myself uncomfortable, I decided to have the skin removed."

She nodded, some of the anxiety clearing from her scrutinizing stare, but she still looked worried.

Sighing, I placed a kiss on her lovely lips. "Do you still want to shower?"

Emily continued to nod, pulling away to undress, her gaze still somewhat conflicted. I moved to the glass shower and turned on the water, waiting until the temperature was just right before removing my pants, wishing I'd told her about this weeks ago. I didn't want the fact that I hadn't told her to be made into something it wasn't. At one point, I'd made it a big deal, I'd made the skin important, I'd allowed it to symbolize something for me. But now, it just simply didn't.

Emily walked past me as I pulled off my shirt, and I paused, the arms of the shirt still at my wrists because I was momentarily caught, mesmerized by the sight of her naked body beneath the spray of the water.

"You can watch," she said conversationally, having caught me staring. "Or you can join me."

"Join you."

She grinned, backing up to make room for me as I tore the constraining cuffs from my wrists. Her gaze moved over my body and I stiffened a little but forced myself to keep moving. I wondered what she saw when she looked at me. The scars? The loose skin still between my legs and under my upper arms? The stretch marks all over my body? They'd never disappear but might eventually fade until they weren't as noticeable.

Grabbing the soap behind her, I waited for her verdict, growing more uncomfortable the longer her eyes moved over me.

But then, she closed the distance between us, her hands reaching, grasping, like she couldn't wait to touch me. "Can we be naked for the rest of the day? Can I kiss you everywhere? Will you kiss me everywhere? How do you feel about nudes? I mean, photos?"

"Photos? What?"

She grimaced. "I'm sorry. Too soon? Should I put a ring on it first?" Emily lifted to her tiptoes, the front of her body sliding against mine such that all those unpleasant ponderings and questions vacated my brain in an instant.

In fact, what were we even talking about?

"I can be patient," she said, her hands slipping down along with the water's current. "I will be the picture of patience and the portrait of prudence until you're ready to send me nudes."

A laugh erupted from my chest as I finally caught up with what she'd not-so-subtly been implying. "You're joking."

She merely smiled, gazing up at me, her hand coming between us to slide along my cock with an open palm.

"God. Em." My body shuddered as I gripped the wall

behind her for balance. My lungs on fire, I released a shaky breath.

"I think you underestimate how obsessed I am with you. Honestly, you should be afraid," she said as she stroked me, sounding completely reasonable, if not a little amused.

"Obsessed? Really?" My voice gruff, I glared down at her where I caged her in. My hips rolled reflexively as I thrust into her hand.

"Yes. Obsessed." She placed a kiss on my chin. "And I have a superactive imagination. I think I've actually imagined this moment before."

Fuck.

I couldn't think. I could only . . . glare. And try not to come, yet.

"It would've been that week after you had the advocate appointed, when I was taking your class."

Shit shit shit shit.

I couldn't look at her anymore, I was so close, and her words were electrifying.

"I think the subject being covered was quasi-experimental designs, and you were standing at the front of the class, doing that thing where you pinch your bottom lip while someone was talking, trying to answer your question. I imagined *this.* Doing this, to you, in the shower." Her voice grew husky, and she leaned forward to whisper in my ear, "But before you come, I want you in my mouth."

I shook my head, because it was too late. I was coming. My limbs trembled with the force of it, of the picture she painted with her words, and that I believed her. I believed her when she said she'd been fantasizing about me, wanting me all this time.

Headless to the mess I'd made, I pulled her against me, wrapped her in my arms, and buried my face in her neck.

Emily snuggled closer, and we stood under the warm spray, breathing deeply, catching our breath, until she spoke.

"It was your sass, back then, that got me hot." Her voice sounded distant, absorbed with the memory. And then she laughed. "You were so sassy!"

I sighed, pulling away just far enough to find and claim her lips, kissing the bottom one first, and then the sweet cupid's bow on the top.

When I came up for air, her gaze snagged mine as did her smile. She looked happy.

"You're so beautiful," I said, my attention moving between her happy smile and her happy eyes. Her happiness was stunning.

"Thank you," she said, her grin growing. "So are you."

I returned her smile, somehow intrinsically knowing she meant the same, that she found my happiness beautiful too.

EPILOGUE

VICTOR

-One year later-

"Nobody looks good naked." Emily crossed her arms, lifting her eyebrows in one of her classic *I dare you to disagree with me and my superior logic* looks. It was one of my favorites.

"False." Or, as Andy might say, *Fake news.* "You look superb naked."

She shook her head in a quick movement, rebuffing my attempt to kiss her cheek by flattening her palms against my chest. "First of all, I look superb naked *to you,* just like you look superbly, magnificently naked to *me*. But all human bodies are Monets, not Rockwells. You get up close and *no one* looks good naked. Body perfection is a myth perpetuated by airbrushed magazine covers!"

I squinted at her and her impassioned words. I could remember the path we'd taken to arrive at this present moment, but for the life of me I couldn't understand why we were talking about this.

Wracking my brain, I reviewed the events of the evening.

We'd gone to Anna and Luca's engagement party. As far as I could tell, everything had gone well, she seemed happy, fine. We stopped by Rain City Café for coffee and a biscotti, discussed our weekend plans, and then drove home.

"Remind me, what does this have to do with anything?"

Her hands dropped, and then settled on her waist. "Naked sex."

Naked sex.

Emily's eyebrows arched over her gorgeous brown eyes, like she was waiting for me to defend myself, or argue.

Instead, I shrugged. "What about it? Do you want to do it? Now?" I made a show of tugging at my suit tie. "Let's go."

My words seemed to both fluster and frustrate her, and she crossed her arms, her chin lifting stubbornly. "See? This is the problem."

"You don't like my tie?" I teased, pulling it completely free from its knot and walking past her to the closet.

She followed. "No. I love that tie. The problem is, when I bring it up, you're happy to do it—or you seem happy to do it. But then, days pass, we get busy, and when it's time for happy-sexy-fun-times again, unless I *specifically* ask you to take all your clothes off, you keep your shirt on."

"What? I don't do that." . . . *do I?*

"Yes. You do. I've been charting it on my phone and you never take off your shirt unless I ask."

"You've been charting it on your phone?!" I turned completely around to find she'd pulled out her cell and was showing me the screen.

"Well." Her arm dropped and she looked caught between embarrassment and determination. "I know how you like data, and it was only a suspicion at first. But now . . ." She lifted the phone again, giving her hand a little shake. "Look."

Dividing my frown between her and the phone, I plucked it out of her hand and examined the screen. Sure enough, she'd tracked my shirt-wearing habit, which both impressed and irritated me. Also, as an aside, her tracking also proved that we had a lot of sex, which just impressed me.

Heaving a sigh, I gave her back my eyes. "I'm not really sure what to say."

Emily seemed to be bouncing between frustrated and worried. "Okay, I am sorry I tracked it. I'm sorry. Do you forgive me? I'm not tracking anything else, I promise. But this is important to me. I love you and your body, and I want *all of it!*"

I rubbed my forehead with stiff fingers. "I honestly had no idea. I guess I'll try to make sure I take my shirt off from now on."

"Good." She stepped closer, into my space, her gaze hopeful. "Good. Thank you."

We studied each other for a long moment. Or rather, she gazed at me while I studied her, and her words from earlier struck out at me, still ringing false.

"But, Emily." I grasped her upper arms lightly, gazing deep into her eyes because I wanted her to believe me. "You truly have a *superbly* naked form. Top rate."

"Thank you. So do you."

Something inside me cringed away from her words. I recognized the impulse for what it was. I also recognized it for what it wasn't. I didn't consciously think of myself as anything other than attractive to her. The cringing was an instinct, years of evidenced-based, negative reinforcement and punishment training that taught me appearance didn't and shouldn't matter to self-worth. Therefore, compliments about external attractiveness were cringeworthy.

She must've seen something change behind my eyes, because her fingers gripped the front of my shirt and gave me a little shake. "Argh!"

"Look." I covered her hands, giving in to a grin. "I know you love me, and want me, just as I am."

"Good!"

"And, like I said, I didn't realize I was always wearing a shirt. I don't want to be, I don't need to be, so I don't mind taking it off."

"Double good!"

"But Em, although I admire your dedication to evidence-based arguments and solid data collection practices, you could've just told me how you feel."

"Really?" Her voice was high and belied her disbelief, but her hands did relax on my shirt.

"Yes. Really. I love you and your body, and if you were hiding it from me—consciously or unconsciously—I'd be upset too."

She was nodding enthusiastically. "Yes. Exactly. That's exactly right. I love everything that makes you uniquely you. The shape of your calves and that freckle on your right shoulder." Her eyes moved to the spot, like she was searching for it under my clothes.

"So, you admit you were wrong?" Gently, I pried her hands away and smoothed the front of my shirt.

"About the tracking?"

"No. I mean, yes. Don't track, just talk to me. I mean about your earlier statement."

Her stare became laced with suspicion. "Which one?"

"That nobody looks good naked."

Emily opened her mouth, as though a protest were on the tip of her tongue, and then she snapped her mouth shut and nodded. "Yes. Fine. All right. I concede the point. *You* look good naked. So you should probably get naked."

I chuckled. "Stage five naked? Or—"

"Stage one naked." Her fingers moved to the buttons of my shirt and she pressed a quick, urgent kiss against my lips.

"Not stage three?" I teased, moving my hands to her thighs and lifting her long skirt.

"You want to wear a garter belt? I wouldn't mind. You'd look hot in it."

Now I laughed. "Oh? You think so?"

"I know so." Her enthusiastic nod made a reappearance. "Because I've fantasized about it."

That had me snapping my mouth shut and standing straighter, which gave her plenty of time to finish undoing the buttons of my shirt and pushing it from my shoulders.

But then I blurted, "You've fantasized about me in a garter belt?"

Emily laughed, low and husky. "More like, I've fantasized about you being the lingerie model and me coming in for a private showing."

"Oh."

Well.

Okay.

I nodded, not minding the sound of that. Even more, I liked that I'd lifted her long skirt to her hips and now had free access to her backside.

"What would my name be? Fuchsia?"

She grinned, and then she laughed in earnest. I loved her laugh.

"Um, what about Cyan? Or, I know, *Slate.*"

"Slate? Like the stone?"

"Or maybe Navy?"

"Navy?"

"What?" She sounded indignant. "I like Navy. Navy is better than United Nations Blue."

I barked a laugh, letting her skirt fall in favor of capturing her cheeks and bringing her mouth to mine for a deep kiss.

I'd learned a lot from Emily Von over the last eighteen months. Some of the knowledge had focused on areas I'd previously considered myself to be ignorant. Some had opened my eyes to my ignorance in areas I'd previously considered myself an expert.

But mostly, Emily had taught me how to be brave.

"Okay. Call me Navy. Do you want to see a robe?"

She shivered, using the tip of her index finger to draw a line along the outside of my zipper to my belt. "Stage five naked?" She made a clicking sound with her tongue.

"What's wrong with stage five naked? Then you can touch me everywhere."

Leaning an inch backward, Emily's lips curved into a small smile. "As someone wise once told me, 'Just because a thing is allowed, doesn't mean it should be done.'"

~THE END~

Subscribe to Penny's awesome newsletter for exclusive stories, sneak peeks, and pictures of cats knitting hats. Subscribe here: http://pennyreid.ninja/newsletter/

ABOUT THE AUTHOR

Penny Reid is the *New York Times, Wall Street Journal,* and *USA Today* Bestselling Author of the Winston Brothers, Knitting in the City, Rugby, Dear Professor, and Hypothesis series. She used to spend her days writing federal grant proposals as a biomedical researcher, but now she just writes books. She's also a full time mom to three diminutive adults, wife, daughter, knitter, crocheter, sewer, general crafter, and thought ninja.

Come find me -
Mailing List: http://pennyreid.ninja/newsletter/
Goodreads: http://www.goodreads.com/ReidRomance
Email: pennreid@gmail.com ...hey, you! Email me ;-)

OTHER BOOKS BY PENNY REID

Knitting in the City Series

(Contemporary Romantic Comedy)

Neanderthal Seeks Human: A Smart Romance (#1)

Neanderthal Marries Human: A Smarter Romance (#1.5)

Friends without Benefits: An Unrequited Romance (#2)

Love Hacked: A Reluctant Romance (#3)

Beauty and the Mustache: A Philosophical Romance (#4)

Ninja at First Sight (#4.75)

Happily Ever Ninja: A Married Romance (#5)

Dating-ish: A Humanoid Romance (#6)

Marriage of Inconvenience: (#7)

Neanderthal Seeks Extra Yarns (#8)

Knitting in the City Coloring Book (#9)

Winston Brothers Series

(Contemporary Romantic Comedy, spinoff of *Beauty and the Mustache*)

Beauty and the Mustache (#0.5)

Truth or Beard (#1)

Grin and Beard It (#2)

Beard Science (#3)

Beard in Mind (#4)

Dr. Strange Beard (#5)

Beard with Me (#5.5, coming 2019)

Beard Necessities (#6, coming 2019)

Hypothesis Series

(New Adult Romantic Comedy)

Elements of Chemistry: ATTRACTION, HEAT, and CAPTURE (#1)

Laws of Physics: MOTION, SPACE, and TIME (#2)

Irish Players (Rugby) Series – by L.H. Cosway and Penny Reid

(Contemporary Sports Romance)

The Hooker and the Hermit (#1)

The Pixie and the Player (#2)

The Cad and the Co-ed (#3)

The Varlet and the Voyeur (#4)

Dear Professor Series

(New Adult Romantic Comedy)

Kissing Tolstoy (#1)

Kissing Galileo (#2, read for FREE in Penny's newsletter 2018-2019)

Ideal Man Series

(Contemporary Romance Series of Jane Austen Re-Tellings)

Pride and Dad Jokes (#1, coming 2020)

Man Buns and Sensibility (#2, TBD)

Sense and Manscaping (#3, TBD)

Persuasion and Man Hands (#4, TBD)

Mantuary Abbey (#5, TBD)

Mancave Park (#6, TBD)

Emmanuel (#7, TBD)

Printed in Poland
by Amazon Fulfillment
Poland Sp. z o.o., Wrocław

63495442R00163